THE SCHOOL

Tor books by T. M. Wright

THE
SCHOOL

T. M. Wright

TOR
HORROR

A TOM DOHERTY ASSOCIATES BOOK
NEW YORK

c.1

THE SCHOOL

Copyright © 1990 by T. M. Wright

A Tor Book
Published by Tom Doherty Associates, Inc.
49 West 24th Street
New York, N.Y. 10010

ISBN: 0-312-85042-5

Printed in the United States of America

First edition: June 1990

0   9   8   7   6   5   4   3   2   1

For my mother, MarieAnne Aubin,
with love and gratitude

"We are watched and judged and manipulated by other people all of our lives, but I think the people who most watch and judge and manipulate us are the people we once were, the people we were twenty years ago, ten years ago—the children we were, the adolescents, the people we were yesterday, this morning. They're all there, invisible to us, watching and judging and manipulating."

"But why would they do that?"

"Because they have a stake in us."

"I'm sorry, I don't understand."

"Because everything comes around again. Everything starts and restarts and restarts and changes. And they—the people we once were—are only looking out for their own pleasure, of course, caught as they are in their moment of eternity."

—Allison Hitchcock, "The Inside"

To the following people, my thanks:

Christine Basile-Wright, for being a superb critic.

My sixth-grade English teacher, whose name I forget, but who gave me a less-than-gentle nudge in the direction of writing as a career.

My seventh-grade home room teacher, Miss Dunn.

My father, for various reasons.

The teachers and students of the Waldorf School in Ithaca, New York, for providing me with a setting for this novel.

Thanks as well to my aged computer, VICTOR, for hanging in there with the pixels and the bytes and the stat commands.

| 1 | What was wrong with being childless? Frank Hitchcock wanted to know. Childlessness was good for the planet, which could not support any more human beings. And it was good for *them*, too—him and Allison. |

They didn't much like other people's kids; they supposed at times that they didn't like kids in general.

But when they thought about it, they realized that that wasn't true. Almost without exception, the *faces* of children were attractive, because even the occasional odd-faced child was attractive. There was no guile or guilt in the face of a child. It had only vulnerability in it, and trust.

Children sought to be molded. How could anyone find that unattractive?

But now, after so very long without Joey, they were childless, and middle-aged, and so they did not think about it much.

The school on Ohio Road had thirty-five rooms totaling almost twenty thousand square feet, plus administrative offices, nurse's station, a huge bus garage, two banks of showers (boys' and girls'), two sets of bathrooms (boys' and girls'), a full kitchen—sans appliances—and a combination gym/auditorium.

Frank and Allison got the school for a song—$75,000. It had been out of use for more than ten years and it was at the edge of decay. From a distance, it looked like a school building still in use—one story, red brick, flat roof, lots of long, rectangular windows. It was the kind of building, in fact, that they both had attended more than thirty years before, a building that was bare and utilitarian—the only bare and utilitarian architecture the 1950s produced.

There were many pastel colors in it, which were so much a part of the 1950s (pastel refrigerators, stoves and washing machines, pastel houses, and pastel hats). Pastels made no statement at all, Frank maintained; and that was the stance the 1950s took, at least during the Eisenhower years. "I like Ike!" was such a pastel statement. Why not "I love Ike!"? Simply because "like" rhymed with "Ike"? That was a pastel way to think.

The pastels in the school on Ohio Road were orange and light blue green. The orange was used in most of the schoolrooms, and the light blue green in the large gym/auditorium. These pastels were supposed to prettify the big cinder blocks the school's insides were made of, and, Allison pointed out, it was very durable paint because it had lasted all those years and had withstood the hands of ten thousand children without wearing down.

When Frank and Allison were looking through the school and giving good serious thought to buying it ("Show us something *unusual*," they said to the real-estate agent), Frank imagined the children who had attended the school in the fifties being told what to do in case of a nuclear attack, that they should crawl beneath their desks and shield their heads with their hands— "duck and cover." Assumedly, the red brick on the outside of the building and the pastel orange cinder blocks inside were going to shelter them from instant oblivion. And he thought it was reasonable to expect that the children of the fifties would believe this, because those were pastel years, after all. The world was pastel.

Bombs were pastel.

Frank remembered that he had been working in his study, figuring out the quarterly taxes, which were due in a week. It was a job that Allison usually did; she was better at it, but Frank, declaring that it was about time he learned about "such venal things," took the job for himself. He was having a hell of a time with it—he had never been good with figures.

He remembered a soft knock at the door. Joey's voice. "Dad, can I get some of that wood?"

"What wood, Joey?" Frank called back, and noted the hint of impatience in his tone. But it was all right to be impatient. The boy was interrupting him, after all. He—Frank—had a right to sound impatient.

"The wood out next to the driveway," Joey answered through the door.

The branches Frank had cut up. The branches that had fallen from the huge willow during the freakish mid-October snowstorm a week earlier. Lots of branches had fallen. The willow had still held its full complement of leaves, so the wet snow had done a job on it.

"I want to bring a piece of the wood into my room, Dad."

One huge branch still hung precariously, broken at the trunk of the willow, but connected by the bark.

"No, Joey. You'll have to wait until we can go out there together."

His son's voice came back through the closed door; "Please, Dad?"

"I'm busy, Joey. In a few minutes." Still impatient.

His son's voice came back again. "When won't you be busy?"

Frank said nothing.

Nostalgia, they told themselves, was partly responsible for Frank and Allison's decision to buy the school on Ohio Road. (They knew they wanted to live away from the ocean, where they had maintained a beach house for fifteen years; the place where Joey had lived and died. They knew they wanted to be somewhere in the Finger Lake region of upstate New York, where they had both been raised. They spent a couple of months driving and looking, and talking to realtors, until they saw the school on Ohio Road, in Danby.) If their years together in elementary school were not the best of times, then they were secure times, at least. They were times when there were no real questions being asked, and, so, no hand wringing over answers.

Boys had crew cuts and girls wore their hair the way girls were *supposed* to.

Nuclear power was something that was easily sold to the masses in public-service cartoons starring Mickey Mouse and Goofy.

Mommies cooked all the meals, and they cooked them on their pastel stoves. Daddies did not. Daddies had jobs.

Blacks were not called "blacks." And they knew their place.

Rock Hudson was the supreme male hero.

Allison and Frank knew that they had been marked by those times, and molded by them. They both wanted very much to be the true liberals that they knew they weren't. The stereotypes of the fifties—the cooking mommies and working, crew-cut daddies—existed as strongly within them as did the children they were then.

Because children existed forever. They died, they grew up. But they existed forever. Because the only true function of life was to watch itself grow. Life found expression in watching itself grow and change. And when those processes stopped, childhood stopped.

Joey was dead. And though, for complex reasons, they rarely discussed him anymore, he still grew inside them both.

It was not too hard for Frank and Allison to tell themselves they knew exactly why they bought the school on Ohio Road, with its aging red-brick walls and leaking flat roof, pastel orange cinder blocks and brown-speckled linoleum floors. Ugly thing.

So hard and gritty. And real.

They bought it because there were things in it that were still in that wonderful, life-fulfilling process of growth and change.

They bought it, they maintained, because they saw it as a time machine.

Danby—five miles south of the school—appealed to them, too. They had both grown up in a similar small town, and they saw Danby—through eyes glazed by nostalgia—as representative of a rapidly dying breed, an isolated community filled with independent, curmudgeonly people who had not allowed their quiet, antitrendy life-styles to be corrupted by fast-food joints, video rental stores, and BMW dealerships. Even cable TV had yet to make an appearance in Danby, and most of the town's simple frame houses sported big roof-mount antennas.

It was not a picture postcard sort of town. There was no white clapboard church, no covered bridge. The only church, in fact, was a squat, sturdy-looking structure made of brownstone that called itself the Danby First Church of the Deliverance and Resurrection.

If Danby had, indeed, been a picture postcard sort of town, Allison and Frank would have found it offputting. Such towns carried an oppressive old-style conservatism, values based somewhere in the late nineteenth century. Danby, with its big, roof-mount TV antennas and its hardware store that sold only hardware, its drugstore—"Sy's Drugs"—that sold only drugs, and its supermarket—"Hearst's A&P"—that sold only groceries, seemed somewhere in between. Externally, it was trapped in the thirties or forties, but the people sitting in those old frame houses were obviously much aware of the fictional worlds that existed outside their little town—the worlds of "Miami Vice," "Dallas," "Murder, She Wrote."

Geographically, Danby was appealing as well. It sat on the shores of pristine Otter Lake, not quite half a mile wide, a mile long, and one of the deepest lakes in New York State. It was surrounded, on the other three sides, by high pine-covered hills (the locals did not call these hills "mountains," and Frank and Allison found that refreshing), so all roads in and out of the village were steep. In winter, the realtor said, the town was actually cut off from the rest of the world for whole days at a time.

Allison was forty-five years old and wonderful to look at— tall, gray-eyed, lithe, and graceful. People often asked her if she had been a dancer. She told them no, although it was a gentle lie. She had spent several years in her late teens and early twenties studying dancing and had decided at last that she simply did not have the wherewithal to pursue dance as a career.

In her late thirties, she took up writing as a hobby. It was a response to decades of reading and storytelling and a love of "things made up" (a phrase she had used often as a child). Since taking up writing, she'd completed several novels, unpublished, and a couple dozen short stories—a few of which had seen publication in literary magazines of almost nonexistent circulation.

It would not have been hard to guess that she was forty-five, at least that she was in her forties. She had the presence and self-confidence that forty-five-year-olds should have. And she had stopped wanting for very much outside herself. She had left such needs behind her. The last material thing she had wanted badly was a vintage Corvette. That was eleven years before she and Frank came to Danby, two years after Joey's death. They were able to buy the Corvette, and in the first week that she owned it she totaled it. The experience made her see how transient such things as vintage Corvettes really are.

Frank remembered his son's voice from so long ago. From yesterday. From now. "Dad, I want to get a piece of wood and put it in my room."

"Wait for me. I'll go with you." A premonition. The huge limb hanging precariously from the willow. The gusting wind.

But premonitions were stupid.

"How long are you going to be, Dad?"

"A few minutes. Just wait, okay."

Silence.

"Joey?"

Joey's voice through the closed door. "Okay." Clearly, he was exasperated with his father.

Frank said, "I'll only be a minute. I promise."

A minute passed.

Two.

Five.

"Dad?"

"Only a little while longer, Joey. Please don't keep bothering me. This is very difficult work I'm doing here."

Silence.

"Joey?"

"Can I come in and see you, Dad?"

"For heaven's sake! I told you I was working, Joey."

"Can I watch you work?"

"Joey, I'll come and play with you in a minute. Please be patient. And stop bothering me, okay?"

Silence.

"Joey?"

Silence.

"Joey, I promise."

The wind pushed at the bay window on the other side of the room.

"Joey, you there?"

A loud whumping noise from oustide.

"Joey?"

The wind pushed again at the bay window on the other side of the room.

"Joey?"

*Allison's voice. From outside. "*Joey!*"*

Sitting. Shaking. Eyes wide. Knowing *what had happened.*

*Allison's voice. "*Joey, my God, Joey!*"*

Breathing stops. Starts.

"There's one very big problem," Allison said on the afternoon of their first day at the school.

"Oh. What's that?" Frank said.

"I've looked into half of the rooms in this place and I don't know how I overlooked it when the real-estate man showed us through—maybe I was just assuming they were there. . . ." She paused.

"Assuming *what* were there?" Frank asked.

"Closets. There are no closets."

Frank thought about this a moment. "You know," he said, "you're right. These rooms weren't built with closets. Remember the school we went to, it was the same way. There were clothes hooks along the wall, but no closets."

"It's very inconvenient, Frank," Allison declared.

"No. It's a challenge. We'll *build* some closets. What can it take, after all? Some pine, some nails, some screws, maybe a little wood glue, some hinges, a couple of doorknobs. Big deal. We can do it in an afternoon. We just need two or three of them. One for our bedroom, one for the guest room, maybe one more for . . . just for the hell of it, I guess."

"There's no bathtub, either, you know."

This took Frank aback. He loved baths. Loved to linger in them with a good book in hand, or—which was something Allison got a real kick out of—with little windup boats and fish to play with. He told her that he didn't so much *play* with them as simply wind them up and watch them move in lazy circles in the hot water. It was a form of self-hypnosis, really, and wasn't that good for relaxation?

"No bathtub," he said. "You're sure?" He remembered touring the school with the real-estate man; he was sure that when they had looked into the locker rooms and shower areas he had seen a bathtub. He shook his head. "No," he went on, "of course there's no bathtub. Why would there be a bathtub in an elementary school?"

"Why indeed?" Allison said. "Only showers. Lots of showers."

"Uh-huh." He was glum. "Showers are better for you anyway, I guess."

"They get you cleaner."

"I'll just have to make a life-style adjustment. Unless we buy a bathtub and have it installed."

"We could do that. Do you want to do that, Frank?"

He thought a moment. He very much wanted to have a bathtub installed, but he didn't know how to say it without sounding as if it meant as much to him as it did. "I don't know," he said. "We'll talk about it."

Frank had been a free-lance photographer for twenty years. He was very talented. His subjects ranged from people to landscapes to cities, and he had been able to make a very respectable living. He had even acquired a name for himself as a first-class "shooter." He had seen several books of his photographs published, and most major magazines had regularly bought his work. Then, at age forty-six, he had picked up his camera and had realized how unhappy he was, that he had never really *wanted* to be a photographer, that it was something his father—who had also been a photographer—had forced him into. For two decades, he had contented himself with the knowledge that he made a living doing something he was good at. But the happiness this brought him was only a kind of intellectual happiness, the happiness derived from a job well done, and he realized that he had been living all these years in a state of suppressed depression. At last, it had caught up with him. (He was not willing to entertain the idea that his newfound disenchantment with his career might have been related to the fact that his vision was slowly failing. When he brought his eye to the viewfinder, there was a long moment of adjustment as his eye refocused. Often, the adjustment was imprecise, and he'd have to lower the camera, wait, try it again. He'd always been proud of his visual acuity. If there was something wrong, then surely it was temporary.)

He needed a rest, he told Allison. He needed to be away from his work, if only for a year or two. He didn't want to *look* at a camera for a while. He needed, he told her—feeling like the archetypal middle-aged man undergoing midlife crisis—to find out who he was exactly, and what he *really* should have been doing all these years. *Would she indulge him in this foolishness?* he wanted to know. *Do we have the money for it?* she asked. *You

know better than I, he told her, because she had always been the
one to manage their money. *Yes,* she said, *they did. Barely.* And so
the search for a house in upstate New York began.

They spent a sleepless first night at the school. Both of them
were aware, as they lay awake—eyes closed, as if in active invitation to sleep—of just how much *edifice* there was around them,
how many big and empty rooms there were, how much artificial
space, how many memories that were not their own.

Well into that first night—he had no idea what time it was;
close to 3:00 A.M., he supposed—Frank wondered aloud why they
had bought the school in the first place. He had thought that
Allison was asleep. Her breathing was even and shallow, as if she
were asleep. So, when she answered, "Because we thought it was
nostalgic. And because it was cheap, remember?" it startled him,
and his body lurched a little.

After a moment, after the adrenaline had pushed through
him and sapped his strength, and after he was no longer nearly
breathless because of it, he said, "It's very . . . big, isn't it?"

"Very," she answered.

They did not speak again that night, each out of deference to
the other's need to sleep, though they both supposed that the
other was not going to fall asleep, anyway. They were, after all,
much aware of the needs of the other, and much aware of their
fallibility when it came to judgments of the other.

They thought, at various times that first night, that there
should be more noises in such a large buiding. It would have been
oddly comforting if there had been creaks and groans and strange
little tap-tapping sounds, all of which would have been much like
noises they had grown accustomed to in their big wood-frame
house by the ocean.

But this, they knew, was a very different building from that.
This building was made of brick and cinder block. Any settling it
had had to do had probably concluded years ago.

It was, literally, a rock-solid place.

And it was very quiet.

Which is why, when the furnace kicked on early that first morning, Frank noticed—even though it was little more than a distant hum, like a bee's nest high up in a tree. And when the radiators flooded with hot water minutes later, he lurched again and exclaimed, "Jesus Christ, what's that?" But he realized what it was even as he said it.

"It's the radiators," Allison told him calmly, though they had startled her as well.

"Yes, I guessed that," Frank said.

"Do you think we're ever going to get to sleep?" Allison asked.

"No," Frank answered at once. "Not tonight, anyway." But they lay in bed, hoping in vain for sleep, until the big windows colored over with the rust of dawn. And when daylight arrived, they climbed out of their queen-sized bed.

Frank stifled a yawn and exclaimed, "I sure as hell hope *this* doesn't keep up."

"It won't," Allison said with certainty. "Tonight will be better."

2 When he was a seventh-grader at Woodrow Wilson Junior High School, Frank believed that his social-studies teacher despised him. He was sure of it. It was a given, then, that teachers were not supposed to despise their students, or if they did, that they weren't supposed to show it. But, as far as he was concerned, she made no bones of how she felt about him. At one point, she jabbed a stiff finger at him and proclaimed, "This boy needs help! He's going to be a bum for the rest of his life. He's shiftless and lazy and will do himself no good at all."

She had been dead for ten years when Frank moved into the school on Ohio Road. She was old when she was his social-studies teacher, and she lived a good long time. Her name was Miss Dunn, and Frank grew to understand, over the years, corresponding with her from time to time, that she had had his best interests at heart all the while, but that she was convinced, as were many people, that children would "do their worst if they're allowed to." So she had taken it upon herself to show him the right path, to keep his "internal demons from destroying him" before he got out of puberty.

If asked, he would have maintained grinningly that his internal demons were still with him. Puberty wasn't, thank the good Lord.

> We cannot go back.
> How can we go back?
> We are constantly rushing headlong into the present and we don't have the time or the wherewithal to go back.

Which is why it's good that a part of us does not
go forward.
                          —Allison Hitchcock, "The Inside"

Allison proclaimed during their first week at the school that
it was "as spooky as a tomb," and Frank had to agree with her.
All the pastel orange cinder block and water-stained acoustical
tile and wide, low-ceilinged hallways—gritty and anachronistic
and comfortingly nostalgic things during the day—were unnerving at night, even with the overhead fluorescent tubes switched
on. The coverings for these fluorescents were dirty, and many of
the lamps themselves were dim or burned out, so the light was
iffy, or stark, or missing altogether. As a consequence, walking
the school's hallways at night was like walking in a mirage.

But, regardless of this, Frank got a sniggering delight out of
walking naked down these hallways, from the room they used as
a bedroom (they had put a couch, two chairs, a coffee table, and a
couple of floor-standing lamps in the adjoining room, but rarely
used it. Allison had set her word processor up in a corner of the
bedroom) to the bank of showers near the gym, towel around his
neck. What eyes were there to watch him, after all? Only eyes
that were caught in moments long past; what they saw of him
now could hardly interest them.

At Woodrow Wilson Junior High School, more than thirty
years earlier, Frank had hated gym because he had hated taking
showers, en masse, with the rest of the boys. It was an embarrassment. There they were, all naked and white (all of them very,
very white) with their pubescent parts crowing their male
sameness. Frank thought that he was more than simply that—
more than simply a male body—so he made excuses about why
he couldn't take gym, or failing that, about why he couldn't take
a shower that day; or he would dawdle and take his shower when
everyone else had finished theirs (and, invariably and inevitably,
the gym teacher—who wore a crew cut that was slick with
Brylcreme, spoke sharply to everyone, was hard and taut-muscled,

and who expected each of them to do the things that everyone else did (which, Frank imagined, signified male oneness and unity)—came in and stared at Frank a moment or two, with his mouth set on the verge of speech, as if Frank were something very strange; but he would always go away without saying a word). That boy was still at Woodrow Wilson Junior High, too. Naked forever. Embarrassed forever.

On their ninth day at the school, while they were unpacking boxes in the bedroom, Allison nodded to indicate an open box on the dresser in front of her and said, "Are we going to put his pictures out, Frank?" There were photos in frames lying face-down in the box.

Frank came over to her and looked into the box. After a moment, he said, "Why wouldn't we?" It was designed to be a rhetorical question, but he realized that it didn't turn out that way. Everyone displayed pictures of their kids, whether the kids were alive or not, so why shouldn't they continue to display Joey's pictures? Because, Frank answered himself, Joey's pictures had always brought him to tears; in their last house, he had stopped looking at them altogether. They might as well have been in this box.

"Because," Allison said, "I know how they affect you."

"And they don't affect you?"

She looked accusingly at him. "That's unfair, Frank. Why would you ask such a question?"

"I'm sorry," he said, "it wasn't meant to be . . . to sound the way it sounded."

She continued looking at him a moment. He noticed that he could smell her perspiration. It wasn't offensive. It was almost sweet smelling. She perspired when she got angry. She said, lifting out one of the pictures and turning it over to look at it, "Of course they affect me." The picture showed Joey at age four, two, years before his death, in a sandbox that Frank had built. Joey was looking at the camera and smiling, a red shovel in hand, sand flying from it. The picture was a little out of focus, and Frank remembered that when he developed it, he had thought of putting it in the "discard" pile—pictures to be put away and never looked at again because they had turned out poorly. He said now, "I remember taking that." He looked away. His memory carried him back to the moment the picture was taken; his memory built up an image of his son for him. He heard Joey's bell-like laughter, heard the camera shutter click, the hum of the motor drive advancing the film to the next frame, felt the sand hit his legs, because, the moment after he had taken the picture, Joey had thrown a shovelful of sand at him.

He sighed. "It's hard for me to remember simply a moment," he said. "Like the moments in these pictures. I remember the moments around them. And I relive them."

"I'd say that's good, Frank."

"No. It's not good. It's hellish. It's nightmarish. Because those moments are so . . . static, so unchanging, and so . . . unchangeable. Do you understand?"

"I don't know."

"What can we do with them? Share them with Joey himself? No. That's impossible. What we can do with them is remember them in the context of his life. We can remember, *Yes, this happened a year before he died.* Or *This happened a week before he died.*" He paused. "I think that's one of the reasons I'm taking this little hiatus from my work, in fact. Because it—and I've always thought this—because it really has so little to do with reality. Because it's a . . . a hoax, really."

Allison nodded, her gaze still on the photographs. "Yes. I understand that, Frank." She looked at him. "But I would still like to put these pictures out."

He said nothing for a moment. Then, laying his hand on hers, which was holding the edge of the box, he said comfortingly, "Go ahead, then."

A light, short-lived snowfall came to the Danby area during their second week at the school. Allison, on her way from the bedroom to the kitchen, down one of the school's long, wide, window-lined hallways, said to Frank, "You know what just occurred to me?" Her gaze was on the parking lots and fields beyond. "It occurred to me that I should be getting my coat on and heading for the bus."

"Your brain playing back a moment from childhood," Frank observed sagely.

"Well, I know that," Allison said. "The impetus is right. The school, the parking lots, the snow . . . We were allowed to go home early on the first day of snow." She was talking about a time before she and Frank met, when she was in fourth grade, nine and ten years old, going to a different school than Frank. "Pretty nice, huh? It was the principal's idea."

"They used to let us out to play in it," Frank said.

She turned her head and smiled at him. "We were luckier." She looked out the window again. "This is a nice snowfall. Lazy and fat. Like an old tomcat."

"Rhymes," Frank said.

"Rhymes," Allison whispered.

Silence.

Frank said, "That's one of the signs of growing up. We stop thinking that rhymes are . . . something special."

"And we stop telling knock-knock jokes," Allison said.

"And using night-lights."

"And homemade modeling clay."

"Homemade modeling clay?"

Allison nodded. She was still looking out the window at the falling snow. "My mother used to make it for us out of flour and water and salt. I think she used salt. I'm not sure."

"My mother never did that."

"We were luckier."

"Yes, I think you were."

The snowfall increased. A little breeze came up and pushed the big flakes around. "It's getting frisky now," Allison said.

"Why do we need to grow up?" Frank said.

"It's tradition."

Frank nodded. *"Fiddler on the Roof."*

"Fiddler on the Roof?"

"'Tradition.' That was one of the songs, remember."

She nodded, slipped her arm around Frank's waist, gave him a little squeeze. "I like being here with you, Frank."

"This is the very best place to be," he said.

The snowfall stopped a few minutes later.

The school on Ohio Road, viewed from above, was like a headless, four-legged spider, with the two-story gym/auditorium at the center—its abdomen—and the classrooms, administrative offices, cafeteria, kitchen, showers, toilets, and storage areas in the north and south legs. On the north and west of the school there were parking lots, and on the south and east there were lawns, tennis courts, and a playground. The playground was still functional when Frank and Allison moved into the school. The swings were still hanging, the teeter-totters still usable. Frank and Allison used the playground several times, in fact. They had also used the tennis courts, though only twice, because the asphalt was pitted and therefore dangerous to people—like themselves, they joked—who got their feet tangled up in their legs.

Ten acres of lawns surrounded the school. Weeds had crept into some of this acreage, of course, but—probably due, Frank supposed, to the seasonal use of some noxious chemical when the school was used as a school—most of the acreage was still covered only by tall grass. There was a huge riding lawn mower supplied with the school when they bought it, but neither of them cared much for compulsively manicured lawns, so they agreed that they would simply let the grass continue to grow. This violated a clause in the mortgage agreement, which stated that they were to "maintain the grounds in a pleasing manner," but their lawyer assured them that the clause was ambiguous (tall grass might, after all, be pleasing to *them*), and that they were the owners of the property, as well, so they could do what they wanted with it, within reason (they could not turn it into a brothel, in other words, or make the grounds into a landfill, or paint the bricks some garish color that would be offensive to passersby, or, in general, "transform the place into a public nuisance"). Besides, their nearest neighbors were half a mile away and were not likely to complain.

One of the first projects that Allison assigned herself was to make plans to cover all of the huge, rectangular hallway windows, and they spent quite a while deciding how to do this— with curtains, or venetian blinds, or (Frank's facetious suggestion) with whitewash. Allison wanted to cover the windows so they would have privacy. Frank said that they *had* privacy by virtue of the fact that their nearest neighbors were so far away, and on the opposite side of the school from the hallways, besides. But this logic did not satisfy Allison. She argued that visitors might get quite a show indeed if they were to come over while Frank was parading naked from their bedroom to the showers—a practice she found amusing. And, besides, windows as large as theirs were *meant* to be covered, she said.

They decided, at last, on venetian blinds, which would be easier to open and close, and cheaper, Allison pointed out, than the curtains she had been thinking of, as well, a virtue that was not lost on them. They had applied much of their life savings as a down payment on the school. Frank did not like venetian blinds, but Allison was very persuasive—people simply found themselves wanting to do what she asked of them. This was because, in part, she was the kind of person that other people found themselves spilling their guts to a minute after they'd met her; and it was due, as well, to the fact that there was nothing overtly judgmental about her. She was a listener, and if someone wanted to confess naughty secrets to her, secrets they would tell no one else, then she had the added virtue of making it seem that she had naughty secrets, too.

The first naughty secret Frank told her was that he suspected he was homosexual. He told her this in high school, when he was sixteen years old.

"Why do you think that?" she asked. It was a simple question, asked simply; she was acknowledging that he thought it, and acknowledging, also, that if he thought it, then possibly it was true. Other people would have dismissed the idea, for his sake, almost at once. "*Why* do you think *that?*" they would have asked.

He told her, "Because I don't like to take showers with the other boys."

She nodded smilingly. It was a pretty, noncondemning gesture. "I don't like to take showers with the other girls," she said.

He nodded. "Sure. But the times that I *have* taken showers with them, I've found myself . . . you know, *looking* at them."

"With interest?" she asked.

He nodded again.

"And you feel that means you might be homosexual?"

He thought about that a moment. Then he shook his head. "Not that in itself."

"Do you look at girls with interest?"

He thought about that, too. They'd been going out for a couple of months and it came to him that the question might be something of a trap. But such a trap would be out of character for her, he realized, so he answered, "Sure."

"The same kind of interest?"

Which was the question that exploded his self-doubt. Of course he looked at the boys in the shower in a very different way than he looked at girls.

During their second week in the school, while Frank was reading to Allison—a book called *The Enchanted,* by Elizabeth Coatsworth—he stopped reading and said that he had heard noises from somewhere else in the school. *What kind of noises?* she wanted to know. He shrugged. He didn't know. Noises. He reflected a moment. Actually, no, he said. Not *noises* at all, but vibrations through the tile floor, as if something very raucous, but strangely silent, were going on somewhere else in the school. She told him that she had felt it, too, and explained that she had felt it before, when he had been away, and when she had checked, she had seen that there were large trucks moving on the road in front of the school.

"What kind of trucks?" he asked.

"I think they were going to a landfill," she answered. "Those kinds of trucks. Landfill trucks."

Allison was writing a story about people and their internal torments. She had been writing it for quite a while—a year. More. The story was set up much like a dream, where any or all of the characters could actually be themselves, and where the person they saw as themselves could be someone else altogether.

It was a very tricky story to write, and Allison did not always like the way it moved from scene to scene, but she did like the characters themselves, and the conflicts they found themselves in. These conflicts were soul-wrenching. They had to do with time, with decay, with the passage of events, with aging, and with dying. Classic, eternal, timeworn subjects that she felt she dealt with, in the story—called "The Inside"—in a new and engaging manner.

This is what I saw; I saw tentacles coming out of him and wrapping him up. Smothering him. And then the tentacles grew and lengthened and moved about in the room, went through the open doorway and out the windows and then the whole house was wrapped up by them.

But they weren't tentacles. I knew that. They had no suckers on them. Tentacles, real tentacles, have suckers. These were not like that. These were like thick strands of his own hair.

And he had *power.* He was not simply strong, not simply able to lift more weight than other men, or make love all night long, but real, geography-shattering *power.* The power to *create,* and to *change.* And to renew. He was a magician.

—Allison Hitchcock, "The Inside"

In several places in the school on Ohio Road, the cement holding the red brick and cinder blocks together was under great stress. The bricks themselves, and the cinder blocks, were under great stress, too. And it was not the stress of gravity, or of water, or age.

Some of the cinder blocks, bricks, and cement had developed cracks, and, in places, there were walls that threatened to crumble before too long unless the stress could be relieved. But it was not the kind of stress that a team of engineers could come in and fix.

In a corner of one of the rooms, a mother field mouse and its family had made a home for themselves in a wide fissure in the cinder-block wall; the fissure had developed because of the stress.

The cement slab the school had been built on was slowly but inexorably giving way. It was not giving way because the school had been constructed on a wetland—which it had, but the builders and architects had made all the necessary corrections—or because the cement itself was substandard—it wasn't—but because of the stress.

It was everywhere.

It reached into every corner of the school. Like tentacles.

It reached beyond it, into the surrounding countryside.

Into the village of Danby itself.

And, in places, it caused change.

The man driving the station wagon—his name was Harold—was getting damned sick and tired of listening to his twins and his two daughters fighting in the back of the car and he had given serious thought to strapping them in, which was the law, anyway (stupid though it was). But he decided that that would waste time. He'd have to stop, bawl them out, give them a swat or two, and then try to get them strapped into seat belts that, without a doubt, were lost beneath the seat. So he decided to bellow at them, instead. It usually worked. He had a very powerful bellow, full of a disdainful kind of authority, and very threatening, the kind of bellow his father had possessed and which had worked so well with him and his own brothers and sisters.

"Shut the *fuck up!*" Harold bellowed. "And if you don't—" He felt a twinge of pain in his throat.

"Harold, please!" Marilyn, his wife, admonished. "Your language!"

"And if you *don't,*" he repeated, ignoring her, "then there are going to be some red backsides real quick!"

His four children fell silent at once.

"Do you have to use the 'F' word?" Marilyn asked.

He glanced at her. She was buckled in on the passenger's side and was looking straight ahead (because, he knew, she did not like looking at him when she was trying to correct him).

He said to her, "They hear the goddamned 'F' word every day at school, so don't get on *my* case for using it."

"No, we don't," his daughter, who was twelve and unafraid of him, offered from the second seat.

"And *you* keep out of this discussion," he said, glaring at her in the rearview mirror.

"Look out!" Marilyn shouted.

His gaze snapped back to the road. There was a dog not more than thirty or forty feet away. Harold slammed on the brakes, pulled the wheel to the left. The dog, which had been sitting in the middle of the lane, watched the car veer past.

It took a moment for Harold to bring the big wagon under control again. When he did, he glanced in the rearview mirror, first at his daughter, who looked scared—"That was *your* fault, young lady!" he told her—and then at the dog, who was still sitting in the road and had turned its head to watch the car. "Damn thing!" Harold said. "Goddamned thing! Sitting right there in the middle of the goddamned road. Do you believe it?"

He took his eyes off the dog, focused on the road again. There was a long, gradually sloping hill ahead, and fields alive with tall golden grass to either side of the car. His brow furrowed. "Marilyn, where by bald-headed Christ *are* we?"

She had a map folded on her lap. She unfolded it, while he slowed the car—unsure that he was on the right road—studied the map a few moments, and said, "Isn't this Route 36?"

"Damned if I know," Harold said. "There aren't any damned route signs."

There was a connecting road just ahead. Harold slowed the wagon to thirty, and when they passed the road, he said, "Look that up. Chelmsford Road. Look it up."

Marilyn checked the map's index. "It's not here."

"Not there? It has to be there." He glanced at the map on his wife's lap as he drove.

"Harold," Marilyn complained, "don't do that. Watch the road. That's how you almost hit that dog, remember."

"No, it isn't. I almost hit that dog because I had to tell your daughter there to mind her own business."

"Just keep your eyes on the road, okay?"

"Jesus, it's not like this is the New Jersey Turnpike or something, Marilyn." He glanced at the road, then back at the map. "I mean, we haven't *seen* any other cars, have we?" He reached over, pointed at a route printed in red. "Wait a minute, what's this?"

She slapped his hand. "That's ten miles away, for God's sake! Now will you watch the damned road, Harold!"

He withdrew his hand, looked at the road again. "What the hell is going on?" he bellowed.

Chelmsford Road was coming up on the right.

"Didn't we just pass that road?" Marilyn asked.

"Yeah," said one of the kids, "we did. I remember."

"Dammit to hell!" Harold breathed, and pulled over to the shoulder, a hundred yards past Chelmsford Road. He threw the station wagon into park and grabbed the map from his wife.

"We're going around in goddamned circles!" He spread the map on the steering wheel.

"I don't see how that's possible, Harold," Marilyn said, perplexed, but certain. "We haven't made any turns. We've been going absolutely straight."

He looked at her, clearly awestruck. "Marilyn, how *can* we have been going *straight* and come upon the same road we passed five minutes ago? I know you're limited, but I never thought you were actively stupid."

"Damn you!" she breathed.

He realized he had gone too far, although he was not about to apologize. "All I'm saying," he told her, his tone suddenly even and controlled, "is that it's clear we made a turn somewhere, otherwise—"

"Daddy!" one of the children called out.

He glared into the backseat. "Can't you goddamned kids see that I'm talking to your—" He stopped. The black dog they had nearly hit was moving toward them over the rise behind the car, mouth open, tongue hanging out and waving right and left with each step. Harold looked at the child who had called out. "Well, it's only a *dog,*" he said, but he put the car in gear and pulled onto the road.

Minutes later, and much to Harold's relief, they found the route they were searching for.

They took it.

Five minutes later, Danby was behind them and they were on their way to the Thruway entrance, fifteen miles north.

When Danby was far behind them, Harold said to Marilyn, "Next time we go to see your parents, let's find a different route, okay. Christ, I felt like I was in the freakin' Twilight Zone!"

They never came through Danby again.

3 For instance, you're walking in the woods, it's autumn, and the trees are brilliant with color, you're enjoying the hell out of it because you're all alone—there's no one around for miles, and there never has been. And you come upon a door in the woods, under the brilliant autumn colors and the bright blue sky. The door's standing upright and you can't tell if it's embedded in the earth because there are leaves on the forest floor and they cover the bottom of the door.

—Allison Hitchcock, "The Inside"

"Do you like this room?" Frank asked. He could feel Allison's elbow against his as they lay in the darkness; the room was cool, good for sleeping. He thought of taking hold of Allison's hand, but if he did, she might suppose it was a prelude to making love, and he wasn't up to it tonight.

"What's to like or dislike?" Allison said. "It's a room."

"Well," Frank said, smiling, "it's certainly not your regular sort of bedroom, is it? I mean, it's *orange,* for God's sake."

"It is orange!" Allison said.

"We can change it if you'd like."

"I think that would be good. But in its own time. There are other things to consider first."

"Of course, painting on cinder blocks is tricky," Frank said.

"You've done it before?" Allison asked, and Frank could hear amusement in her tone.

He hesitated, remembered. "Yes," he said, "I have. A long time ago. My father and I—"

"I've been thinking about Joey quite a lot," Allison cut in. Her tone was oddly flat, as if she were fighting back emotion.

Frank said nothing. He did not want to broach the subject of Joey. As far as he was concerned, it was a subject that they each dealt with in their own way. It was not a subject that they had been able to share without both of them breaking down.

Allison said, "I believe it's this school that makes me think about him, Frank." There was more emotion in her voice now. It quavered a little, as if she were on the verge of weeping.

"I understand that," Frank said.

"He went to a school like this."

"So did we."

Silence. Frank could dimly hear the furnace running. It was in a room near the gym, a good distance off, but it hummed loudly when it was heating water. In a few moments, he knew, they'd hear the water pushing through the radiators. It was a sound that never failed to startle them both, even though they knew it was coming. He thought that it was a sound that would always startle them, that they would never grow accustomed to it.

There were other things, he realized, that they would never grow accustomed to. Being without Joey, for instance. Even though it had been a decade since his death.

Allison said, "Do you think about him, Frank?"

"That's a silly question," he answered, realizing that he sounded testy, but unwilling to apologize for it.

Allison said nothing for a moment; then, "Yes, I'm sorry—it was a silly question. Forgive me."

"I think about him," Frank said. "Yes. How can I help it? I'll think about him when I'm on my deathbed, I'm sure. You don't stop thinking about someone who was a part of you—"

"He was his own person, Frank." It was an admonition, the recollection of past disagreements.

"Yes," Frank said. "He was. And he was an extension of us, regardless of how distasteful that sounds to you."

"I never said it was distasteful. I said it was unfair. To him."

Frank sighed. She was right. But, after all, he was only trying to get in touch with his instincts, only trying to tell her that
denying those instincts was foolish and self-defeating. She had
always wanted to think of Joey as distinctly separate from them,
distinctly his own person, had always wanted to believe that their
blood relationship was of absolutely no importance. Joey was not,
she had told him more than once, a miniature Frank, or a miniature Frank and Allison. He was himself. Joey. It was an argument
that Frank did not want to have now. The night was too peaceful, too good for sleeping. He looked forward to the rushing noise
of the hot water in the pipes, no matter how much it might startle
him at first. He hadn't been thinking about Joey, she had started
him thinking about her, and he resented her for it.

"We have the rest of our lives to think about our son, Allison," he began, and realized at once how callous he sounded. He
felt certain she would come back with some biting comment, and
she would be entitled.

But, instead, she whispered, "Yes. It makes living a little
more bearable, I think. Remembering him."

Frank glanced at her in the darkness. He didn't see much—
her gentle profile, the suggestion of an eye; it gleamed a little in
the light that filtered into the room from God knew where. Suddenly he was concerned for her. Concerned for her well-being.

The night was very quiet and very dark. It always was, at
the school.

Allison swung her bare feet off the bed. She felt the cold
floor, the chill air on her exposed arms. The darkness embraced
her and she was thankful for it.

Frank slept soundly on his side of the bed.

Allison rose, moved gracefully to the closed door, opened it,
looked out. She could dimly see the long, wide hallway to her
right and left, and the big windows in front of her.

Frank slept soundly on his side of the bed.

She moved very quickly to her right, down the dimly lit hallway, toward the gym.

She saw a woman walking toward her. She stopped. The woman was tall, as she was, and graceful, as she was. But the woman's face was lost in shadow.

"Who are you?" the woman called down the hallway.

It was her own voice, Allison realized.

"Who are you?" Allison called back.

And darkness swallowed the woman up.

Frank snored softly on his side of the bed.

Light flooded over her.

Morning. The Baby Ben alarm sounded and woke them.

Frank looked over at her, his large, drooping eyes heavy with sleep. "What time is it?" he asked.

She nodded at the buzzing alarm clock. "Turn that off, would you."

He turned it off. "Did you sleep all right, Allison?"

She didn't answer at once. She was remembering, fighting to remember, losing the fight. "I don't know," she answered, at last. "I think so."

"Whose turn to make breakfast?" he asked.

She didn't answer. Apparently, she hadn't heard him.

"Allison?" he coaxed.

She didn't answer.

He got out of the bed. "I'll make it," he said.

4

Very early on the morning of the Hitchcocks' eleventh day at the school, the furnace shut down. It was in a large room next to the gym and Frank knew that it had shut down because when he woke he was very cold. The cinder blocks transmitted cold well, as did the big windows in the school, and their first few nights, when the furnace was working, were cold enough, but that morning Frank woke as stiff as a stone.

He turned to Allison, asleep beside him in the double bed—the room held their double bed, a mahogany chest, a tall cherry chest, Allison's desk, desk chair, and word processor—and he said, "Allison, it's damned cold!"

But she was asleep. He chose to let her stay asleep while he did what he could with the furnace.

It was out of fuel oil. They had contracted with the local fuel-oil supplier—who had also refurbished the furnace, which had not seen use for several years—to keep the tank filled, so Frank called him and bawled him out. An hour later, the tank was full and the delivery man was showing him how to relight the pilot.

Allison woke shortly after that. Frank was walking back to their bedroom down the wide hallway from the area of the gym when he saw her. Daylight bounced almost painfully off the floor and the walls, and it was that, Frank supposed, which made Allison look illusory at first, as if he was not seeing *her* but some dim *idea* of her that was taking shape as he walked closer to it. Then she resolved into the Allison he knew and loved, smiled, and called down the thirty feet of cinder-block hallway that still separated them, so her words echoed, "Well, good morning. It's very crisp!"

He nodded, and a moment later they were standing in front of each other. "Crisp isn't the word for it," he said, and made a show of hugging himself for warmth, although it wasn't that cold, and he had put on a warm velour robe that Allison had gotten him the previous Christmas.

"C'mon," she said, and took his arm. "Let's see what we can whip up for breakfast in that cavern they call a kitchen."

"We are watched and judged and manipulated by other people all of our lives, but I think the people who most watch and judge and manipulate us are the people we once were, the people we were twenty years ago, ten years ago—the children we were, the adolescents, the people we were yesterday, this morning. They're all there, invisible to us, watching and judging and manipulating."

"But why would they do that?"

"Because they have a stake in us."

"I'm sorry, I don't understand."

"Because everything comes around again. Everything starts and restarts and restarts and changes. And they—the people we once were—are only looking out for their own pleasure, of course, caught as they are in their moment of eternity."

—Allison Hitchcock, "The Inside"

Frank and Allison decided that their first two weeks in the school had been pleasant, if strange. A big building with only two people in it can be very forbidding; there was also the slippery atmosphere of decay and premature aging that, Allison said, the place "oozed." All of it quickly added up to melancholy. Fortunately, they agreed, they had each other, so the melancholy was usually short-lived.

They made love quite a lot in those first two weeks. It cheered them up. They made love in lots of places. They made love in the gym, under one of the basketball backboards (the baskets and nets had been taken down long ago); they made love in what had once served as the principal's office, on a big gray-metal desk that Frank hoped had been used by one of the school's principals; they made love in the kitchen, although, for some odd reason, it was not as satisfying as they'd hoped it would be. (It occurred to Frank that making love in the hallway would be an interesting thing to do, but Allison nixed that idea. "What if the Welcome Wagon hostess should come over?" she said.

"Well then, she'd get a hell of a welcome," he said, and though Allison laughed at that, they did not make love in the hallway. They made love in the cafeteria, several times, on one of the long cafeteria tables that had been left behind; they placed pillows strategically, to avoid back strain and pressure on their knees.

After a few days of this, they decided that the school had been "christened," and that they could make love in more natural and comfortable places again.

At the end of the second week, Frank called the realtor, Mr. Atkinson, and asked if he—the realtor—could supply them with history on the school.

"What kind of history?" Atkinson asked.

"Whatever's available," Frank answered. "When it was built, how long it was used as a school, that sort of thing."

"If you check your deed," Atkinson said, "I think you'll see that it was built in 1951. And I know from personal experience that it was closed twenty-seven years later, in 1978. That was the year my daughter went to sixth grade there." He paused. "If I can give you any more information, please feel free to call."

Frank realized he was being dismissed, and he didn't like it. "Thanks, I will," he said, and hung up.

He did indeed want to know more, because he was convinced that there *was* more. He could feel it. Something other than elementary education had happened in the school on Ohio Road and he wanted to find out what it was.

He shared that idea with Allison on the night that he called the realtor. They had just moved a big mirror into their bedroom—it was a tall, rectangular mirror, and they had found it in a large room off the gym—the room had once been used to house janitorial supplies—and Allison was standing in front of the mirror in her bra and panties. She was trying to decide if she was getting fat. She glanced at the reflection of Frank's face in the mirror and smiled, clearly amused. "Do you have some theory as to what exactly happened here?" she asked.

"Sure," he answered.

"Okay," she coaxed after a moment's silence. "What?"

He shrugged.

Allison moved her right leg so she could get a good look at her inner thigh. She mouthed a curse, which was unusual for her.

"Anything, I guess," Frank answered. "Murder, mayhem. That sort of thing."

Allison looked at his reflection once more. "Murder and mayhem? Here?" She smiled again, shook her head. "I doubt it, Frank."

"This school has secrets, Allison, and I'm going to find out what they are."

She looked at him, still smiling. "That sounds like an adventure," she said; then, dismissing the subject, "When are June and Rick going to arrive?"

He didn't answer at once. She was shutting him up, just as the realtor had, and he didn't like it. At last, he said, "I don't know when they're going to *arrive*, exactly. But they said they'd be here at seven." He checked his watch. "A half hour."

"You think June will bring that stupid little dog?"

"Of course. She takes it everywhere, doesn't she?"

Allison nodded grimly. "I've seen her feed it at the dinner

table." She paused. "It's a prop, I think. The dog's a prop. It draws attention away from her."

"Why would she want to do that?"

"Why does anyone want to draw attention from themselves? Because they lack self-confidence, of course." She looked at her other thigh. "I used to do the same thing, Frank. When we started going out."

"Back in high school?"

She nodded. "If you get people to talk about themselves, then it takes the spotlight off you. That's a pretty simple concept." She paused, stood up straight, smiled; she was pleased with her reflection. "I still do it. I listen. I've been a listener for forty-five years because I don't believe I have much to say."

"Of course—" he began to protest.

"And now," she interrupted, "I think I'd better get dressed. They'll be here before long."

June and Rick were friends from their years at the beach house, and they were younger than Allison and Frank by a decade. Rick was black, June white, and June was never without her wire-haired terrier, Miklos. The dog had bitten Frank three times and had nearly bitten Allison once. June was fond of forgiving the dog before its victims had had time to acknowledge that forgiveness was forthcoming. "He's high-spirited," she proclaimed. "He was abused as a puppy." Frank and Allison thought it was a reasonable excuse, but they secretly hoped that the dog would meet with some grievous and fatal accident.

"Maybe that dog of hers will be muzzled," Allison suggested now.

"No," Frank said. "She's teaching it to talk."

Allison smiled. She had heard the story before. She said, off the subject, "I think something happened here, too, Frank. Something . . . melancholy."

June and Rick were a half hour late, which was not unusual. Their excuse was that they had had trouble finding the address, and when they actually found it, they sat outside in the circular driveway for ten minutes, asking each other, "Do you think they actually *live* there?" Frank and Allison had told them nothing about the building they lived in other than that it was "unusual," and that when June and Rick found the exact address, not to be surprised.

Rick, who was tall and very sturdily built, with a wide nose, flaring nostrils, and short hair, said, "This is great," and looked about. They were standing in the west entrance, a pair of double glass doors halfway down one of the spider's legs. A covered walkway, supported by thick black iron posts, led to this entrance from the front parking lot. Rick continued, smilingly, "This is really great. A relic of the Eisenhower years. A reminder of white flight." Frank could not tell if Rick was joking. Rick smiled quite a lot—a thin, self-amused sort of smile, as if he were playing a secret joke on the world.

Allison, who had never really known how to react to him, said, "It's good you're here."

"Why on *earth* did you buy this place?" June asked.

And for several moments, both Allison and Frank were stuck for an answer. It occurred to them simultaneously that there was no clear-cut answer, that all their talk about nostalgia and expenses and the school's "uniqueness" was just talk. *This* was not the kind of house they had been looking for. They had been looking for a little Cape Cod—a smaller version of the house they had moved out of. Something away from the ocean. Something manageable. But, instead, they had bought this monstrosity, and it was suddenly, glaringly obvious to them both that they had no real idea why.

"Well," Frank said at last, "we like it. We do like it very much."

A couple of days after June and Rick's visit, Frank learned from a neighbor that there had been several deaths at the school in the late fifties. These deaths—four students and a biology teacher—had been the result of food poisoning. Frank wanted to know more—the students' names, their ages, the name of the teacher, the particular sort of food involved, whether other students had fallen ill—but the neighbor he spoke with, a man named Bowerman, who lived in a farmhouse half a mile away, said that he had forgotten the "nasty details" and would prefer never to remember them. The whole affair had aroused quite a lot of ire in the community.

Frank did learn that the culprit was not the school itself— improper food handling, unsanitary conditions—but a meat supplier who was, subsequently, forced into bankruptcy.

Frank went alone to the cafeteria after hearing the story. He tried to imagine the place on the day that the actual poisonings happened. In his mind's eye, he saw the huge room filled with children, all of them yammering with their mouths full, or complaining about tests, ogling "the new girl," throwing paper airplanes or spitballs or paper clips.

He heard one kid say to another, "Jeez, you eat *this* stuff and it'll kill ya!"

And the other kid nodded his agreement, which was to say that the food wouldn't *really* kill him, it just tasted lousy; school food was like that. It looked awful, and it tasted awful. It was the way of things. Trees were green in the summer and school cafeteria food tasted lousy. So the kid ate it, and several hours later, he felt awful. He couldn't remember ever feeling quite so awful in all his young life. So he went to the nurse. The nurse didn't know what to do. State law said that she couldn't even give him *aspirin.* So she told him to lie down on the little green cot that she had there, in her office. So he lay down. But it didn't help. After a few minutes, he felt even worse, and the nurse started worrying that maybe something was really wrong with him. Then another kid showed up with the same problem, and another kid, and another. . . . Until all hell broke loose at the school on Ohio Road. A week later, there were funerals and memorial services, and someone prattled on under a bright spring sun about "young lives snuffed out in their blossoming."

Frank shared these thoughts with Allison, but she told him again that the subject was distasteful to her, so he said no more about it.

Frank looked blankly at the line of polished, cream-colored urinals—each one reflecting the white light of the overhead fluorescents—and Allison, seeing his lack of expression, said, "Is something wrong?"

He didn't answer at once. His blank look changed slightly, became one of subtle anger or, Allison thought, regret—it was hard to tell. Then he said, looking at her and trying for a casual smile, "Have you ever thought what a really . . . unprivate place this is?"

She shrugged. "What school bathroom is private? The girls' bathroom is a little more private, but still there are those awful open shower areas." She paused, continued, "These are the kinds of places where we were supposed to learn to be part of the group, I think."

"Yes," Frank whispered. "Bathrooms, showers, urinals—it was their way of showing us how alike we really were, under our clothes." He gestured to indicate the urinals. "I hated these things. I still do." He grinned as if embarrassed. "You probably don't know this—hell, how *could* you know it, but when I use public rest rooms, I avoid these urinals if I can. I go into the stall and I close the door." His grin grew a little lopsided. "And if someone else comes in . . ." He stopped, continued, "I don't know why I'm telling you this."

"Something about the child being father to the man?" Allison offered.

"Yes," he said. "That's a good thought." He paused. "Anyway, when I use the stalls in public rest rooms, and someone comes in, I scroonch down a little so they won't know that I'm only peeing in there."

"*Why* do you do that?"

"Because that's not something men do, is it? I mean, they don't go into public rest rooms to pee and then hide out in the toilet stall to do it. They pee where they were meant to pee, where God *intended* them to pee. In the urinal. They saunter up to it and they whip out their . . . cock, and they pee. And if someone else comes in and stands next to them, so what? They're both doing their particular masculine thing. I think it's all part of the mystique of being a man. I certainly couldn't imagine women doing the same sort of thing—"

"Well, we can't, can we?"

He smiled. "It would be difficult, I guess." A pause. "But I hide out in the toilet stall. I even imagine, to this day, that some guy is going to come in and he's going to notice that all I'm doing is peeing in there, in the stall, and he's going to say something like, 'Hey, you're supposed to pee out here. What kind of fruit are you, anyway?'"

"Oh, I don't think anyone would say that, Frank. It's all in your imagination."

"Sure it is. Of course it is." He gestured to indicate the urinals again. "But it's just that these . . . things bring back memories that are uncomfortable."

She patted him on the rear end. "You're just a little shy. Big deal."

"Yeah," he said. "I'm shy."

The old couple had driven through Danby and its environs many times before, on their way south from their home near Buffalo, New York, but now, the man, who was driving, turned to his wife, who was sitting quietly beside him, and said, "I think we're lost, Gracie."

Gracie reached out and gently touched her husband's arm. "Of course we're not lost," she assured him. "We can't be lost. How can we be lost?" She patted his arm. *Need more be said?*

"But I don't understand. . . ." He stopped. He was very confused. It was not the first time. Confusion had gripped him more than once in the past couple of years; he and Gracie knew the reason for it, and accepted it. But he was sure, now, that his confusion had an external cause. "We've been down this road before, Gracie," he said.

"Of course we have," Gracie told him. "Thirty-two times, now"; which was the number of years they had journeyed south in order to escape Buffalo's fierce winters.

"I don't *mean* that," her husband snapped, and immediately regretted it. In their forty-five years together, he had rarely spoken harshly to his wife. "I'm sorry, darling," he said. "I'm just . . . Look there!" He pointed at a connecting road coming up. "We've passed that road before. I *know* it!"

"Of course we have," Gracie said. "Don't you remember?" She was still speaking sweetly, but there was an edge of impatience in her voice. "It was just five years ago that we went down that road during a storm and we found a bed-and-breakfast inn, and we stayed there for the night."

Her husband shook his head earnestly. "No. It wasn't that road. I remember. It was another road."

Again, Gracie touched his arm reassuringly.

"Look at him!" he said.

"Who?" Gracie asked.

"Him there!" He pointed to indicate the fields to the left of the car. The fields were high in golden grass that crowded the road, and the old couple could see, standing just inside the grasses, a man's broad, smiling face. The man was wearing a suit, apparently; they could see the top half of the jacket, a garish tie. Then they were past him. Ten minutes later, they found themselves passing the connecting road again, and the man began to weep because he was sure that his own internal confusion was being compounded, now, by a strange confusion or anarchy in the world itself.

He pulled over and begged his wife to drive. She was reluctant to do this. He had been the driver for nearly all of their

married life, and she thought that she simply wouldn't feel *right,*
somehow, chauffeuring him around. It was a *man's* duty, after all.
And it would not be right, either, to make him feel dependent
upon her for anything. At last, however, she agreed—"But I'll
expect you to let me know when I'm doing something wrong,"
she told him—and got behind the wheel.

Within minutes, they had found the route they had taken so
many times before, and Florida was just two days away.

The man standing quietly in the tall golden grasses continued crookedly smiling.

"You know what I really wish, Frank?" Allison said. "I
wish there was some woodwork in this school. There's no woodwork, and I miss it. Remember the woodwork we had in the
beach house? Oak banisters and cherry molding. And the
wainscoting. I loved that wainscoting." She glanced at Frank,
across the table. He was looking down at his bowl of Raisin Bran
as if there were something foreign in it. "Are you listening to me,
Frank?"

He nodded, head still lowered, and pushed desultorily with
his spoon at the Raisin Bran. "You don't like it here?" He seemed
hurt.

"I do, Frank. I like it here very much. I was just saying that
I miss the woodwork we had in the beach house."

He looked up at her suddenly. "We had a lot of things in the
damn beach house, Allison. Some of them we had to leave behind."

She stared at him for a long moment. "I am only too aware
of what we had to leave behind at the beach house, Frank."

He sighed. "Of course you are. I'm sorry." Clearly, he meant
it.

*"Joey, I'll come and play with you in a minute. Please be pa-
tient. And stop bothering me, okay?"*
Silence.

"Joey?"

Silence.

"Joey, I promise."

The wind pushed at the bay window on the other side of the room.

"Joey, you there?"

A loud whumping noise from outside.

"Joey?"

The wind pushed again at the bay window on the other side of the room.

"Joey?"

Allison's voice. From outside. "Joey!"

Sitting. Shaking. Eyes wide. Knowing *what has happened.*

Allison's voice. "Joey, my God, Joey!"

Breathing stops. Starts.

Frank rises. Walks slowly at first. Walks faster, Runs. Throws the front door open.

There is Joey.

Asleep beneath the willow branch.

| 5 | During their third week at the school, there was an incredible electrical storm that shut the electricity down and, therefore, the heat again. |

There were few places in the school that had no windows and, hence, complete isolation from the out-of-doors. All of the classrooms had windows, and the outer hallways had windows on one side, rooms on the other. But the principal's office had no windows—it was next to the gym—and the showers didn't, of course; nor, remarkably, did the gym itself. It was a huge, cinder-block room with bleachers on one side—flanked by two sets of double doors—and a stage on the other. When the double doors were open, daylight filtered in from the hallway beyond. But the gym itself was completely without windows.

Allison and Frank went there during the lightning storm because storms of such violence had always frightened Allison; she could not remember a time when they hadn't. In their previous house, which had no rooms that were completely cut off from the out-of-doors, she had retreated to the closet several times during violent storms. If she couldn't *see* the storms, then she was all right. And it was not simply a matter of turning away, or keeping her eyes closed. Violent storms *invited* witness. Something deep inside her begged her to look.

So she went with Frank to the gym/auditorium, where they could not see the storm. They could not hear it, either. Every few seconds, the building vibrated a little, as if the landfill trucks Allison claimed to have seen were moving past on the road out front, but they actually *heard* very little, and this pleased Allison immensely.

They shut the double doors because the doors opened onto a hallway and, so, to the outside. They were thick, solid wood doors and were excellent sound insulation. The room had, after all, been designed as a place where basketball games could be played, and gym classes taken, so it was reasonably soundproof.

They went to the middle of the gym. The electricity was not off, and there were hanging lights that burned brightly in black wire cages above them and turned the light blue/green/lavender cinder blocks nearly white.

Allison and Frank did not huddle there, at the center of the gym. It was, under the circumstances, the most distant place from the storm, and because they could not see or hear the storm there, they did not need to huddle from it.

They stood side by side. They faced the bleachers—made of dark wood on which names had been scratched here and there— on a frame made of flat, black steel.

Frank said, "It was nice seeing June and Rick again. I miss talking to them—to Rick especially."

Allison, clearly just for something to say, responded, "Yes, they're good people."

A few moments' silence followed, then Allison continued, "Do you think the storm has ended?"

Frank shook his head.

She repeated, because she hadn't been looking at him. "Do you?"

"No," he answered. "I don't think so. A few minutes."

"I think it's stopped." She looked at him. "I'm sure that it's stopped." She was smiling a little.

"Let's give it a while longer, Allison."

Her smile vanished. She looked away, at the bleachers again, and nodded once. "That would probably be wise."

He looked at her. In profile, she was very still, and her mouth hung open slightly, as if she were on the verge of speech. He thought, not for the first time, that she had a striking pro- file—strong chin, straight nose, high forehead.

"You're very attractive," he told her.

"I'm very scared," she said; it was the kind of remark that would usually have been accompanied by a quivering little grin. But she did not grin. "Not because of the storm," she added, and her words were sure, and measured. "It's not that." She shook her head. "I just don't much like it here. In this gym. It's so big, but it feels so . . . close. I can't explain it."

"Yes," he said. "I can sympathize with that."

The lights went off. Allison gasped, Frank lurched, and they stood quietly side by side in the darkness for a long while. Then they embraced.

The following day, while he was looking through a classroom on the opposite end of the school from the room they had made into their bedroom—they'd decided to convert some of the other rooms into guest rooms—Frank came across a batch of student reports. They were drawn up by someone named Mrs. Hastings, and they were dated October 1956. There were several hundred of the one- and two-page reports stored in a cardboard box that he found in a metal storage cabinet. The reports were grimly thorough. Apparently, Mrs. Hastings saw herself as an amateur child psychologist.

"Lynn," one report began, "is a girl who bears watching. She is too quiet, too passive, too wary of her classmates. She is hiding something from us, perhaps even from herself, and this guilt she carries could be very destructive. Perhaps a meeting with her parents is in order. Such passiveness and malleability as this child manifests can only breed ill will among her classmates." Frank paused because he had a very good idea what was coming next. Mrs. Hastings's handwriting was flowery, and large, done in blue ballpoint pen. He read on. "She must learn to fit in." He whispered a little curse at Mrs. Hastings for her presumption that the introspective Lynn indeed *wanted* to fit in.

Another report, on a boy named William King, age eleven, dwelt at length on the boy's "numbing obesity, which can only

lead to a lifetime of closed doors and missed chances, if left un-
checked and unattended to."

Another report said that Jerry, age twelve, "spends entirely
too much time talking with the girls in the class, which is an
unhealthy pastime for a boy his age who should be developing
male friendships that will be the bulwark of his life experience in
the coming years."

There were some desks piled up in a corner, near the windows, and when Frank looked up from the student reports, he
wondered if some of the students he was reading about had actually used those desks. They were sturdy wood-and-steel desks that
were open at the front; he had used such desks, himself, many
years before. It was a sunny day, this morning after the storm,
and the sunlight bathed the desks in a warm yellow light.

He went over to the desks. There were six of them, three
sets of one turned over on top of another, so their bright metal
legs pointed straight up, as if they were some strange dead animals. He turned one of these desks over and set it on the floor.
He expected to find graffiti on it, but there was none. It would, he
realized, have taken quite an effort to scratch a name or an
obscenity into the hard, lacquered oak.

He was unsatisfied. He searched the desks themselves. He
found a paper clip and a fragment of notepaper.

He looked under the desks but found nothing.

Late the following morning, Allison came into the cavernous
kitchen, where Frank was making himself bacon and eggs, and
she asked him, "Are we going to replace those broken windows
in the north wing?"

Frank was surprised. "What broken windows?" he asked.

She answered, "In the north wing. In the doors to the rooms.
They're broken. Glass everywhere."

Frank set his skillet to the side of the stove; the eggs still
were runny, but he could see that his breakfast was going to be
interrupted. "When could that have happened?" he asked. "We

inspected the place before we moved in. Those windows weren't broken then."

Allison shrugged. "They're broken now."

"Shit," Frank breathed.

"We don't use those rooms," Allison observed. "So why don't we just let them be."

Frank shook his head. "How can we do that? This is our home, for God's sake. We can't leave windows broken willy-nilly."

"Who's that?"

"Who's who?"

She smiled. "Willy-nilly."

He smiled back. "Very funny." He sighed. "Let's go take a look at those windows. It'll probably cost an arm and a leg to have them replaced. Dammit!"

The windows that were broken were in the doors to rooms 8 through 12. All of the windows had been smashed from the inside, apparently, because shards of frosted glass lay on the floor outside.

Frank fingered one of the window frames. "It looks like someone did this purposely," he said.

Allison shook her head. "I don't think so. I think it was caused by some sort of pressure change. I mean, why would someone break into the school just to go into these rooms and break the windows from the inside? It doesn't make any sense."

Frank said, "It doesn't need to make sense, does it? You're assuming that whoever would do something like this thinks the way we do, and that's not necessarily true. Whoever would do something like this is nuts, pure and simple."

They were standing in front of room number 9, halfway down the north corridor. There were tall windows behind them that looked out on open, gently sloping fields, and woods at the horizon. The midmorning sun was shining brightly, but since it was at the southeast end of the school, much of the spacious lawn beyond the windows was in shadow cast by the school itself.

Allison glanced out the windows. "How'd they get in?"

"Who?" Frank asked. "The vandals? Hard to say. But this is a big place, isn't it. Lots of doors and lots of windows. It'd be hard to keep it completely secure."

Allison nodded uncomfortably. "I don't like hearing that."

"We could install some kind of security device, if you'd like. I mean, this"—he gestured to indicate the broken glass by his feet—"indicates that we probably need to. I hadn't thought it would be necessary. After all, our nearest neighbor is what—a mile away, and no one ever goes down the road in front of the school."

Allison asked, "What kind of security devices are you talking about? Burglar alarms?"

"Sure. I don't know. Burglar alarms. Sound sensors. Of course, you've got to attach them to all the exterior windows and doors, and that would be a real job. There must be four or five hundred windows and doors in this place."

"That many?"

"Two or three hundred, anyway. I haven't counted them, but if you figure thirty-five rooms, eight or ten of those push-out windows per room, that's three hundred, three hundred and fifty windows right there. *Then* there are all the doors—"

"So putting these 'sound sensors' up would be awfully expensive, wouldn't it?"

"I don't know." He shrugged. "Probably. A couple thousand dollars, anyway."

"We could get a dog. Two dogs."

Frank nodded a little, clearly not enamored of the idea. "We could. But dogs are . . . they're like children, aren't they. You've got to take care of them. Feed them. Make sure they don't get sick, make sure they don't get depressed, that they're loved—"

Allison could see what he was driving at. A dog, two dogs, would, in many ways, require of him what Joey had required of him. And while he had been only too happy to provide Joey with the love and care and attention that he needed, a dog was another story entirely. Perhaps if Joey had never been born—and died— Frank's attitude would have been different.

She said, "I understand."

"Yes," he said. "I know you do."

She let a silence hang between them for a moment, then she nodded at the shards of glass at their feet. "I'll clean this up."

"I'll help," he said.

The man behind the counter at the *Danby Press and Sentinel* was, Frank guessed, at least eighty years old. Surely a man that old would be able to give him the information he needed.

"Good morning," the man said. "Help you?" He adjusted his wire-rim bifocals—which had been perching at the tip of his short, thin nose—so they were at his faded blue eyes again. He smiled. "New here, aren'tcha?"

"Yes," Frank told him, smiling back, "I am. My wife and I moved into the school on Ohio Road just two weeks ago."

The man continued staring at Frank. His smile faded slowly. At last, he said, as if feigning disinterest, "Didja now?" He paused. Frank nodded, started to speak, but the man went on, "Why in hell didja wanta do a thing like that?"

Frank's smile increased. He was nervous. "I guess my wife and I felt it would be an interesting place to live."

The man nodded gravely. "I'm sure it's all of that, and more, Mr. . . . ?"

"Hitchcock." Frank stuck his hand across the counter. The man took it. His grip was firm, his skin cool. "Plaine," the man said.

"Sorry?" Frank said, misunderstanding what the man had said to him.

"Plaine," the man repeated. "My name is Plaine. Gregory Plaine." He smiled crookedly. "Whad'joo think I was saying?"

Frank shook his head, shrugged his shoulders, knew he

looked bemused, which he disliked. Too many men his age looked bemused because it was a pose. "I don't know, Mr. Plaine."

Plaine spelled his name for Frank. Frank thanked him, then asked, "What do you know about the deaths at the school?"

"Nothing," the man answered.

"Simple as that?"

Plaine nodded. "Simple as that. I wasn't here when those deaths happened, awful as they were. I moved here ten years ago. Had a newspaper in Ithaca, that's downstate. Beautiful country."

"Yes, I've been there."

The man nodded. "Somethin' else, then?"

"Actually, yes. Even if you weren't here when the deaths happened, I assume you have access to newspaper articles about it, isn't that correct?"

Plaine nodded. "Yes, I do, Mr. Hitchcock. But it'd take me a while. Files are in bad shape, 'specially files that old."

"I understand," Frank said. "Perhaps I could look at them myself."

Plaine shrugged. "Suit yourself. But like I said, the files are in bad shape. We had a fire ten years ago. Destroyed a lot of the files, but I think those are okay. Trouble is, putting 'em back together was sort of a hit-and-miss thing. Lot of the files aren't in any particular order."

Frank shook his head. "That's all right. I'm a very patient man."

"Okay, then," Plaine said, and motioned for Frank to come around the counter. Frank came around the counter, and Plaine led him toward a back room.

"You like living in that place?" Plaine asked.

"In the school? Sure."

"Awful big damned place to make into a home, don'tchoo think?" Plaine opened the door to the back room.

"We like big. We were thinking of making it into a kind of bed-and-breakfast inn." It was a topic he and Allison had dis-

cussed briefly, as, he supposed, a concrete rationale for buying the
school.

"Sure," Plaine said. "Well, there's big, and then there's too
damned big, if you know what I mean. What's it got—thirty,
forty rooms?"

"Thirty-five rooms. Plus a gym. And offices—the old nurse's
office, and the principal's office, you know. But it's all right.
We're going to close off the areas we're not planning on using."
Frank nodded to indicate the room. "Can I go in?"

"Sure. Take all the time you need," Plaine answered, and
Frank walked past him into the dark room.

"Light switch?" Frank asked.

Plaine reached around the corner and switched on an overhead fluorescent. He smiled. "Place as big as that school would be
a hell of a place to have a party, don't you think, Mr. Hitchcock?"

"I guess so," Frank said. There was a row of tall file cabinets
along one wall. Frank went to the first cabinet, looked at the
label.

"Is that what you're planning," Plaine asked. "A hell of a
party?"

"We're not partying people, Mr. Plaine." He opened the first
file cabinet, labeled "1953–56." The cabinet was empty. He
looked over at Plaine, who was still grinning. "This is empty," he
said.

Plaine took off his bifocals and cleaned them with a wad of
Kleenex he pulled from his pants pocket. He said as he cleaned,
with his eyes on the glasses, "I hear you had a son. Lost him. Isn't
that right?"

Frank tried unsuccessfully to fight back the anger that
welled up in him. "Who told you about Joey?"

Plaine looked up from cleaning his glasses. "John Atkinson.
The realtor." He was clearly taken aback by Frank's anger. "It
wasn't my purpose to anger you, Mr. Hitchcock. I had a son,
too—he was killed in the Second World War—so I know what
you felt . . . what you're feeling." He paused, seemed suddenly ill

at ease. "It's just that a person in your position . . ." He faltered, shook his head. "*I* would never have bought that building, Mr. Hitchcock." He paused. "Having lost a child, too, *I* would never have bought that building."

He left the room, closed the door behind him.

Frank stared silently at the closed door for a long moment, then turned his attention to the file cabinets again. He pulled open a drawer marked " '62–'65." There were newspapers from 1973, 1974, and 1952 packed inside. He opened another file cabinet—marked " '50–'52," found it empty, opened another cabinet—" '70–'72"—and found several papers from the late forties. He cursed. "Christ. What kind of filing system is this?"

But an hour later, he had the names he needed.

One of them was William King.

6

Frank pulled into the driveway, a stretch of weathered blacktop barely wide enough for the car, and sat looking at the modest, white Cape Cod for a minute. He wondered what he was doing here. He wasn't sure. Surely the least he would be able to accomplish would be the calling up of the grief these people had felt so long ago. He had no right to do that simply because he wanted to know what had happened at the school—*why* those children had died.

They had died from bad food. It was simple. It happened somewhere every day. People ate a turkey sandwich that had been sitting around collecting death to itself, and so they ingested death, and so, they died.

He *knew* why those children had died.

They had been poisoned.

But that fact did not satisfy him. Those children had died because they had been poisoned by the food they ate, but it was not the *reason* they died, not the reason they had been *selected* to die.

What did that mean? he wondered. What *could* it mean?

He hit the steering wheel with his fist.

He knew why he was here. He was here because these people shared the grief that he and Allison had felt.

He was here because his son was where their son was—lost, in limbo, out of reach.

He got out of the car, closed the door gently so as not to announce his presence (he cringed at the idea of these people peeking out at him from a break in the curtains, wondering what the hell this balding, middle-aged man wanted).

He went to the door. There was no buzzer, only a small tarnished brass knocker. He used it. It produced little more than a slight tapping noise.

He heard nothing from within the house, so he used the knocker again. Still nothing.

He knocked softly.

A chubby white-haired woman wearing a yellow dress and a blue apron with the words "Janet's Kitchen" emblazoned on it in red opened the door. She smiled, her cheeks round and flushed and her eyes afire with warmth and good feeling. "Yes?" she said. "What can I do for you?" She said it as if she meant it, as if her day would be improved by being of service to this stranger at her door.

Frank nodded. "I'm Frank Hitchcock. We're neighbors, sort of." He inclined his head to the north. "I bought the school on Ohio Road. . . ."

The woman's smile vanished at once, and Frank understood why. Suddenly he did not want to be here. Suddenly he felt like an ass, a meddler, like someone who had no feelings. But he could think of no excuse for being here, other than the real reason he was here, and it was clear from the look on the woman's face that she wanted an immediate explanation for his presence at her door.

"You're Mrs. King, isn't that right?" he asked.

"I am," she said.

He cleared his throat. "My son," he began, and did not finish because he realized what he had been about to say—*My son is dead. Like yours*—and he was astonished that he had been about to say it.

"Your son?" Mrs. King prompted.

"No," Frank said, "I'm sorry." He hesitated, felt his mouth move in preparation for speech, but could think of nothing coherent to say. At last, he said, "I'm here about *your* son, William."

"William is dead," Mrs. King said flatly.

"Yes, I'm aware of that, and I'm . . . I'm very sorry for your grief. You see, my son is dead, too—"

"Is there a point to all this, Mr. Hitchcock?"

Frank shook his head, not in denial that there was a point to what he was saying, but in apology for his clear confusion.

But Mrs. King misunderstood. "Then I don't understand the purpose of your visit," she said.

Frank smiled. Too broadly, he thought. *I must look like a clown.* "I would like to talk to you about your son, if you don't mind."

"No," Mrs. King said.

"I can appreciate your feelings, of course. As I told you, I, too, lost a son—"

"William is dead. Please leave me alone."

It sounded final; it even sounded vaguely like a threat, but she did not close the door, so Frank hurried on: "You see, I . . . feel something very . . . strange at the school."

"My son died," Mrs. King cut in, "and Mrs. Lewis's son died, and Mr. Green's daughter, and Mr. and Mrs. Lincoln's daughter. And the biology teacher, Mr. Blom." Her eyes were afire again. *What are you doing here?* they said. *Why have you brought me this pain again?* "And there is no reason to mention them ever again, because they do not exist. They *can not* exist." She stopped talking. She still did not close the door.

Can not exist? Frank wanted to ask. "Believe me, Mrs. King," he said, "I don't want to bother you, and the last thing I want to do is open old wounds. I *know* about those wounds. Joey taught me about them. . . . That's my son. His name was Joey. Joseph Dean Hitchcock. 'Dean' after my wife's father. We thought it was a strong name—" He realized he was babbling, but it confused him that this woman seemed to be listening. "I'm sorry. . . ." he began.

Mrs. King cut in, "You miss him terribly, I can see that, Mr. Hitchcock." She hesitated. The whisper of a smile came to her lips and she continued, "But don't miss him too much. Especially there. In that school."

"I don't understand—"

"You will." She closed the door.

*   *   *

Allison woke him very early on the morning of their twenty-first day at the school and said that there were people walking about in the hallway.

It was dark in the room; Allison had not turned a light on, but when he looked across the room at the big, frosted window in the closed door, he saw that there was a strange sort of greenish light beyond it, and he said, "My God, Allison, I think the school is on fire."

"It's not on fire," she said. "There's someone out there—there are *people* out there."

"Turn on the light," he whispered.

"No, I don't want to do that." She sounded hesitant, uncertain.

"You don't want to do that?" He glanced at her. He could see little more than the dark outline of her head, a small greenish gleam reflected from her eye. "Why?"

"Because then they'll know we're in here," she answered.

He thought about that and decided that it was reasonable. He got up, stood silently next to the bed.

"What are you going to do?" Allison asked.

"I'm going to go and look out into the hallway," he whispered.

After several moments, Allison said, "Then why don't you do it?"

"Because I'm letting my eyes adjust to the darkness."

"Oh."

There were shadows being thrown on the frosted glass, as if people were moving past the door, but Allison and Frank could hear nothing. All around them, the school was quiet.

Frank started toward the door, his eyes on the greenish rectangle of light. When he got halfway across the room, he stopped.

"What's the matter?" Allison whispered.

"They're gone."

"No, they aren't."

"Yes. They're gone."

He heard her get out of bed and cross the room to him. She grasped his arm. "Where'd they go?"

He didn't answer.

"Let's take a look," Allison suggested.

"Yes," Frank said, and they crossed to the door. He put his hand on the knob, hesitated, pulled the door open.

The hallway beyond was empty.

He stuck his head out, looked right, left; the hallway was a rectangle of darkness. He pulled his head back into the room and closed the door. "I think it was cars," he said.

"Cars?"

"Out on the road. Their headlights reflect and refract through the windows and hallways, and we see what we saw." A pause. "I think it's reasonable."

Allison said nothing.

"Can we have some light now?" Frank asked.

Allison said, "Yes, okay," and Frank turned on the overhead fluorescents. They flickered into life, bright white with a touch of green.

Allison was naked. She looked silently at him for a long moment; she shivered; it was a quick but violent shiver, and he went to her, put his hands on her waist. "You're cold. Come back to bed."

She shook her head. "No, it's okay. I'm not cold." She sighed, managed a little smile. "Thanks for being chivalrous," she said, and put her arms around his shoulders, clasped her hands behind his neck.

"You have a wonderful body," he said.

Her little smile broadened a bit. "For a forty-five-year-old, you mean?"

He thought about her question. "Sure. For a forty-five-year-old. For me."

She gave him a quick, moist kiss on the chin. "That was an odd answer, Frank. It sounded like a piece of dialogue."

He nodded. "Yes, it was. It was a piece of dialogue between you and me. It fit, don't you think?"

She stepped back from him, so her nipples were just touching his bare chest. "No. It didn't. It was too abrupt."

He glanced at her breasts, brought his hands up over them. They were warm, soft. "You have lovely breasts," he said.

"You've told me that before," she said. "I like to hear it, but just now it sounded like another piece of dialogue." She paused. "Are you somewhere else, Frank?"

He continued gently massaging her breasts. They were large, white, and he found it difficult to keep his hands off them. "I'm with you," he said. "Here. In this school." He smiled. "With the spooks." He tilted his head backward to indicate the hallway.

"Is that what"—a pause; a sigh; she enjoyed having her breasts caressed—"you think?"

He shrugged. "Is it what *you* think?"

"I prefer not to believe in ghosts."

"I prefer not believing in lots of things, Allison. Unpleasantness, murder, spit on the sidewalk."

"But they exist?"

"They exist. Yes."

"You're speaking in dialogue again, Frank."

His thumbs passed across her nipples. She squirmed. "Please, Frank—"

"Please what?"

"Please don't do that. It's annoying."

He sighed. He liked passing his thumbs across her nipples, and he had always assumed that she liked it, too, even though she'd told him more than once that it annoyed her.

"Sorry," he said, and let his hands fall to his sides.

She grinned an apology. He thought what a wonderful face she had; it was almost completely free of age lines, and her eyes seemed to possess the same density of color as when they had first met. Her mouth was full and sensual and promised pleasure. "Let's turn off the light and make love," she said.

"Yes," he said, "let's." He went to the door and turned off the fluorescents. He looked at the rectangle of frosted window. He hesitated.

Allison asked, from halfway across the dark room, "What's wrong?"

"They're back," he answered.

After a moment she whispered, "Yes. I see them."

He reached, grasped the knob, hesitated, threw the door open.

He stuck his head out, looked right, left. He saw nothing. He stepped back in. The door was still open.

"My God!" Allison gasped behind him. He glanced at her, saw only her dark silhouette against the gray early-morning light through the windows. He flicked the fluorescents on. She had her hand to her mouth; her eyes were wide. She backed away, toward the bed.

"Allison?" he coaxed.

She shook her head.

He went to her, put his arms around her. One hand was still at her mouth, so her arm was folded between them. "What do you see?" he whispered.

She shook her head. She said, "I saw them."

"Who?"

"I don't know."

"Children?"

"I don't know. I don't know, Frank." She was having trouble speaking; she was beginning to sob. "They were looking in here. They were walking past and they were looking in here."

He asked again, "Who?"

She repeated, "I don't know."

"What did they look like?"

"I don't know. I don't know." She was frantic. "They were looking in here, into this room, at me."

He held her.

7

The following morning she told him that she was mistaken and that she had seen nothing.

"It's not what you said at the time," he reminded her.

"Of course it wasn't. I was in . . . turmoil. Sexual energy does that to me, Frank." She paused, sighed, went on, "It makes me see things."

He fought back a smile. "I wasn't aware of that."

She nodded. "I've been seeing things all my life. Well, since puberty, anyway. I just never told you about it."

He gave her a sidelong glance. "Are you joking, Allison?"

"No," she answered, and shook her head earnestly. "It's true. When I'm . . . aroused, I see things. Sometimes."

They were making breakfast. Allison had charge of the toast and coffee. Frank was making a cheese omelet, and it was shaping up into a god-awful mess.

The kitchen was huge, but almost totally empty. All of the school's appliances had been removed years before, so their big Kenmore range and brown side-by-side refrigerator, which they had brought from their oceanside house, were dwarfed by the dimensions of the place. They did not eat in the kitchen; just after moving in, they had both spent a whole day scrubbing it, but an odd, musty odor remained, and it was unappetizing. They ate their meals in the cafeteria, at a long cafeteria table near a set of steel doors that led to the playground.

Frank said to Allison as he struggled with his god-awful omelet, "I didn't know that the threshold of your sexual energy was so high that it actually caused you to have hallucinations. I think it's fascinating. Titillating, too."

"Don't get carried away," she said. She poured two cups of coffee, one with sugar, one with cream. "I doubt that my sexual energy is anything to write a medical paper about."

"What sort of things do you see?" he asked, and gave her a mock leer.

She frowned. "The sort of things I saw last night, Frank. Phantoms."

He did not believe her. She was a consummate storyteller. She'd been telling stories all her life. She made things up to fit the occasion, or simply to entertain. It was part of the reason she had become a writer. She had told him about salesmen who'd visited while he'd been away, and who had done or said very odd things, or who had been odd, themselves—one-legged, or transsexual, or as she had once told him, "abysmally ugly, as if the parts of his face had been borrowed from various animals." But these people had never existed, except in her imagination. She had told him elaborate stories about her childhood, about visiting eccentric aunts and uncles who lived in exotic places, but these people had never existed either. It was to her credit as a storyteller that all of her stories had the ring of truth to them—the people and events she spoke of *could* have existed. And although Frank had been listening to her tell these stories for over three decades, she was, occasionally, still able to trick him into believing her.

But he did not believe her when she told him about her sexually induced hallucinations. It was an acceptable story, a believable story; he even supposed that he had read similar tales in some long-forgotten magazine. But the very fact that she had never shared her "hallucinations" with him before made the whole thing suspect from the start.

He thought, instead, that she *believed* she had seen something passing by their open bedroom door. The fact that he had seen nothing meant little. His vision wasn't what it once was.

He went into Danby later that morning to do some food shopping. Allison took the time alone to look for a good place to plant a garden the following spring.

She found a spot north of the school, a place that would get good sunlight, where the soil seemed rich, permeable, and relatively free of stones.

Her plan was merely to stake out an area. It would do no good to actually turn earth over until she was ready to plant seeds, even though she very much liked the physical act of digging in the earth. It was such a real thing and had such an immediate and visible effect and significance, unlike writing, which was mostly in the head, even when it was on paper. The ideas and images that gave form and reality to a piece of writing meant nothing unless the reader understood them, and reacted to them.

Everyone had a reaction to a carrot freshly plucked from the earth, or to a beet, or an ear of corn. Such things did not need interpretation or explanation. You ate them, enjoyed them, or spit them out, or packed them into canning jars for later use. Spending six months tending to a garden, and then harvesting it, was a far different experience than spending the same amount of time on a piece of writing. One experience brought you closer to God, the other, inevitably, brought you closer to yourself.

It was a bright, unseasonably warm day she chose to scout out her garden area. She had brought a half-dozen thin bamboo stakes that Frank had bought for her at the Danby Hardware Store, and a ball of twine. She planned to stake out the perimeters of her garden, then fence it with the twine. It was a purely symbolic gesture, she knew. The twine would probably not last until spring. But if she came out here in a couple of months, in the dead of winter, and saw the tips of her bamboo stakes peeking above the snow cover, it would give her renewed hope that the winter would not last forever.

Winter was a season for grieving. And it had been for a very long time.

She took the plastic wrapping off the ball of twine and smiled as the earthy, faintly stinging smell of the twine rose up to her.

* * *

She staked out an area thirty feet wide by forty feet deep. A larger garden than any she had tended before. It would require much work.

Her bamboo stakes were four feet tall. They reached nearly to the middle of her shoulder. Tall enough, she told herself. She planned to push them into the earth a foot or so with her bare hands; the stakes were thin enough, the earth permeable enough. Unless there was a real humdinger of a blizzard, the winter's snows would not cover them.

She sighed. She wished there were more that she could do today, under this pleasant sun, amid these tall brown grasses swaying lazily in a cool morning breeze.

"Hello," she heard from behind her. She swung around, startled. A tall, thin, dark-haired woman of about her own age was standing a few feet away, smiling cordially. "Hello," the woman said again, and extended her hand.

Allison took it and smiled back. "You startled me," she confessed.

"I'm sorry," the woman said. Her gray eyes were large, expressive, kind. "I didn't mean to." She let go of Allison's hand. "My name is Sandra. You must be the new owner here. Your name is Hitchcock, isn't that right?"

Allison felt uncomfortable having to look up into the woman's eyes; she had always been taller than most of the women she encountered. "Allison, actually," Allison said.

"Of course," the woman said. "I live nearby. I thought I'd come over and introduce myself." She gestured with her arm to indicate the school, which formed a backdrop to her. "I knocked on several of your doors and got no answer. I was about to leave when I heard talking back here."

Allison shook her head a little and smiled confusedly. "I wasn't talking."

"No," Sandra said, "I imagine you weren't. Who would you be talking to, after all?" She paused, though not long enough for

Allison to respond to her rhetorical question. "It was probably someone in those woods there." She nodded to indicate the woods a good quarter mile behind Allison. "Sound carries awfully well on cool, windy days like this. Probably some hunters in there." She scowled a little. "Man shot himself last year while he was hunting. It was an accident, of course." She smiled. "But that's a depressing topic, isn't it, Allison? I think a much more interesting topic would be you. And this school. What brought the two of you together? It's such an unlikely place to live, isn't it? So many big empty rooms. So many hallways. Really not very homey, I can imagine. And so sterile, besides. Not in the sense that it's clean, though I imagine you keep it more than spotless. But in the sense that it has no character. No atmosphere."

"To the contrary," Allison began.

But Sandra did not seem to hear her. "Basic cinder block and acoustical tile. Like living in a fallout shelter, isn't it?"

"No . . ."

"Of course. *I* remember fallout shelters. My father built one when I was in college, and when I came home, why, there it was. What did you say your husband's name was?"

Allison noticed that the woman's kindly gray eyes had hardened. They were no longer kindly. They were like marbles. "Frank," she said.

"What a coincidence, my husband's name was Frank." Sandra scowled. "He's dead, I'm afraid, so he and I do not do very much together anymore." She smiled. "That was a joke. A poor one, I admit, but I'm trying very hard to reestablish my sense of humor. I lost it, you see, when he died. When was that? Oh, seven years ago, now. He's buried behind the house. Had to have a zoning variance declared. He cooled his heels at the mortuary while that was going on, I'll tell you." She smiled again. "Another joke. Better, don't you think—"

"It's getting a little chilly," Allison observed, and hugged herself to illustrate what she was saying, in case Sandra chose not to hear her. Allison was actively avoiding the woman's eyes, now. Looking into them made her nervous.

"Let's go inside, then," Sandra said, surprising Allison. "You can make us some coffee, if you're up to it, and we can chat some more. I love to chat. It is one of the few really inexpensive things a person can do anymore." She smiled. "Another joke. They're getting better, wouldn't you say?"

Allison smiled weakly. "Actually, Sandra, there were some errands I had to do—"

"I'll help you with them, how about that? What are they? Laundry, dusting, cleaning?" She stopped. She looked nervously to her right, her left. "I'm sorry," she said. Her tone had changed. Her words were slow and measured. "Excuse me, please. We'll talk again." And with that, she turned to her right and walked through the knee-high grasses until Allison lost sight of her as she went down a slope to the east of the school.

The night was very dark and quiet, as it usually was at the school, so when Allison swung her bare feet off the bed, she felt the cold floor against the soles of her feet, the chill air on her exposed arms, and she cringed. Then the darkness embraced her and gave her a strange kind of warmth. She was thankful for it.

Frank slept fitfully on his side of the bed. Small noises of pain or discomfort came from him. He was on his back. She could barely see him; only his slightly open mouth, lower teeth gleaming dully.

He was an anchor, something gritty, and real.

She rose and moved gracefully to the closed door, opened it, looked down the long, dimly lit, wide hallway to her right and left, and then at the big windows in front of her.

Frank was sleeping soundly, now.

She moved very quickly to her right, down the hallway, toward the gym.

She saw a woman walking toward her. She stopped. The woman was as tall as she was, and moved as gracefully, but her face was lost in shadow.

"Who are you?" the woman called down the hallway.

It was her own voice, Allison realized.

"Who are you?" Allison called back. "What are you doing here?"

"I belong here," the woman called. "I live here. This is my home."

The woman moved forward. Allison saw her own face staring back at her.

Then darkness swallowed the woman up and she was gone. Frank snored softly on his side of the bed.

Light flooded over her.

Morning. The Baby Ben alarm had not been set, but Frank was sitting up on his side of the bed. "We should install a bathroom in the room next to this one," he said.

"Why?" Allison asked.

"Well, it's a long walk in the middle of the night, isn't it?"

She looked questioningly at him. "Neither of us gets up to use the bathroom in the middle of the night."

"You did."

"I did? I don't remember."

He grinned. "I believe it."

8 For instance, you're walking in the woods, it's autumn, and the trees are brilliant with color, you're enjoying the hell out of it because there's no one around for miles, and there never has been. And you come upon a door in the woods, under the brilliant autumn colors and the bright blue sky.

The door's standing upright and you can't tell if it's embedded in the earth because there are leaves on the forest floor and they cover the bottom of the door.

You think, *Well, someone has stuck this door here, that's obvious.* But you're not sure. It has a *look* to it, like it's been stuck there, certainly, but not by anything human or, at least, not by any human you can walk up to and talk about politics with.

What kind of a door is it? A wooden door, I think. A solid wooden door. There's a peephole in it for people to look out of so they can see what visitors have come to call. But it's solid wood and it's very sturdy looking, which is ludicrous, of course, because it's clearly not a door that *leads* anywhere, it's clearly not a door *into* anything, because you can walk around it and look at the other side.

—Allison Hitchcock, "The Inside"

Frank did not much like cold weather—a complaint that, he realized, he had been making with increasing frequency as his fiftieth birthday approached—so in their first month at the school, he stayed inside as much as possible, because those late

October and early November days were marked by much unseasonable cold.

But a day came in the first week in November when the temperatures hovered in the upper sixties and the sun was bright, a day when Allison decided to try to get the washing machine working properly—a task Frank had told her he'd help her with, but a task at which, they both knew, he would be less than useless ("You've got the mechanical sense of a snail," she told him once, and he glumly nodded his agreement)—so he went for a walk by himself.

He had never much liked being by himself, especially since marrying Allison, whose company he considered necessary to his very sanity. But he thought of the walk as therapy. Certainly it was not a good thing that a man his age disliked being alone. Hell, before long, he would be alone for all eternity. In twenty years, thirty. Maybe more, if he watched his weight and didn't take up smoking again. But it didn't matter when, really. The time would come, inevitably, and he would be gone to God knew where, and he would surely be alone. That was the awfulness of death. It was why people avoided it for as long as they could.

His walk took him north, behind the school, past the spot that Allison had staked out for her garden, where the lawns sloped gently into rolling fields and woods a good distance away.

He soon found himself off the lawn—which was a good two hundred feet wide—and in the fields of brown quack grass beyond. The grass was waist high and he wondered, after a minute, if he was enjoying pushing through it on his way to wherever his feet carried him.

He decided quickly that yes, he was enjoying it, that the sun was pleasant, and the brown grass had the look of warmth to it, that this day could easily be a day late in spring instead of the middle of autumn; that comparison drew him back, first, to his own childhood, when the temperature of the air didn't matter much, when fields of golden grass that joined with a fluid blue sky meant freedom, youth, and strength. Then the comparison had him thinking about Joey, and he saw in his mind's eye Joey's profile against the blue of the ocean; then he saw Joey moving gracefully through the saw grass around the oceanside house—a child being alone and loving every moment of it.

The memory was delicious on Frank's tongue. But it bit going down.

So he turned back toward the school.

When he looked up at it, when it was still a thousand feet off, he thought that it beckoned to him for the first time, the way a home does when it's winter, and the home's inhabitants are approaching. His memories of Joey were somehow more comforting there. Safer. As if Joey himself were hiding somewhere inside the school, playing games with them both.

It was a grim, and fanciful, and appealing notion, and he dwelt on it until he was back in the school and watching as Allison took a wrench to the washing-machine motor. "It makes all that damned noise either because the belt's old, or the pulley is loose, or the motor is loose," she explained.

Frank smiled. "I'm always amazed that you know about such things."

She glanced at him, a small glint of condemnation in her eyes. "Because I'm a woman, you mean?"

He thought only a moment about his answer. "No. Because you're the woman you are—a woman who was raised when such things as washing-machine motors were things that men were supposed to be concerned with. I'm amazed that you overcame that mind-set, that's all."

She continued looking at him for a few moments, and her vague look of condemnation vanished. Apparently she had accepted his explanation, for the moment. "Where were you?" she asked.

"Out for a walk."

"Oh?"

"Yes. Behind the school."

"Did you enjoy it?" She started to work on the washing-machine motor again.

"I enjoyed it. Yes." He paused. "I started thinking about Joey and I came back."

She looked at him, said nothing, started working on the motor again.

"I like to think that he's here, sometimes, Allison. In this school."

She nodded as she worked. "He is, Frank. He's here. With us. He'll be with us wherever we go."

Their second visitors at the school on Ohio Road were a brother-and-sister acting team named Iris and Sam Pfeffer whom they had met several years earlier, while attending the Tanglewood Arts Festival, in Massachusetts.

Iris and Sam—on their way south to Pennsylvania to visit relatives—were an unlikely brother-and-sister team. They didn't look at all alike. He was very tall, and painfully thin, and she was not; she was short, chunky. But they were full of love and compassion for one another, especially for the tangled skein of their love lives, about which they were constantly consoling each other. Over the years they had drawn to themselves all sorts of odd characters, people who were apparently titillated by the idea of sleeping with someone who was not classically attractive, people who were stimulated by the idea of having sex with the deformed, or the deranged, the grotesque, or the simply unattractive.

They arrived on Frank and Allison's thirty-fifth day at the school.

The fissure in the cinder-block wall that the field mouse and its family lived in was in an outside corner of room 22. The fissure was a yard long and three inches wide, at its widest point. It ran diagonally up from the corner, near the floor, to an area just below the windows. The wall itself was askew by three inches, though this was not visible from the outside, because the red brick built up over the cinder block had remained intact.

Room 22 was in the north leg of the four legs of the school. The principal's office, gym/auditorium, and showers were only a short way down a corridor, and the nurse's office—into which much of the paraphernalia that could not be sold had been put when the school was closed—was next door.

The floor in the corner where the fissure had appeared was covered by several inches of black water. The water had churned up from beneath the cement slab that supported the school.

On the first day that Allison and Frank played host to Iris and Sam Pfeffer, the wall where the fissure had appeared collapsed another couple of inches—under the increasing stress—which opened the fissure even further, buckling a window frame and causing one of the acoustical-ceiling tiles to fall.

Sam Pfeffer, who was, at the time, using the shower room not far away, felt the wall give and did not know what to make of it. He decided to ask Allison and Frank about it later, but by the time his shower was done, he had forgotten.

That night, while Iris and Sam were asleep in room 7, at the opposite end of the school, and after Allison had fallen asleep, too, Frank went to Mrs. Hastings's room and opened the box of student reports. He was looking for more information on Lynn, William, and Jerry. He needed to *know* them as they had existed in the school so many years ago.

But after he had finished searching through the box, he found nothing more than the five sheets he had already found— two on Lynn, two on William, and one on Jerry—which told him only what Mrs. Hastings's prejudices were, and nothing more about the children themselves.

He was disappointed. He wanted to be able to *see* them in the school, to hear them talk, and laugh, and cry, but now he wouldn't be able to because he didn't know enough about them to mentally call up their ghosts. He knew only their names and something of the torments they must have been experiencing in their twelfth or thirteenth years.

Torments that Joey had never been allowed to experience.

Frank left Mrs. Hastings's room and went down the long hallway that led back to the bedroom, where Allison was sleeping.

He did not like the sounds his slippered feet made on the linoleum. They were too loud, a kind of *scuff/slap,* pause, *scuff/slap,* pause, that was unnerving because it was in such sharp contrast to the silence and the darkness.

He decided that the hallway needed a series of night-lights and that he and Allison would go and buy some the following morning. He thought that Mickey Mouse night-lights would be nice. The school had been built during Mickey Mouse times. How much fun it would be to walk down that hallway and see a series of smiling Mickey Mouse night-lights softly illuminating his way through the darkness. Surely Allison would think the idea was great.

She did. He shared it with her the following morning, but when they went looking for Mickey Mouse night-lights, they couldn't find any. Only Rambo and Masters of the Universe and Hellcats night-lights, which simply would not do.

It was on the thirty-sixth day, while Iris, Sam, and Allison were in Danby, shopping for supplies at Hearst's A&P, that a strange and unidentifiable odor developed in the school.

At first it reminded Frank very much of the odor of worms that have come out by the thousands after a rain to escape being inundated in their little tunnels in the ground. He was, in fact, quite certain that that was what was causing the smell, and he spent a considerable amount of time searching for the worms. Heaven knew there were any of a number of places worms could hide in a building that size—in corners, under bleachers; there were probably numerous hidey-holes in the school. Hadn't lockers been built into one whole hallway wall, and couldn't worms have gotten into them?

He didn't mind the smell overly much when he first noticed it. Worm smell was something he remembered from his childhood; he remembered running out after a rain to the blacktop road in front of his house and marveling at all the living and dying and dead worms there. And though, in and of itself, the smell of the worms was, at the time, not something he found pleasant, the associations he had with it now—the anarchy of storms, the adolescent thrill of seeing all those small, untidy deaths—made it a smell that was almost pleasurable.

But the smell quickly altered. It became something else— lilac perfume splashed onto old cheeks, lipstick and pancake makeup bleeding together into a puckery, orange mass, breath made sour by insides falling apart.

It was everywhere in the school, even outside it, on the playground and the tennis courts, in the moist, November chill. He could not escape it, and he desperately wanted to. He thought of leaving the school grounds altogether, but there was no place to go. Allison had the car, and Iris and Sam had the keys to theirs.

But, before long, that smell altered, as well, and for a while there was no smell at all in the school, not even the dank odor of waterlogged acoustical tile and old linoleum. He was concerned about this. Places without smells were static and changeless. Cemeteries, for instance, have no particular odor.

He put his nose up to the pastel cinder blocks, but he smelled nothing. He went to the gym and wrapped himself in the aged, thick brown curtains on the stage, hoping that their comfortingly musty and theatrical odor would overwhelm him. But it didn't. He got down face-to-face with the gym floor. He hoped that the odor of ten thousand rubber-soled sneakers would penetrate the varnish on the blond wood. But he smelled nothing.

He was beginning to worry. Perhaps he was witnessing some catastrophic and immutable change in the very structure of matter.

But then a new smell came to the school. If he were to try to pin it down, he supposed, he would say that it was a mixture of three smells—the smell of wood burning, which he found pleasant; the smell of formaldehyde, which he had encountered first in high-school biology; and the smell of spring flowers. It was an odd and unpleasant mixture that was reminiscent of nothing in particular, and yet it was discomfortingly *prodding,* too, as if it were a smell he had once encountered in a nightmare he had long-since forgotten.

"That's an awful smell, isn't it?" he said to Iris, Sam, and Allison when they got back from buying supplies.

"What smell?" Sam asked.

Allison sniffed conspicuously and shook her head. "I don't smell anything," she said.

Iris did not join in the conversation. She was busily putting food away in cupboards, a job that seemed to give her pleasure.

"*That* smell," Frank insisted, and he too sniffed conspicuously. But the smell was gone.

He encountered Iris later that night in the hallway. He was on his way to Mrs. Hastings's room and Iris was on her way to the bathroom. She startled him at first. The hallway was dark, as always, and when he saw her, he had no idea who she was. He saw only a shimmering gray blob suspended in the darkness at the end of the hall, and as he stared at it, transfixed, it grew larger and wobbled toward him.

At last he saw that it was Iris, and he called hello to her.

"Hello," she called back, and a moment later they were standing together in the dark hallway. He could see little of her—only her round face, eyes glistening with some anonymous reflected light. Her body was covered by a huge dark robe, but he sensed the presence of it. Her skin was dark orange, and her arms, too, which were exposed, and which she crossed over her massive breasts, so she looked like the Cheshire cat.

They spoke of little that was consequential. She had some

thoughts about the story that Allison was writing, and she said that she was pleased, also, that they had bought the school. "It's really quite perfect, isn't it?" she enthused, and he agreed.

"It is perfect," he said. "It's a perfect place to live in because it wraps up a life so well. It caresses the present and exudes the past and is unsure of the future, so it is a perfect reality."

She said, then, what Allison had said a couple of nights earlier: "You sound like you're writing dialogue."

"I'm sorry," he told her. She said it was okay, she wasn't criticizing, and excused herself to find the bathroom.

Later, in their double bed, Allison complained that he was too cold to sleep so close to her. But he had to sleep close to her because *she* was warm, warmer than he was, at any rate, and he liked the touch of her skin in the cool darkness. She slept in a satin nightgown, and he was constantly rolling it up to expose her body so he could throw a leg over her and get himself warm. There were other reasons he rolled her nightgown up. Nothing was quite so stimulating as running his hand over her while she slept, to steal long moments of pleasure from her unconscious self.

But that night she complained that he was too cold, that he had awakened her and had made her shiver, and that if he wanted to throw his leg over her or put his hand on her, he should go and warm himself up.

"Where am I going to do that?" he asked.

"I don't know," she grumbled. "Go and sit on the radiators."

They weren't radiators, in the strict sense, he told her. They were baseboard heaters. But he took her suggestion and went and sat on one of them for a while, with his back against the cold window.

In room 22, the fissure widened again, causing the cinder block that the field mouse and its family were using to pitch forward, into the black water.

*   *   *

Five miles north, on Route 43, near Chelmsford Road, a man
named Marty Nappersteck was driving through the Danby area.
He was looking for a route to Elmira, New York, fifty miles west,
and he was cursing himself for having gotten so far out of his
way. He thought it was true what the comedians said—that
"real" men were imbued with a gene that made it impossible for
them to ask directions.

He was already a day late for his meeting in Elmira and had
been driving for nearly eighteen hours straight (up from
Charleston, South Carolina). His eyes were trying very hard to
close, and his imagination was producing devils on the dark country road in front of the car. These devils were visible on the
periphery of his vision—like ghosts standing just beyond the
glare of the headlights—but when he turned his head to look,
they stepped away. They reappeared a moment later, somewhere
above the car, where his tension made them into birds intent on
destroying themselves against the windshield; his fear always reacted to this before his head did, so he swerved the car left and
right.

He supposed that he should find a place to rest. A motel, a
bed-and-breakfast inn. Even a parking area. The night was cold,
but he was dressed warmly enough. Even if he pulled over and
shut his eyes for a few minutes, it would be enough to refresh
him until he found his way back to civilization. He was flirting
with disaster, he knew. Already, he had let his eyes close a couple
of times, and when he had forced them open, he had found that
the car was bumping along the shoulder, on its way into the fields
of tall grass beyond.

"Damn!" he whispered. How many times had he gotten
himself into this kind of situation? A hundred? A thousand? Too
many. *If you don't know where you are,* he began to tell himself,
but he did not complete the thought because he saw a grinning
man standing in the road fifty feet ahead.

The man was not in his lane and Marty was, at first,

thankful for that. Then, in the next fraction of a second, he realized his eyes were so tired that he couldn't be sure *what* lane the man was in, or, indeed, what lane the *car* was in.

He hit the brakes. The rear tires locked, the car spun around, so it was sliding sideways. He felt a sickening *whump!* from the car's rear end.

He brought the car to a stop. He got out. The car had spun around completely and now was pointing back to where the man had been standing. The engine was still on; the headlights were bathing the area in white light. Twenty yards away, at the center of the road, he saw a dark smudge on the gray asphalt. He stared at it for a long while, the last nightmarish half minute playing at fast speed over and over in his head. Then he got back into his car and drove off.

When he arrived in Elmira, he told the people he had come to meet that he had hit a deer while driving up from Charleston.

9 The first big snow came on November 22, the third day of Iris and Sam's five-day visit.

The snowfall was a surprise because the day had dawned cloudless and bright and as warm as a day in late November can be.

The storm came from the north, out of Canada, and it did not begin as such snows so often did—tentatively, as if testing the territory. It started all at once, like a sneeze, and it kept up for a long time, depositing half a foot of snow before moving on and dissipating in the southern counties.

It brought a numbing cold with it that traced a puzzle pattern of frost on all the school's big windows. Frank and Allison turned up the heat and, with Iris and Sam, stayed in the school's interior sections—the gym and the cafeteria—because the cold penetrated the school like a fog. They read to one another there—each of them taking a turn. Allison and Frank often read to each other. They also played games. Battleship and Parcheesi were Iris's favorites.

Allison wondered aloud if their first winter at the school would be only too memorable because of the cold, and Frank assured her that the reason they were feeling the cold so intensely was that it was unseasonable and their bodies were not yet ready to make the transition to winter. She accepted that explanation, which made him feel good because he liked his spur-of-the-moment explanations to be believed.

The snow was gone within a day, and a warm spell settled in. They were happy for it because it gave them a chance to install weatherproofing on many of the school's north- and west-facing windows, which would, they found later, make the whole place much warmer.

It was while Frank was helping Allison put up a sheet of
weatherproofing plastic on a window that looked in on Mrs. Hastings's room that he saw what looked like a young girl looking
out at him.

He saw her through the sheet of plastic and the window,
and there was a glaze of late-afternoon sunshine on both, besides,
but he supposed that the girl was smiling at him in a shy way
from the center of the room. And though she took him very
much by surprise, he eventually smiled back, and nodded.

"What are you doing?" Allison asked.

He glanced at her. "Nothing," he said, unaccountably nervous.

"You nodded at someone," Allison said. "I saw you."

"No, I didn't." He realized that his voice sounded shrill, so
he cleared his throat and tried the denial again. "I didn't. You
were seeing things."

She raised an eyebrow at this. "I don't *see* things, Frank. You
nodded and you smiled as if someone was in that room."

He cocked his head at her. "You don't see things, Allison?
Of course you do. You told me so."

"I didn't," she protested. She nodded at the electric tacker
they were using to put the plastic up. "Give me that, would you?"

He handed it to her. "You did," he said. "When you are . . .
you said that when you're aroused—"

"Oh, Frank, didn't you understand that that was a conve-
nient lie?"

He had thought as much, he said, and added, "But I
wasn't nodding and smiling at anyone. Who *would* I nod and
smile at in there?"

Allison didn't answer at once. She leaned over and peered
into the room through the plastic. She straightened. "Her," she
said.

"Her?" Frank said. "Who?" And he looked into the room
again and saw Iris standing in it in the same spot where the
young girl had been. As he watched, Iris came forward and pre-

pared to open the window they had just put plastic on. "No," he called, "don't do that," and he tapped on the taut plastic.

Iris nodded. "Lunch is ready," she called.

"Oh," Frank called back, and turned to Allison. "Iris says lunch is ready."

Iris and Sam went into town later that day and found the night-lights Frank had been looking for. They were not all Mickey Mouse night-lights. Some of them were Goofy and Daffy Duck, and Pluto too, and when Frank tried them out in the long main hallway later that evening—there were wall outlets every three feet or so—the subtle spray of color delighted him. Never again would that hallway be a place of darkness and mirages. He had captured in it the spirit of an era with his Walt Disney night-lights, and when he went down it much later that evening, he found himself singing Jimminy Cricket's song, "When You Wish Upon a Star," and lingering there, with that soft spray of orange and blue and yellow transforming the place. Transforming him.

He saw the young girl, again, in that hallway. She stepped out from where the hallway connected with another, smiled shyly, and stepped back. She was barely more than a slim shadow, but he could see her eyes, which were large and bright, and her mouth, which was full. He did not go after her. She seemed a very shy girl and he did not want to do anything that would frighten her. Perhaps she was the girl named Lynn, whom Mrs. Hastings had talked about in her report—the girl who was painfully shy to the point of being antisocial. Perhaps she was merely some strange sort of wish fulfillment, one of his middle-aged fantasies of returning to simpler times.

He went back to the bedroom. Allison was awake, reading.

"Iris and Sam are leaving tomorrow," she said.

"Are they?"

"Yes. They'll be back before long."

"Good." He paused. "Are they comfortable here, do you know? Have they had any complaints?"

"They're not complainers. But I think they were uncomfortable."

"Cold, you mean?"

She hesitated, then answered, "Maybe. I don't know. This is a cold building, but I think they were uncomfortable in other ways. More subtle ways."

"It's that smell, isn't it? They didn't want to mention it. Like going to someone's house where there's a cat and you don't want to mention that the place smells like kitty litter."

Allison shook her head. She was dressed in her blue satin nightgown and her breasts were stretching it wonderfully as she sat up in the bed, her nipples erect and perfectly outlined. "There is no *smell*, Frank. I told you that. It's all in your imagination."

"That would be a pretty serious thing, if it were true, Allison. But it isn't. There *is* a smell; at least there *was* a smell. You didn't smell it because your nose isn't as good as mine."

She gave him a bemused smile. "My nose is *better* than yours. It always has been."

He nodded. "Yes. Maybe when we were younger . . ."

"Age has nothing to do with it. My nose works better than yours, and if you're smelling some obnoxious odor that I'm *not* smelling, then, yes, it is a serious thing because it means you're losing your mind."

He frowned. "If that were true, then I hope you would be much more sympathetic than you appear to be."

She sighed. "Yes, of course I would be. And of course I don't think you're losing your mind." She paused, sighed again, shook her head. "It's this place, I think."

"You don't like it here?"

"I like it here, yes. But you can't deny that it has its eccentricities."

"You mean the . . . things you saw the other night?"

"Yes. Precisely. And there is an ambience that would get anyone's imagination going."

*   *   *

She did not want to make love that night. She lay back, and made herself available to him, but he could tell that she did not want to make love.

Her body, he thought, was not the body of an eighteen-year-old, it was true. It was the body of a sensual and exciting forty-five-year-old, and she had a forty-five-year-old's knowledge of how to use it, even when she was not in the mood for lovemaking.

He realized how giving and generous it was for her to consider making love when she didn't want to. And he did not insist. When he approached her, and she did not respond with her usual enthusiasm, he said, "Yes, I understand, I'm sorry," and turned his back to her.

"Are you going to kiss me good night?" she said.

"I did," he said.

"No. You turned away from me. You didn't kiss me."

He thought a moment. He felt sure that he had kissed her, but realized quickly enough that he hadn't, so he turned back to her. He could not see her well, only her face and the soft blue of her nightgown. He put his hand on her breast. He didn't caress it, or massage it, or squeeze it. He simply let his hand rest on it, said, "Good night," and leaned forward to kiss her.

She kissed him back.

They lingered on the kiss for several moments, and then she pulled away and said, "Good night, Frank."

"No lovemaking?" he said.

She did not answer.

"Maybe I could convince you," he said.

She sighed, but said nothing.

"Do you mind if I try?"

"Could I stop you?"

He smiled his reassurance, though he realized she could not see his face. "Well, yes, of course you could. All you've got to do is say 'No, I don't want to make love.'"

"I don't want to make love."

"Oh," he said, took his hand from her breast, and rolled over again.

"Are you angry?" she asked.

"Why would I be angry? I understand why you don't want to make love."

"Do you?"

"Yes. You find me unattractive."

She sighed. "Frank, for God's sake—"

"Are you denying it?"

"You aren't unattractive."

He said nothing.

"You're very attractive, Frank."

"Thanks," he whispered.

He felt her small, warm hand on his shoulder. He waited a moment and put his hand tentatively over it. There were a few moments of silence, then he rolled over and faced her. He could see her better, now. She wore a look of apology and submission that he had seen more than once in their long relationship. He reached, found the bottom of her nightgown, lifted it. It caught where her knees touched the mattress. She hesitated, then lifted her knees so he could continue with what he was doing.

She rolled to her back and lifted her hips and before long, with her help, he had the nightgown off her.

He hesitated. "You don't want to do this, do you, Allison?"

She said nothing.

"Allison?"

"No," she whispered.

She was almost luminescent in the dark, and he stared silently at her nakedness for a long while. At last he said, "I understand," kissed her, reached, found her robe, and handed it to her.

"Do you, Frank? Do you understand?"

"Yes," he answered.

He rolled away from her.

"I do understand," he said.

"Good."

The young girl he had supposed was Lynn stood just inside
the doorway. He could see her slim gray form, nothing more. He
stared at it, saw it shimmer and disappear into the surrounding
darkness.

Iris and Sam left the following morning, after protracted
thank yous, hugs, and good wishes. Frank told himself that he
would miss them, because they were good company, and whenever they had visited them at their oceanside house, he had missed
them for days after they'd gone. But he knew that he was kidding
himself. He would not miss them. He wanted the school to be his
and Allison's alone. He wanted to share it with no one else. It was
their little universe that had its own peculiar, reticent, and amazing inhabitants, and anyone who visited—June and Rick, Sam
and Iris, the meter man—was a trespasser on that universe.

So Iris and Sam drove off, their old Volvo wagon belching
blue smoke into the late November dawn. Frank watched as a
raccoon ambled across the road just in front of them, saw the
Volvo's brake lights come on in response, whispered a thank you
that Iris's reactions had been quick enough.
    Then the car disappeared over a rise and he and Allison
turned to go back into the school.
    She put her hand on his arm and stopped him after a couple
of steps.
    He looked at her. "What's up?" he said.
    She looked at him. There was question and pleading in her
gray eyes. "Are you happy here, Frank?"
    "At this school?"
    "Yes. Living here. Are you happy?"
    He nodded. "Very. And you?"
    She shrugged. "It's a place to live."
    "That's not high praise, Allison. What's wrong?"
    She shook her head. "Nothing."
    "I don't believe you."

"Nothing's *wrong*, Frank. I'm uncomfortable here, that's all, and I thought that you . . . well, you've been acting strangely, and I thought—"

"I'm exquisitely happy here, Allison. I'm sorry you're not." He paused. "Do you want to leave?"

"How can we do that? We've made plans—"

"We can do anything we want, Allison. We're all grown up. If you'd like, I'll call the realtor and we'll have a 'For Sale' sign on the front lawn by the afternoon. And while the school's on the market, we can rent a house somewhere."

"No." She shook her head quickly. "No, that would be stupid."

He smiled at her. "Do you think the school is haunted, Allison?"

She looked momentarily stunned, then she nodded vigorously. "Of course I do."

He put his hands firmly on her shoulders. He said, "Allison, I'm a guest here, you're a guest here. Let's try to get along with the people who really belong here." It was a fanciful remark, a fact he hoped she realized.

She looked silently at him for several moments. He could tell that she was shocked and dumbfounded by what he had said. He thought of explaining himself; he tossed a few phrases around in his head, but by the time he had something that sounded reasonable, she had turned and was walking quickly into the school.

He called after her, "Well, I was only joking. Weren't you joking, too?" But she was too far away by then to hear it.

She told him later that she hated taking showers at the school. They were using the girls' shower room. "It's such a big place," she said, meaning the shower room. "And it's so empty. It *echoes!*"

"Do you feel that there are eyes moving over you?" he asked.

"That's a ludicrous image, Frank."

She was right, he realized. It was a ludicrous image. He felt momentarily cowed.

She went on, "What I *feel* is that there are people watching me."

"People?"

"Children, Frank. Adolescents."

"God, that would make anyone squirm."

She looked curiously at him. "You think this is funny, don't you?"

"No, I don't."

"You're *titillated* by it. My God—"

"Oh, Allison, of course I'm not titillated by it."

"Yes, you are. I can see it in your eyes. They positively shout lasciviousness."

"They do?"

"Yes."

"I'm sorry."

She rolled her eyes.

"I am," he said. "Honest."

"Frank, it's not worth discussing. I wanted you to know that I'm uncomfortable using the showers, and I was going to ask if we could erect some kind of stall so I could have a little privacy."

"From the spooks?"

She glared at him. "Yes, dammit. From the spooks."

He nodded. "I'll see what I can do."

That night, before Allison and Frank went to sleep, while they were sitting up in bed next to one another, silently deciding whether they wanted to make love, Frank felt the same sort of vibrations that he had felt a month earlier, as if something raucous but strangely silent were happening somewhere in the school. He glanced at the alarm clock, on an oak nightstand beside the bed, then looked at Allison. "There," he said, "do you feel that? You can't tell me that that's landfill trucks. They wouldn't be dumping stuff at 11:30."

She looked at him and frowned a little, as if puzzled. She shook her head. "No, it couldn't be trucks, could it?" She glanced toward the bank of windows—heavy curtains drawn—which faced a parking lot and several acres of lawn beyond. The lawn was covered by a shallow blanket of snow. "I think it's coming from out there, Frank," she continued.

He looked at the windows. "Maybe you're right," he said, swung his feet over the edge of the bed, and stood. "I'll go and take a look."

He went to the windows, parted the curtains a bit, peered out. He saw darkness. "I can't see anything, Allison," he said, frowned, and looked back at her. "Turn the light off, okay?"

She turned the light off. He looked out the window again. Again, he saw nothing. But slowly, the landscape resolved as his eyes adjusted. The snow was nearly luminescent. It covered the parking lots and the lawns. The trees, up a short slope, near the spot where they had planned to put a garden, were great black clumps against a gray sky.

A squat, black object the size of a small car was moving silently on the lawns. It moved in a pattern, the way a tractor does; it moved east fifty feet or so, then west fifty feet, then east again.

Frank motioned with his arm for Allison to join him. "Come look at this," he whispered.

"What is it?" she whispered back.

"I don't know. Come here."

He heard her get out of bed and pad across the floor to him, felt her put her hand on the small of his back, felt first her breast and then her shoulder against him as she leaned forward to look out the window. "I can't see a thing," she said. Her breath smelled of Listerine.

"It's right there," he said.

"There's *nothing* there, Frank." She paused. "Wait. Yes. I see it." She was clearly puzzled.

"What do you think it is?" Frank said.

"I don't know." She shook her head; he felt her hair brush against his cheek. "I don't know. It could be anything. Maybe some kind of animal. Do you think it's some kind of animal, Frank?"

"It's too damned big to be an animal," Frank said.

"Well, don't snap my head off. It was only a suggestion."

"Sorry."

"And I can *see* now that it's not an animal, anyway." She sounded hurt. "I couldn't see it very well before."

"I said I was sorry, Allison."

"I heard you."

"And I am. I'm sorry. I didn't mean to snap at you."

She stepped back. "Aren't there floodlights or something out there?"

He thought a moment, then nodded. "Yes. I think so."

"Then why don't we turn them on?"

He sighed. "It's not that simple, Allison. I can't remember where the switches are for those floodlights. Can you?"

"Dammit, Frank, you're doing it again—"

"Wait," he cut in. "It's gone."

"It's gone?"

"Yes."

"That thing is gone? Just like that?"

"Yes."

"That's sort of strange, isn't it, Frank?"

"It's very strange. It just vanished. *Poof.* It's gone. I can't see it."

She shouldered in next to him again and peered out the window. "You're right. It's gone."

"Thanks for the vote of confidence. I'm not blind, Allison. Not yet, anyway."

"Well, I know you're not blind, don't I?" Allison said. "It was just an expression. *You're right.* Just something to say, like, 'Oh, really?'"

"Yes, I understand."

She looked at him. "I think we should go out there and see if there are any tracks, Frank."

"Tracks from what?"

"From that thing. Whatever it was. If it was there, it's bound to have left some tracks in the snow."

But there weren't any. They found some flashlights and went out to where the thing had been, but the snow was unsullied.

Allison aimed her flashlight toward the school; its beam caught one of the windows. "Is that our bedroom, Frank?"

"Yes," he answered, and pointed out that it had to be their bedroom because it was the only room with curtains installed.

"And this," Allison went on, gesturing to indicate the area around them, "is where the thing was?"

"I think so."

She shrugged. "Then the bald and unattractive fact is that we were hallucinating, Frank. Chalk it up to horniness, advancing middle age, to being lonely; but we were seeing things."

"I don't believe it," Frank proclaimed.

"You have no choice," Allison said flatly.

The woman in the school said, "I think there are people out there."

"People?" the man said. "What people?" He paused, got up from his chair and joined his wife at the window. "What would people be doing out there at this time of night?" He peered out. A spotlight illuminated much of the parking lot. He saw moving shadows just beyond the perimeter of the light. "It could be deer," he suggested.

The woman shook her head quickly, as if annoyed. "No. It's not deer. How could it be deer? Deer aren't that tall."

The man put his face to the window and cupped his hands around his eyes to block reflections from the room behind him.

"I'm sorry," he declared after a moment, "but I don't see as much as you apparently do." He stepped back from the window.

"It's your damned eyes," she told him. "You're going blind, and you won't admit it."

"I am *not* going blind," he said, and his tone betrayed his sudden anger. "Must you always—"

"There!" the woman cut in. "There they are!"

The man looked again. "Yes," he whispered, because he could see them now; though they were still little more than shadows, he could tell that they were indeed human. "What the hell do you think they're doing?"

The woman shook her head, bewildered. "I don't know. I don't know." She paused, looked at her husband. "I think they're coming here. I think they're coming to the school."

"Yes," the man said, "I believe you're right—"

The woman gasped.

The man glanced quickly at her, then out the window again, then, once more, at his wife: "What is it?"

She shook her head quickly, clearly in sudden confusion and fear. "Can't you *see*? Damn you! Can't you see?"

He looked again.

He saw.

He backed away from the window, head shaking, sweat starting, throat dry. "It can't *be*," he whispered.

10 "I used to wonder," Allison said, "what it would be like if we lost him. Sometimes I would consciously wish that he had some . . . obnoxious flaw. That he wasn't so impossibly lovable."

"Could we please not talk about this, Allison?"

"But I think even if he had had some flaw, if he'd been a brat, or whatever, it wouldn't have been any different. We would still have known and loved the child beneath."

"Allison, please!"

"He was so much . . . there, Frank. He was so much in need of us. So vulnerable. And so in love with living."

"I'll leave the room, Allison. I really will."

She sighed. "I'm sorry." She thought, then, that if it could be said that one of them was the weaker one, it was Frank. She glanced at him. "I'm sorry," she repeated.

That afternoon, he made a shower stall out of chemically treated lumber and thick black plastic, with a flower print, white shower curtain for a door. Allison was pleased with it, and very thankful.

"You can watch me use it," she invited.

"I'd like that," he said, and she stripped—making quite a wonderful and prolonged show of it—and got into the shower stall, turned on the water, lathered herself up, paying particular attention to her breasts and the area between her legs, and while he watched, he thought that there were others watching him, that he could see them out of the corner of his eye. He turned his head. The blue-white tiles that the room was made of had begun to collect moisture from Allison's shower; little rivulets of water were running down them.

"Are you enjoying yourself?" Allison called above the white noise of the shower. He looked at her again. She was facing away from him. The suds had worked their way down her back and between her buttocks. Her head was turned his way but her eyes were closed to keep the lather out.

He reached, put his hand on her waist. She shivered a moment, then smiled.

"Want to join me, Frank?"

He did want to join her, yes.

"Why don't you join me, Frank?"

"I can't." His hand moved from her waist, forward, to her breast. "The water's too hot."

"Oh, c'mon in, Frank."

He took his hand away from her breast. "Thanks. No. I can't."

She opened her eyes, looked at him. "What's wrong?" she asked.

"I can't join you. I'm sorry. I . . ." *want to,* he wanted to say.

"You don't know what you're missing," she coaxed.

"I can see what I'm missing," he said.

Suds got into her eyes. She closed them, reached toward him. "Towel," she pleaded. He had installed a towel rack on the right-hand side of the shower stall; he got a towel from it and handed it to her.

He saw the wraith he called Lynn in a far corner of the room. She was standing very straight, but she had her hands clasped in front of her. She was wearing a brown dress. Her eyes sparkled. She smiled at him. He smiled back.

"Thanks," Allison said, and he felt her pushing the towel against his stomach. He took it, put it back on the towel rack.

Lynn moved forward.

Allison said, "Thank you for building this, Frank."

"I enjoyed building it," he said. "I'm glad *you're* enjoying using it."

"I am. A lot. The stall makes it hotter in here, too, and I like that." She gave him a coy smile, her eyes still closed. "You know that I wasn't serious about the spooks, don't you?"

"You weren't?"

Lynn stopped moving forward.

"Of course not. I was having some fun. You should know when I'm having fun by now."

Lynn moved back.

"I thought you were serious," he said. "I took you at your word."

Allison opened her eyes and gave him another coy smile. "*Everything* I say"—her coy smile altered—"is a lie, Frank." She turned away.

He forced a little chuckle.

Lynn vanished.

Allison's shower was done.

He had begun to look forward to nights at the school. Very cold nights were the best, because they were like nights from his childhood, when he would get out of bed while the rest of the house was asleep, dress warmly, and go out into below-zero weather to crunch around in the frozen snow in the woods near his house, to feel the sting of the frigid air in his lungs. It was a time of solitude and sanity, that time of cold.

At the school, he often waited until Allison was asleep, and he got out of bed, wrapped himself in his velour robe, put his slippers on, and went to the hallway where he had installed the night-lights. He did not do much there. He brought a chair in from a room nearby and put it halfway down the hallway, against the wall that faced the windows, and he sat in it. He sat very straight, sometimes with his hands folded in his lap. The venetian blinds had been installed, but on very dark nights, when there were clouds and no moon, he raised the blinds so there was a reflection of the night-lights on the windows to his left and right, while, at the same time, out of the periphery of his vision, he could see the actual night-lights themselves. It gave him a comforting feeling of separation. He was suspended in time, caught in a cold night of clouds and Walt Disney night-lights and darkness. And there, in that chair, with his eyes straight ahead, he could see children around him, dozens of them moving about like shadows. And if he turned to look, they were gone, like smoke. Those were comforting and peaceful nights at the school on Ohio Road, and he recalled them later with a little pang of sadness, the way he recalled so many other nights, from much deeper in his past.

Nights so deep in his past that they were veiled and changed by time into being more what they should have been than what they actually were. For he realized that those nights were always too cold, and his teeth always chattered too loudly in the frigid woods, and he was always certain that there were beasts who searched out midnight fools like himself and made quick work of them.

But there was magic in those nights nonetheless, because they transformed the future without knowing it. The boy who walked those cold midnight woods was the man who sat quietly among the reflections of Mickey Mouse night-lights, remembering the boy. It was like a time-travel paradox. As Sam Jaffe used to say, it was "life, birth, death, infinity." But he could not know, then, how very much they were all intertwined.

In Toronto, Canada, a young woman named Eileen Shute was planning a trip south to visit her parents fifteen miles south of Danby. She did not want to make the trip alone. (The last trip she had made alone, north to Ottawa, had been nightmarish; her car had broken down, she'd gotten a ride with two men whose car she had nearly had to jump from, and then the police had given her a summons for hitchhiking. At the end of her ordeal, she had found that her car, which she had left on the shoulder, had been vandalized.)

She called her friend, Victoria Shephard. They had gone to

college together—both had graduated two years earlier—and
though they had not been in touch for many weeks, their friend-
ship still was strong enough that Eileen had no qualms about
asking her to come along. "It's just for a weekend, Vicky," she
said. "You won't miss any work." She hesitated. "And besides, we
could use that great car of yours."

After some coaxing—"Oh come on, Vicky; it'll be an adventure. You like adventures, right?"—Vicky said yes, and the trip
was planned for two weeks later.

*"Joey, I'll come and play with you in a minute. Please be pa-
tient. And stop bothering me, okay?"*
Silence.
"Joey?"
Silence.
"Joey, I promise."
*The wind pushed at the bay window on the other side of the
room.*
"Joey, you there?"
A loud whumping noise from outside.
"Joey?"
*The wind pushed again at the bay window on the other side of
the room.*
"Joey?"
Allison's voice. From outside. "Joey!"
Sitting. Shaking. Eyes wide. Knowing what has happened.
Allison's voice. "Joey, my God, Joey!"
Breathing stops. Starts.
*Frank rises. Walks slowly at first. Walks faster. Runs. Throws
the front door open.*
There is Joey.
Asleep beneath the willow branch.
*Frank stands very stiffly in the doorway. If he stands stiffly, not
breathing, this . . . thing will not have happened and time will go
backward and he will open his door to his son and go out with him to*

collect a piece of wood and avoid the gust of wind. And the branch falling.

"Call the ambulance, *for Christ's sake!" Allison screams.*

He does not hear her.

"Goddamn you, call the ambulance!"

She has rushed to her son, is trying to pull the branch off him.

11 You think, *Well, someone has stuck this door here, that's obvious.* But you're not sure. It has a *look* to it, like it's been stuck there, certainly, but not by anything human, or at least, not by any human you can walk up to and talk about politics with. What kind of a door is it? A wooden door, I think. A solid wooden door. There's a peephole in it for people to look out of so they can see what visitors have come to call. But it's solid wood and it's very sturdy looking, which is ludicrous, of course, because it's clearly not a door that *leads* anywhere, it's clearly not a door *into* anything, because you can walk around it and look at the other side.

So, just for the hell of it, you open the door.

—Allison Hitchcock, "The Inside"

Two days after Sam and Iris's visit, Frank came in from an inspection of the spot lamps arrayed around the school and found Allison in the bedroom, near the windows, her back to him. She gestured toward the bedside table. "I got the mail while you were outside. There wasn't much, really." He glanced at the table. There was a Land's End catalog, what looked like a utilities bill, and a form letter from one of their congressmen. "That's it?" he asked.

She nodded. "Yes."

He sighed. "We've got a problem, I think. Actually, a couple of them."

"A problem?"

"Which do you want first? The bad news, or the *really* bad news?"

She looked suddenly annoyed. "Frank, don't play games with me."

He nodded. "Yes. I'm sorry. Well, the bad news is that we don't have any spot lamps. We're going to *have* to put spot lamps around this place."

She looked confused. "I don't see why."

"Think about it, Allison. Think how big this place is. Think how many exits and entrances there are. Dozens; hundreds, probably."

"Frank, we're out in the country. People don't break into country houses." She smiled a little, as if at some private joke.

Frank shook his head. "You're wrong. People break into country houses—if that's really what this place can be called—a lot more than they do city houses. It's a fact. Look it up."

"Frank, you're using your condescending tone. I don't like it."

He furrowed his brow. "Condescending tone? I wasn't aware of it." He came forward, picked up the Land's End catalog, began riffling through it.

"And the really bad news, Frank?" she prodded.

He looked up at her, sighed again, put the catalog down. "Yes. Really bad news." He gave a moment to silence. "There's a crack in one of the walls."

She said nothing for a moment. Then, "Inside or outside?"

"Outside. Maybe on the inside, too. I haven't checked."

"Which wall?"

"The gym. In the middle of the east wall of the gym."

They went outside together. It was a cold day, and damp, and Allison had not dressed for it. As she stood looking at the crack in the gym's east wall, she hugged herself for warmth.

The crack was not wide, perhaps half an inch to an inch, Allison estimated, but it extended from two feet up the wall all the way to the top, twenty feet or more high. "Dammit!" she breathed. "Let's go look inside, Frank."

They went into the gym and looked at the inside wall from

a dozen feet away. It seemed intact, and they both breathed a sigh of relief.

They could have looked more closely, but they told themselves that it wasn't necessary. Had they looked more closely, they would have seen that the crack in the exterior wall was mirrored inside by a hairline crack that would have been invisible to the casual observer.

Sandra came over to visit Allison later that afternoon. Frank had driven into town to find out, he told her, about putting spot lamps up, and Allison had shown Sandra into the capacious kitchen and invited her to share a late lunch of grapes and cheese.

Sandra seated herself at a big butcher-block table Allison and Frank had brought from their oceanside house. "You're a writer?" she asked, and popped a grape into her mouth. "I've never met a writer."

Allison smiled sheepishly. "Actually, I'm *trying* to be a writer. I've got four unpublished novels under my belt, and I'm working on a fifth." She grinned. "Actually, it's not a novel yet. It's only a story that I'm trying to coax into *being* a novel."

"Really?" Sandra seemed genuinely interested. "What's it called?"

"It's called 'The Inside.'" She poured two cups of coffee. "What do you take in your coffee, Sandra?"

"Sugar. Two lumps, please. No milk."

"Two teaspoons all right?"

"Sure."

Allison put sugar in Sandra's coffee, brought the cups to the table.

"'The Inside,'" Sandra said, and wrinkled her brow. "It's an interesting title, I suppose."

"You suppose?" Allison sat down.

"Well, yes. I mean, I don't know what it's about, obviously, but I'm not sure from the title that I would *want* to know what it's about, if I didn't know you." She smiled flatly; she was clearly a person who was used to saying what was on her mind, without apology. "So, what *is* it about?"

Allison took a sip of her coffee. She did not much like talking about her writing, even with Frank, who seemed to say only the "right" things. Writing was such a personal affair—especially when it was unpublished. And, much to her chagrin, whenever she started talking about her writing, she went on and on about it and usually had to be subtly directed to another topic of conversation. She said, "I'm not sure, really."

Sandra's smile broadened. "You're not sure? How can you not be sure? I thought writers had everything outlined and mapped out on little three-by-five cards."

"I'm letting the plot develop itself. I start out with the premise that there is a lot going on inside us—"

"Hence the title."

"Yes. A lot going on inside us that we haven't the slightest inkling of, and that some of it, maybe much of it—if we could get hold of it—would let us in on all kinds of secrets."

"Secrets? What kinds of secrets?"

"About ourselves. About the world around us. About the universe. Things that we might not . . . perceive with our five senses but that *something* in us does perceive—"

"Like a sixth sense, you mean?"

"No. Not exactly. I think it's simply a much more highly developed sense of hearing and sight and touch, and that maybe the signals, on their way to the brain, get . . . weakened somehow, maybe because of the distance—"

"The distance?"

"Along the nerves. It really is quite a long way from various parts of our bodies to our brains. So maybe the electrical signal— some of it, anyhow—just peters out, and what we see, or hear, or touch, or smell, is not quite the whole picture. Maybe what's missing—something quite small, actually—would tell us grand and wonderful things about . . . existence.

"It's the same thing that happens to an electrical current

passing through a wire; if the wire is too thin or too long, or both, much of the current is lost."

"Is that right?" Suddenly Sandra seemed to be losing interest.

"Yes," Allison said, ignoring the woman's hint to divert to another subject. "So I think it's logical to assume that the same thing could be true of our electrically operated senses. Something gets in the way of the current, or something makes the current weaker, so some of what we might actually be sensing is lost, and what registers on our brains is only part of what is actually out there to be perceived."

"But we have cameras and microphones and what not, and they don't see or hear anything unusual. Or do they?"

"I don't know. I don't think so. But you have to understand, these things—cameras and microphones, et cetera—have been built with our own senses as models. When *they* perceive only what *we* perceive, then we assume that they're working fine. It's the same with computers. Everyone says that the brain is so much like a computer, when it's the other way around. The computer is patterned after and is much like the brain—"

Sandra cut in, "Do you get this technical in your story?"

Allison shrugged. "To some extent. I mean, I have to in order to explain the premise, so I have my characters engaging in dialogue that's similar to—"

"And what are some of the things your characters see?"

"What do they see?" She felt herself blushing. Sandra, she thought, wasn't really interested in her writing, anymore, or in the story. She was being courteous, and that made Allison uncomfortable. In a strange way, it made her feel put upon. She sipped her coffee, then repeated, "What do they see? I'm not sure really. Truths. Grand and wonderful truths." She grinned. "About life and death and . . . living."

"It sounds fascinating," Sandra said.

"Uh-huh. Well, I'm afraid it's not fascinating yet."

The conversation continued for another hour. It turned from Allison's writing to other, more mundane topics, and at last, to Joey.

*   *   *

As always, the night was very quiet and very dark.

Allison swung her bare feet off the bed, felt the cold floor, felt the chill air on her exposed arms, saw the darkness stretching out forever around her.

Frank snored softly on his side of the bed.

Allison rose, moved gracefully to the closed door, opened it. She sensed the hallway to her right and left, sensed the big windows in front of her, the cold floor, her exposed arms, goose bumps, quiet.

Frank snored softly on his side of the bed. It was pleasant, reassuring. Something real.

She moved very gracefully to her right, down the dim hallway, toward the gym.

The darkness around her was like black water she could breathe. She thought that she could swim in it, float in it, find strange things in it.

She sensed the big windows to her left, the cold cinder-block walls to her right, the chill floor beneath her feet, the goose bumps rising on her exposed arms. She sensed her blindness here, her lungs filling with black water.

Frank snored softly on his side of the bed.

She sensed the massive wooden doors that led into the gym.

She reached, grasped the doorknobs hard, found them as cold as the black water she was breathing. She turned the doorknobs, heard them click. She pulled.

Light flooded over her as if she were newly born.

She was awed, confused, frightened, cold. Hopeful.

Frank snored softly on his side of the bed.

The light abated.

She saw people all around her in the big room, and they were moving like saw grass in a breeze—they were anchored and graceful and animated from without. They were purposeless and real. They saw her and looked through her, as if she were a mirage.

The light ended.

She was blind again.

12 "You need Sylvania A-231s," the electrician said. "You know what they are?"

Frank looked where the man was pointing, at a spot high on the brick wall where it joined the north wall. He shielded his eyes; the bright blue November sky was in sharp, nearly painful contrast to the dark wall. He said, "No. What are they?"

"Well, they're spot lamps, of course," the electrician said testily. "And you need ten of 'em, I'd say. Twelve, if you want to be really safe."

"Really safe? From what?" Frank asked, his gaze still on the wall. He did not like looking into the electrician's face. It was large and lopsided, laced with pockmarks; the mouth was too big, the eyes were too small and close set, and when the man talked, stringy spittle hung between his upper and lower lips, so Frank found him hard to look at.

"From intruders," the electrician answered. "You got a big place like this, it sort of *invites* people to break in, don't it? And the only way you keep them out is to put spot lamps all around. Sylvania A-231s."

"Twelve of them," Frank said, gaze still on the brick wall, eyes still shielded from the bright blue sky.

The electrician nodded. "If you want to be safe."

"Are they expensive?"

The electrician nodded again, gravely. "Yes, they are. They're expensive. But you're paying for security, after all. Your security. Your wife's. Good-looking woman, Mr. Hitchcock. Put Sylvania A-231s up there and you'll keep her safe."

Frank sighed, wanted to comment on the man's observation,

but could think of nothing coherent to say, nothing, at any rate, that would mean anything to the electrician. "Do you have these spot lamps with you?"

The electrician shook his head. "Not in the truck. Be stupid to carry them in the truck. Big things. Got no room for them. Just a van, you know. But I can order them for you."

Frank took his gaze from the wall, rubbed his eyes, looked at the electrician; he could see only the man's chunky, dark silhouette, and this pleased him. "Good," Frank said. "Why don't you do that. How long will it take?"

"Couple days. They come outta Syracuse, you know. Get 'em down here on a UPS truck. So it'll only be a couple'a days."

"And you'll install them, of course."

The electrician shook his head. "Don't do no ladder climbing no more, Mr. Hitchcock. Sorry. Fell off a ladder last year. You want 'em installed, you'll have to get someone else to do it."

"Or do it myself."

The electrician nodded. "Yes sir. Or do it yourself."

They were having dinner three hours later when Allison looked across the table at Frank and said, "Did you feel that?"

"No," Frank said. "What?"

"That vibration. Like something fell over."

"I didn't feel a thing, Allison." He had made Swedish meatballs for supper. He popped one into his mouth and chewed hard; the meatball was rubbery. He had noticed that Allison had stuck to her egg noodles and hadn't touched the meatballs. "I'm sorry they're so tough," he said, swallowed, and smiled guiltily.

"Frank, I really did feel something. I'm surprised you didn't. I think we should check on it."

He shook his head. "It was those trucks. Those landfill trucks. Besides, what could fall over?"

It was a good question, she admitted. The subject was dropped.

*   *   *

The electrician brought the spot lamps over, in four large boxes, the following Friday morning. He helped Frank and Allison carry the boxes to the four points of the school where the spot lamps were to be installed, and then, after taking a check from Allison, drove off.

The morning was cloudy, and threatened rain, and Frank told Allison that he had reservations about climbing an aluminum ladder on such a morning. He talked briefly with her about postponing the whole job, but decided that he was procrastinating, that what he really didn't want to do was climb a ladder at all, especially two stories to where the spot lamps had to be installed. He told her that he had gotten through nearly fifty years of life without having to go more than a half-dozen feet up on a ladder, so he had supposed the chances were good that he'd finish the rest of his life without ever having to go up on a ladder again.

Allison smiled and said, "But you were wrong, weren't you, Frank?"

He nodded glumly, said, "I guess so," picked up the aluminum ladder he had bought at Sy's Hardware, in Danby, the day before. ("No, you don't want a wooden ladder, Mr. Hitchcock. They're heavier than shit, and you're not a young man anymore, are you?") The ladder was unwieldy at best, but he managed to position it—amid lots of grumbling and tottering about with the ladder leaning against him—so its top rung fell a couple of feet below the area where the first three spot lamps were to be installed.

He sighed, looked up at the ladder standing against the wall—it seemed to reach very high up indeed—and began his climb.

"Try not to look down, Frank," Allison suggested.

"I don't intend to look down," Frank said, already ten feet up the ladder, his gaze on the triple sockets above him where the spot lamps were to be installed. He stopped. He looked back at Allison. "I forgot the spot lamps," he said. "I'm coming down."

Allison chuckled, got one of the big lamps from the box near her feet, and handed it to Frank when he was a couple of rungs from the bottom of the ladder.

"Thanks," he said with a sigh, tucked the spot lamp under his arm, and started up the ladder again, slowly.

"It's not really that high up, Frank," Allison called when he was halfway to the top. "It only looks high up from where you are. I think I could reach up and touch your foot. Almost."

"Uh-huh," he managed.

"Really," she comforted.

He almost said, *Then maybe you should do this,* but then, to his surprise, he found that he was within easy reach of the spot-lamp sockets. He looked at them a moment. They were dark blue, pitted from weathering; he wondered if they worked after all these years of nonuse. He pursed his lips. "Do you think these are turned on?" he called, without looking down at Allison.

"You mean the spot lamps, Frank?" she called back.

He nodded. "Yes," he said, and chanced a quick look at her. She looked smaller than he liked, foreshortened, all head and breasts, the tips of her beige Wallabees sticking out below. "The spot lamps," he went on. Then he was looking at the spot-lamp sockets again and clinging to the ladder; his right elbow was around the vertical shaft of the ladder, and his right hand had the rung in a death grip; his feet were firmly planted at the instep, his knees against the second rung above his feet. He still held the Sylvania A-231 under his left arm. He noticed that there were multiple spiderwebs attached to the spot-lamp sockets and he wondered briefly if turning the spot lamps on would fry the spiders that had made the webs, or whether these were old webs—it was late in the year, after all—and that the spiders who had made them were long since dead.

"Lots of spiderwebs up here," he called to Allison, without looking down at her.

"I didn't know you were afraid of spiders, Frank," she called back, and he heard a quick chuckle come from her. He looked at her again. "You look odd," he said, and turned his gaze back to the spot-lamp sockets once more.

"Odd?" she said.

"Yes," he said. "Small. Fat," he continued, without looking at her. He maneuvered his left hand so he could grab the base of the spot lamp. It was difficult to do and still hold on to the ladder with his other hand, and he cursed under his breath a couple of times until he was able to get hold of the spot lamp. He smiled, relieved, reached, put the spot lamp up to the socket, turned it.

"I'm not fat," Allison protested.

"I didn't *say* you were fat," he called back, his eyes on the spot-lamp socket. The spot lamp wouldn't go in. "Damn," he whispered, took the spot lamp away, and peered up at the socket as best he could. The sun was behind the school, so the wall and socket were in shadow. He could see little. "I think there's something inside this socket," he called.

"You said I was short and fat," Allison called.

"I said you *looked* small and fat," he called back. "Do we have to talk about it now?"

She did not answer.

He glanced down at her. "It's just my vantage point," he said apologetically. "We both know you're not small and fat."

She closed her eyes for a moment. Clearly, she was hurt. "It was a dumb thing for you to say, Frank."

He sighed. He knew that she was right. He shouldn't have said it; he'd be feeling hurt, too, if she had said the same thing about him. Advancing middle age was responsible, he guessed. Both of them were spreading out, going gray, becoming old, though he more obviously than she, which was all right with him. He nodded. "Yes," he said. "It was a dumb thing to say. I'm sorry." He looked at the socket again, thinking that surely his eyes had adjusted to the darkness. He could see little; there was a whitish crusty substance inside the socket. Without thinking, he reached for it with his index finger.

"What the hell are you doing, Frank?" Allison called urgently.

He stopped what he was doing. "Jesus," he muttered. That was the way people killed themselves. They did stupid things like stick their fingers into spot-lamp sockets while they were standing on aluminum ladders. The brain's circuits got crossed, their priorities momentarily switched places, and they killed themselves. He shook his head. "I don't know. God, that was stupid, wasn't it?"

"You're scaring me, Frank. Maybe you should hire someone to do this."

He shook his head again, more vehemently. "No. That's not necessary. I can do it." He looked at her. "Get me a wooden-handled screwdriver, would you. I think there's one in my toolbox."

"And where's your toolbox?"

"Where it always is, of course. In the bedroom."

"I don't know where it *always* is, Frank." She looked accusingly at him. He looked back, wondering whether he should apologize again. After a moment, he felt something tickling the hairs on his left wrist. He looked. A small brown spider was making its way slowly—logy in the cool November-morning air—up his arm. He shook his arm frantically, in a momentary panic—he was still holding the spot lamp—to get the spider off. The spot lamp flew from his grip and shattered against the brick wall several feet below.

"Jesus, what are you doing up there?" Allison called.

He looked at the remains of the spot lamp on the grass below the ladder. "Making a fool of myself, apparently," he said. He turned his gaze on Allison. "Maybe I should put this off until another day."

"Or until we can hire someone to do it for us," Allison said.

The following day Frank left the school early in the morning, and when he returned late in the afternoon, he had a big, proud-looking German shepherd on a stout leash. The dog seemed to Allison to be quiet and well behaved as Frank brought it in through the school's west entrance and then led it quickly into the big gym/auditorium, where he closed the doors and slipped the dog's leash. The dog stayed put, its gaze straight ahead, on the opposite side of the gym—the stage and the frayed brown curtains.

"Where'd you get him, Frank?" Allison asked. She did not know how to respond to the animal. Her instincts were coaxing her to bend over and scratch it behind the ears, to say the things that people say to animals to keep them contented. But this animal seemed not to need such sweet nonsense. It seemed to be all business, and, she realized, she was a little frightened of it.

"A breeder," Frank answered. "In North Cohocton."

"Where's that?"

"About thirty miles north. I called him a month ago, and I've gone up there a couple of times to train with this dog."

"Train with him?"

"It's necessary. I had to get to know him, and be comfortable with him. And he had to get to know me."

"And be comfortable with you?"

Frank nodded. "That's right."

"And you're saying that when you told me you were going into town in the last couple of weeks, it was a lie?"

Frank shook his head. "Sometimes I wasn't telling you the whole truth. I didn't know what you'd think of me bringing him home."

"And you thought it would be all right to just spring him on me, is that what you're saying?"

Frank sighed. This was not going well. "Yes. I'm sorry. Perhaps I assumed wrong."

Allison shook her head. "It's all right. It was actually kind of my idea in the first place. I just wish you'd shared with me what you were doing. I don't like being lied to, Frank." It was a gentle admonishment, and she didn't want to carry on with it, so she continued, "So this dog is our . . . little pet, now?" She smiled uneasily.

Frank answered, "Not completely. We have to see how he responds to both of us, and to this place. He's trained to . . . he's a guard dog, actually. He should respond well. But if he doesn't, we can bring him back and try another one."

"He's trained to what, Frank?"

Frank did not answer at once, clearly uneasy. Then he said, "Well, he's trained to attack, of course. That's what guard dogs are supposed to do, isn't it? Attack? So that's what they do. At least, that's what they're supposed to do. The breeder himself is coming over on Friday"—two days away—"to continue his 'in-home training,' as he calls it."

"And what are we supposed to do until then? Do we let the dog have the run of the place? How do we know he won't attack *us,* Frank? I mean, how do *I* know that I'm not going to get out of bed in the middle of the night, and go down to the bathroom, and find him . . . going for my throat?"

Frank shook his head. "It can't happen, Allison. The breeder assured me of that. This dog knows you, now. He knows you're not an intruder because of the way *I* responded to you. It's simple. You were here when I came home. I did not react violently to you. So, as far as he's concerned, you're not a threat to his den."

"His *den?*"

"This school. He thinks of it as his den."

"How in the world does anybody know that?"

Frank gave her one of his patronizing smiles. "It's a logical conclusion drawn from years of observation, that's how." He realized that he sounded like a jerk; but, somehow, it was all right. The point he was making was valid. Whether he sounded like a jerk or not was unimportant. This was Allison, after all, and if he could sound like a jerk around anyone and be forgiven, it was her. "There are many conclusions that are drawn the same way."

"Okay, Frank, okay. Can you please just assure me that I'm not going to become his dinner one of these nights?"

"It's not likely." He smiled.

"Is that a joke?"

He nodded.

"Thanks," she said. "I'll laugh later."

"During the daytime, I'll keep him in one of the rooms in the north wing, okay?"

"Fine."

"And at night, believe me, if you get up and move about, then he won't attack you. He *knows* you, Allison. See, he's smiling at you."

She looked at the dog, who had what looked like a sardonic grin on his mouth. "Sure," she said, clearly unconvinced. "Smiling." She paused. "What's his name?" .

"Alex."

"Good name for a German shepherd."

"It is, isn't it?" Frank said, smiling. "Wonderful name for a German shepherd."

The night was very quiet and very dark, as it always was.

Allison swung her bare feet off the bed. She felt the cold floor. She felt the chill air on her exposed arms. She saw the darkness stretching out forever around her.

Frank snored fitfully on his side of the bed.

Allison rose and moved in quick, halting steps to the closed door. She opened it. She sensed the hallway to her right and left, sensed the big windows in front of her, the cold floor, her exposed arms, goose bumps. Talking from far away.

Frank snored fitfully on his side of the bed. It was unpleasant, but reassuring. It was an anchor. Something real.

She moved haltingly to her right, her memory replaying her experience in this same hallway from three nights before.

The darkness around her was like black water, and she could breathe raspingly, at best. She thought that she might drown in it, float in it, find herself dead in it.

She sensed the big windows to her left, the cold cinder-block walls to her right, the chill floor beneath her feet, the goose bumps rising on her exposed arms. She sensed her blindness here, her lungs filling with black water.

Frank snored fitfully on his side of the bed.

She sensed the massive wooden doors that led into the gym, and she reached and grasped the doorknobs hard. They were as cold as the black water she was breathing.

She turned the doorknobs. They clicked harshly in the quiet, fluid darkness. She pulled.

Light stabbed at her and she gasped in awe and confusion and terror.

Frank snored fitfully on his side of the bed.

The glaring light abated.

She saw people all around her in the big room, and they were still and expressionless—anchored and stiff and purposeless. The stuff of nightmares.

They saw her and looked through her, as if she were dead.

13

Frank found an opening to the area under the stage, a door whose knob had been removed, and when he opened it and went in—the area beneath the stage was slightly less than six feet deep (he was six feet tall and had to bend over a little)—he found several dozen boxes filled with costumes from various performances given at the school—*The Mouse That Roared, The Diary of Anne Frank,* and *South Pacific* were a few, according to the labels on the boxes. These costumes were in very good condition because the boxes had been well sealed.

The area beneath the stage was lighted—he had to bring a bulb in and put it in an overhanging socket—and he could see that there was more beneath the stage than simply storage area. There were two small, rectangular rooms, as well, each not much larger than a walk-in closet, and each with a door. When he looked, he found that these small rooms were empty. There was a closed door at the far end of each of these rooms; their wooden knobs wouldn't turn, and when he pulled on the knobs, the doors stayed securely shut. He guessed that they were not doors that actually led somewhere, but that they might simply have been prop doors which had been nailed in place, although he could not find evidence of this.

He told Allison about the rooms and their doors and she was delighted. Perhaps, she suggested playfully, the doors led to another dimension, "Another *place,* anyway," she said, and he realized that she was forming yet another of her complex fictions.

"It would be very hard to open those doors," he told her.

"This school is a big place," she went on. "Who knows what's underneath it."

He knew what was underneath it, a cement slab. There was no cellar, and he told Allison so.

"Oh, don't be an old poop," she chided smilingly. "Of course there's more than a damned cement slab, and I'll prove it, too."

"How are you going to do that?" he asked.

"Well, I'm going to open those doors, of course," she answered.

They got a crowbar from the trunk of the car and pried at one of the doors for a good long time. Finally, they were forced to admit that it was no use.

At last, Frank observed, "Hey, it's *our* school, right? So these are *our* doors. Let's just bash one in and see what's behind it."

Allison thought about this—she didn't like *bashing* things—but at last she agreed that bashing the door in was the only way they were going to get a look at what was behind it. So Frank searched in the school for a long while and finally came back with a length of lead pipe that he had found in the furnace room.

The door was a common panel door, and he focused all his strength on the right-side panel. It didn't take long before he had bashed the panel to smithereens, then he and Allison pulled away the bits of wood remaining and peered through the opening.

There was only another layer of wood just behind it, as if another door had been put there.

Allison wasn't satisfied. She had Frank bash the door that was in the other room, although the results were the same. "Shit!" she whispered, which surprised him because she rarely cursed. "Doesn't that bite the big one!"

"Doesn't that what?" Frank asked.

"Bite the big one!" she repeated. "Doesn't that bite the big one!"

"What big one?" He felt ignorant.

She looked strangely at him. "The big *penis,*" she explained, and smiled; it was an odd smile from her, because it was sarcastic and venomous. "The big *cock!* Understand now, Mr. Nerdo?"

"Sure," he said. "I didn't mean to be so stupid."

Several nights later, Allison found Frank sitting in front of the windows in the hallway, with the venetian blinds up and the night-lights casting their multiple reflections on the windows. He didn't realize that she was standing beside him until she spoke— "Couldn't sleep, Frank?" she said, which startled him; his hands flew into the air, and a low-pitched whooping noise leaped from his throat.

"I didn't know you were there," he said.

She chuckled, clearly pleased that she had startled him. "What are you doing, Frank?"

He shrugged. "Nothing. Remembering."

"Remembering what?"

He shrugged again. He felt foolish. "Whatever there is to remember."

"Uh-huh."

There was a light switch for the overhead fluorescents; it was just down the hall. She went to it, flicked it on. The fluorescents blinked once, then again, then the hallway was bathed in their bluish white light.

Frank looked quizzically at her. "Why'd you do that?"

"Why not?"

"I wouldn't do it to you."

"So what? I just think it's kind of a funny thing for you to be doing. Sitting out here in the dark."

"But it's not dark. I have the night-lights."

She pursed her lips. "You're weird, Frank." She turned the fluorescents off and went back to the bedroom.

Frank thought, *Why is she acting like this?* Moments later, he went back to the bedroom.

Allison switched off her bedside lamp and lay back. "I didn't see the dog," she said.

"He's there," Frank said.

"I hope so." A pause. "I went past the place where he usually spends the night, and he wasn't there."

"Probably patrolling," Frank said.

"Patrolling?"

"Sure. That's what they're trained to do. Patrol. They make the rounds. They go down one hallway, and back again, then down another, and another. They don't sleep much, at least not at night."

She shuddered. "Jesus, that gives me the willies."

"I can't see why. He isn't a ghost. He's a dog. He's doing what he was trained to do."

"Alex?" Frank called, his gaze on the darkened hallway ahead of him. He didn't like the idea of taking the dog by surprise; he still did not trust it completely—a fact he was not about to share with Allison. "Alex?" he called again, and peered down the hallway, hoping to see the dog's gray form emerge from the darkness. But the dog did not appear, and Frank called to him again, without response.

Perhaps the dog was indeed patrolling. It was likely, considering the hour. But he would have heard the dog's nails tap-tapping on the gray linoleum (the breeder had suggested clipping the dog's nails, but Frank decided it was easier to gauge where the dog was if he could hear him).

"Alex, dammit!" Frank called. The dog had phenomenal hearing. If Alex was at the farthest point from Frank—at the end of the north hallway, in the wing they did not use—then Frank had merely to whisper the dog's name and it would come running. The breeder had proven it. "Do you know," the breeder went on, "that a dog's sense of smell is fifty to one hundred million times more sensitive than ours?" It was an amazing statistic, Frank thought now.

"C'mon, dog!" he called.

He would have to fix the overhead lights in this hallway, he told himself. Or put up some wall lamps. That would be interesting. Brass, swing-arm wall lamps on these pastel peach cinder-block walls. It was almost camp.

From a good distance behind him, he guessed, he heard the tap-tapping of the dog's nails on the linoleum. He turned around, looked. He saw a small rectangle of bright light at the far end of the hallway. It was coming from their bedroom, he knew; the light was bright only in contrast to the darkness around it. Beyond that rectangle of light, there was more darkness.

A form emerged briefly from that darkness, into the rectangle of light. Then it was gone.

The dog, of course, Frank told himself. But it had looked too tall, had looked as if it were moving on two legs.

"Alex?" he called.

The tap-tapping noise grew louder. It came from the opposite direction, now—from down the hallway that branched to the left just ahead.

Frank followed the sound.

When he got to the spot where the hallway branched left, he stopped. Someone was standing only a few feet away. Frank could sense the person more than see him; the darkness here was almost total.

"Who are you?" Frank said, voice trembling. "What are you doing here?"

He heard one whispered word in response; he was not even sure he had heard it, not sure it hadn't been merely the rush of water into the radiators. That word was "Please!"

Frank could say nothing. He wanted to see this person who was speaking to him. He did not want to hear a disembodied voice in the darkness. (Joey's last words to him had been disembodied. An entreaty through a closed door.)

He heard very soft footfalls on the linoleum; they could have been the footfalls of a cat. They faded. After a short time, they were gone.

The field mouse and her brood had escaped the black water, though the mother field mouse had had some anxious moments as she pulled and tugged and coaxed her infants to safety.

She had spent a good long time in the fissure in the cinder-block wall and it had been a safe, comfortable, and warm enough home, especially since she had lined it with bits of blankets, old newspaper, and fluffing from a pillow she'd found in an open cabinet near the gym. She had felt secure there, with her babies; life was as it should be for field mice—time passed, there was no pain, she and her brood were rarely hungry.

She had set up a new home, far away from the corner where the fissure had been, in the open area of a desk turned up on its top. She had spent several days building her nest there, and in her feeble, mouse way, she thought that it was an even better home than the fissure in the cinder block had been. It was warmer; the darkness—and therefore safety—was even more intense.

But tonight, all that had changed, suddenly.

There was a strange sort of light in the room that she had never seen before, a light unlike the light of the sun or the moon. It was a light that hurt her sensitive eyes and made her babies burrow deep into her belly. There was a constant, low gurgling noise, too, as if some large creature were angry or sick.

She wanted very much to leave this place.

"I've grown used to the quiet, haven't you?" Allison said from her side of the bed.

Frank answered simply, "No. Not yet." *There was someone in the school, Allison.*

She glanced at him but saw only the hint of his profile against the dark windows that formed his backdrop. "Is something wrong?"

I don't know what he was doing here. He was there one moment, then he was gone. "No. Nothing's wrong." A pause. "I was thinking about Joey."

She turned her head away from him. "Oh," she said.

"You disapprove?"

"How can I do that? It would be stupid, don't you think?"

"Yes," he whispered. *I should be looking for this person now. I don't know why I'm not. He's an intruder. A trespasser.*

In another part of the school, the furnace hummed into life. Frank braced for the inevitable rush of hot water through the radiators.

Allison said, "We'll never know if he's happy." Her voice was trembling.

Frank said nothing. He did not like this topic. She had broached it more than once since Joey's death, and he had told her more than once that it was senseless to discuss; they might as well discuss how many angels could fit on the head of a pin. She had agreed.

"I'm sorry," she said. "I know this is something you'd rather not talk about."

"That's true," he said, and thought he sounded insensitive, uncaring. "It bothers me as much as it bothers you. He was my son, too." A pause. "Allison, I was out in the hallway looking for Alex. . . ." He stopped. Why make her fearful unnecessarily? Perhaps there had been no one. Only his own fears and fantasies and sadness making ghosts out of the darkness.

"*Is* our son, Frank!" Allison said, ignoring the second part of what he'd said. "*Is* our son. That will never change."

He sighed. He said nothing. He wished to God that she would keep these thoughts to herself. For a year after Joey's death, they had propped each other up in their grief—a grief that was overwhelming, and that threatened to destroy them both.

Then, as if through silent agreement, Joey was mentioned only rarely. Time had not been the great healer that they had hoped it would be. The void in their lives that Joey's death had created seemed to grow more vast and more suffocating whenever they talked about him together; they weren't sure why. And so, after a while, they stopped talking about him. They each had their own most precious memories of their child, and each bore a pain that was unique, that could not be shared and, being shared, assuaged.

Frank had always thought that his memories of that last day with his son were particularly painful. What other father who had lost a son had lost him that way?

"I would simply like to know if he's happy," Allison whispered.

"Yes," Frank said.

"Yes, you think he is happy?"

"Dammit, Allison—" he blurted out. "I'm sorry." He sighed. "I don't know. Who can know such things? *How* can you know such things?"

"Sandra says there's a way."

He looked at her again. His eyes had adjusted to the darkness; he thought that she was smiling hopefully. "Who's Sandra?"

She turned her head toward him. Her eyes glistened. "A friend. A new friend. I haven't mentioned her?"

"No."

"She's a woman who lives nearby; I met her when I was staking out my garden. She's told me things . . . wonderful things. I'm sure that I've mentioned her, Frank. Haven't I mentioned her?"

"What kind of things has she told you?"

"Only what I said. That there are ways of knowing what we had always assumed was . . . unknowable."

He was getting angry. Why had Allison kept her meetings with this woman a secret from him? "Goddammit, Allison—" His anger made him suddenly mute.

Allison said nothing.

Frank rolled over, away from her. He thought of getting out of bed, of leaving the room. He did not want to be near her now. She had disappointed him, and he was angry with her for it.

Hot water rushed through the radiators. Frank lurched in the bed. "Jesus!" he whispered, angry now, as well, that he had been taken by surprise.

Allison said, "She told me that we live in a very special place, Frank, that there are only a couple places like it in the whole world. We're so very lucky, Frank." She paused meaningfully. "We can go and visit our son."

Frank could think of no coherent response. Clearly she believed what she was saying, and his mere statement of disbelief was not going to shake her. So, it was true; she had taken Joey's death far harder than he had, and heaven knew that *he,* when he thought about it, still reeled from it after ten years. She was more vulnerable, that was obvious. He was *her* son; she had given him birth, and then, so quickly, he had been taken from her.

Frank turned his head away from her.

"Don't you want to know how, Frank?"

"How we can visit our son? No, Allison." He could hear his voice trembling, knew that he was on the verge of tears. "It's cold tonight. I think that I'd rather sleep."

"I understand that, Frank," Allison said. "I do understand it."

She was so confused, he thought. She grasped at any hope. It was forgivable.

She said, "I'm just so . . . angry. And so frustrated. Please understand."

He said nothing. He listened to the radiators continue to fill up with water, heard Allison turn away from him, thought he heard the tap-tap of Alex's nails in the hallway. He did not feel safe, suddenly. Nor did he feel happy. The woman he loved was slowly, but inexorably, slipping away from him.

| 14 | In Danby, on the last day of November, Frank encountered a woman named Elaine Cryer, who stopped him while he was shopping at Hearst's A&P and asked if he was the man who had bought the school on Ohio Road. She was a tall, firmly built woman of thirty or so, who had a very white, oddly flat face. Her four-year-old son sat in the basket of her shopping cart, playing with a red Matchbox car.

"Yes," Frank told her, "I bought the school."

"And you're living in it?" she asked, clearly astonished.

"Yes, we're living in it."

"We?"

"My wife and I."

She smiled, still clearly astonished. "Isn't it awfully big for just the two of you?"

"It's big, yes," Frank answered, and found that, again, he could not explain exactly why they had bought the school on Ohio Road. "We like big," he went on, smiling cordially. "We've given some thought to turning it into a kind of bed-and-breakfast inn."

Elaine Cryer smiled noncommittally and introduced herself and her son, whose name was Johnathan; the child looked briefly at Frank, passed the red Matchbox car in front of his small gray eyes, smiled, and said, "Zoom!"

"Zoom!" Frank said.

The child's smile vanished abruptly.

His mother explained, "He's not used to people talking to him. He's got no brothers or sisters, and I live alone, and people usually ignore him."

"That's too bad," Frank said, and meant it.

"Yeah," she said, "isn't it." She got a six-pack of Diet Faygo

from the counter behind her and put it into the cart beside
Johnathan; the boy shoved the six-pack toward the front of the
cart. His mother went on, "Kid'll grow up to be an ax murderer
or something unless he starts socializing."

"I doubt it will come to that," Frank said lamely.

She gave him a broad smile, as if she were about to tell him
a joke that she never tired of telling. "You heard about all the
kids that died up there, right?"

"Yes, I have," Frank answered hesitantly, taken aback by
her offhand attitude toward the deaths. "Awful thing."

"Sure," she said, and her smile vanished, "real awful. Mr.
Blom, too. He was crazy."

"Mr. Blom?" Frank asked.

"The teacher who died. Biology teacher."

"Oh. Yes."

She nodded, her long, dark blond hair moving around her
head. "His daughter used to baby-sit for me. When I was a kid, I
mean. She was crazy, too. All the Bloms were crazy. Craziest
people in Danby. Never changed their clothes. He wore the same
suit for ten years, every day. I remember smelling him when he
walked past me in the hall. Smelled of formaldehyde. I didn't
know it was formaldehyde, then. I just knew I didn't like it." She
smiled again. "I guess the Bloms were the craziest people in a town
full of crazy people, Mr. Hitchcock." Then, with a nod, and a "Stay
warm," she walked off, her son Johnathan repeating again and again
as he waved his red Matchbox car about, "Zoom, zoom, zoom!"

The following day, Frank, who was making himself a
tomato-and-lettuce sandwich in the kitchen, told Allison that he
wanted to go up to the roof.

"Why do you want to do that?" Allison asked, smiling.

"Well, I think it's obvious," Frank answered. He cut a slice
from a tomato on the cutting board and gently laid it on the
sandwich he was making. "There's probably half an acre of roof

up there, and the chances are that some of it needs patching. After all, this school has been abandoned for what—ten years?"

"But we haven't seen any evidence of a leak, Frank."

"It hasn't rained or snowed *that* much, has it? And we can't say, either, that we've made a very thorough search. Remember that crack in the gym wall, too." He cut another slice of tomato; too thin. He cut another slice, laid it on the sandwich. "You've got to remember that these false ceilings could hide a lot of damage . . . a lot of potential problems."

"The roof is probably a foot deep in snow," Allison pointed out.

He shook his head. "Snow's mostly melted. Haven't you noticed? And even if there is a slight snow cover up there, I think that will make it easier to spot leaks; there'll be little . . . little shallow areas, you know." He smiled. It was a good theory, especially for having been produced on the spur of the moment.

She looked at him. Her smile widened. "You just want to go up to the roof because it's *there,* don't you, Frank? It's kind of an adventure."

He shrugged. "I don't know. It's flat, so it's safe, and it would be a useful and interesting thing to do."

"Why didn't you say that in the first place? Why are you always trying to convince me that your . . . adolescent cravings have their basis in reason?"

He put the top on his sandwich, went to the refrigerator, looked back with his hand on the door handle. "That's unfair, Allison. All of us have 'adolescent cravings,' as you put it."

"Some of us more than others, Frank. And believe me, I'm not judging you. I think it's cute . . . no, that's not the right word. You stopped being cute a long time ago."

He opened the refrigerator, took out a can of root beer, opened a cupboard, got a glass. "You want to come up there with me?"

She shook her head earnestly. "No way. I don't even know how *you're* going to get up there. You don't like ladders any more than I do."

"There's access behind the gym." He poured the root beer into the glass.

"Is there?" Allison asked.

"Yes. There's a stairway."

But the access—at the end of a long hallway behind the gym—was more precarious than he'd hoped. It was very dark. "There was a light the last time I looked, Allison. It must have blown," he said, flicking a switch at the bottom of the narrow metal stairway. The stairway ascended at a steep angle; the tubular metal railing was very low, so he had to stoop over slightly to keep hold of it.

While Allison watched from below, he went up. It was a clear day and he expected that the trapdoor above, which he had seen on his earlier inspection—would be framed by light. But it was dark, and when he got to it, he found that it was securely shut. "Dammit!" he breathed.

"What's wrong, Frank?" Allison asked from below. He supposed that she couldn't see him in the darkness up here.

"Damned door's locked," he called.

"Well, there must be a key."

"Sure," Frank called back. "One of the three hundred keys"—an exaggeration—"that we got from the real-estate man. Hell, I can't even *see* the lock." He sighed. "I'm coming down. I'll find a bulb, or a flashlight—"

"Frank?" she cut in. Her voice was trembling.

"Yes?"

"Frank, is there someone up there with you?"

"Someone up here? No." He didn't like her tone. It made him nervous. He glanced about below him on the stairway. Allison seemed to be much farther off than he thought she should be. After all, it was only fifteen or twenty feet up here, at most. "How could there be anyone else up here?"

"I don't know. I saw . . . someone there with you."

"Dammit, turn on a light, Allison."

"Where?" she called back.

"Out in the hallway," he called. "Turn on the light in the hallway, for God's sake." He was very nervous now. He could feel that something was with him on the narrow stairway.

"The light in the hallway is already on. Come down, Frank. Please."

"Jesus, yes," he whispered, and started down. He stopped. He couldn't see.

"My God," he breathed.

"Frank?"

"Allison, I can't see!"

The view he had had of Allison, of the lower part of the stairway, of the alcove—all of it was gone.

"Frank, please," Allison pleaded "come down. You're scaring me."

But then she was there again, at the center of a rectangle of dim light. Then she was gone. Then the stairway was visible. Then it was gone. The alcove. Gone. Allison again, looking up at him, wide-eyed. Gone.

And Frank realized that it was as if he was seeing through a crowd of people that was moving around him, up the stairway, blocking his vision.

"Jesus," he whispered. "I'm coming down," he called, and started down, aware of the all-too-loud clank of his feet against the metal stairs.

He could feel them now. People moving around him. People moving up, down, brushing past him, shouldering into him in the darkness. He pleaded, "I can't *see* them, I can't *see* them!"

"Who, Frank?" Allison called urgently. "Who's up there with you?"

He reached out with his free hand. He felt the air moving past him, as if he were feeling an updraft. He shook his head in fear and confusion.

"Frank, I'm coming up there!" Allison called.

"No. Stay where you are!" he called back.

Then he was alone on the stairway.

"My God," he whispered.

"Frank?" Allison pleaded. "For Christ's sake—"

"There's no one here, Allison." he called. "There never was anyone here but me." A pause. "I'm coming down."

The night was dark and quiet, as it always was.

Allison swung her bare feet off the bed and felt the air on her exposed arms. She saw the darkness stretching out in front of her. And, far ahead, a pinpoint of light.

Frank slept soundly on his side of the bed.

Allison rose, moved quickly to the open door, down the hallway to her right, over the cold linoleum, past the big windows. She heard talking from far away. It grew louder. The pinpoint of light grew brighter, and larger.

Frank began to snore fitfully on his side of the bed. It was unpleasant, but reassuring. It was something real.

The darkness around her was warm and comforting and she breathed heavily of it, felt her body absorbing it, absorbing the darkness as if it were nourishment, giving her a strange, knife-edged kind of ecstasy that all but stole her breath away. She thought that she might find herself dead from such ecstasy, and the thought gave her pleasure.

Frank snored fitfully on his side of the bed.

The massive wooden doors that led into the gym were framed by light. She reached, grasped the doorknobs hard, pulled the doors open.

Light spilled over her like fire and she gasped in awe and hope.

Frank snored fitfully on his side of the bed.

The glaring light dimmed.

She saw people all around her in the big room, and they were smiling and nodding at her.

"Welcome," one said.

"You'll love this," said one. "All of it. What an experience you'll have!"

The light ended.

15 The tall figure at the end of the dim hallway was clearly the figure of a woman, and when Allison, drawing closer, finally recognized her, she—Allison—stopped walking; she was both confused and a little angry at the same time.

The figure stood very still, as if expecting that the dog, Alex, would show up at any moment.

"Sandra?" Allison called. "That's you, isn't it? What are you doing here?"

"Hello, Allison." Sandra's voice was soft but steady. "I'm sorry. I didn't know you were up."

"*What* are you doing here?" Allison repeated. "My God, it's past twelve—"

"One-fifteen, actually," Sandra said. "And again, I'm sorry."

Allison started walking again. She was a good thirty feet away from Sandra, and she walked slowly because she was a bit fearful. How well did she know this woman, after all? "We have a dog, you know," she said. "I'm afraid you could be in some danger unless you leave at once. I haven't learned to control—"

"The dog is no problem, Allison. And please, don't be afraid of me. I sense that you are, and there's no need. I . . . we are no threat to you or to your home."

Allison was close enough now that she could see, in the dim light filtering down the hall from far behind her, that there was something very odd about Sandra. She was standing so stiffly, and her face—what Allison could see of it—seemed also to be oddly stiff, as if it were a mask. "Sandra, are you all right? Are you in some kind of trouble?" She didn't wait for an answer. "How did you get in?"

"There are ways in, Allison. You should be aware of that by now. And, please, don't come any closer."

Allison stopped walking. "Just tell me what you're doing, Sandra. This is my home. You're intruding, and I would like to know why."

"No, we . . . I had no intention of intruding. I realize that this is your home. Forgive me, please. As I said, I had no idea you'd be up." Her voice was as oddly flat and emotionless as her face. It was as if she were inside an effigy of herself. "I need to go past you, Allison. I must ask that you turn away so that I may do that."

Allison shook her head. "If I'm going to turn away, I have to have some reason."

"Dammit, Allison, I'm running out of time." Still, her face and her voice betrayed no emotion. "There are . . . circumstances here, in this school, that you cannot yet understand; I've told you that before. Circumstances *we* do not understand."

"Who is 'we'?"

"Please turn away and let me pass, Allison. My time is running out. Please, *please* don't deny me my time here; you have no idea exactly *what* you're denying me—" Her voice betrayed a hint of emotion, and her face—looking at it was like looking at a ceramic mask in a dimly lighted room—seemed to embrace that hint of emotion, as if there were some small insect moving beneath the skin.

"I don't want to *deny* you anything, Sandra. I merely want to know what I have a right to know—I want to know what you're doing here."

"Damn you!" There was great emotion in Sandra's voice now. *"Damn* you!" She turned and moved off down the hallway to her right. Allison went after her. She saw her for a brief moment, far down the hallway, but in the next moment, the woman had vanished into the darkness.

Allison spent a lot of time looking for Sandra, but to no avail. At one point, Alex found her and seemed to regard her presence in his nighttime hallways with suspicion, though she was glad to see him.

When she went back to the bedroom, she did not tell Frank what had happened. She would have to wake him to tell him, and there really was no reason it couldn't wait until morning. She realized at once how foolish that sounded. She realized that she found the whole encounter grimly fascinating, that she found Sandra herself to be someone with whom she felt an odd sort of kinship.

She lay awake for some time, listening to the tap-tap of Alex's nails on the linoleum hallways, the hum of the furnace, the intermittent rush of water into the radiators. She did not sleep. She half expected Sandra to appear in the room. But, at last, the sun rose, light flooded in.

Frank woke reluctantly and looked over at her.

"'Morning," he said.

"Good morning," she said, and was surprised at how rested and cheerful she sounded.

He swung his feet to the floor, stretched with his back to her. He turned his head. "Got to feed the dog." He stood, retrieved his robe from the coat tree near the bed, put his slippers on. "I'll make the coffee, too," he said as he was opening the door. "You go ahead and be lazy if you want."

"That's all right," she said, throwing the blankets off. "How does French toast sound?"

"Great," he said, and went out the door. Alex was waiting patiently for him.

16 Frank went to the north wing of the school that afternoon to gauge how much work would be required to fix the windows there, and when he went back to the bedroom, and then to the kitchen, he could not find Allison. He called to her repeatedly. He looked into all the rooms, the kitchen, and the cafeteria, but without luck. At last, in the gym, he called, "Allison, where in the *hell* are you?" and she called back, "I'm in here. Under the stage." She was in one of the little rooms there. Over the space of an hour or so, she had removed one of the doors that he'd bashed in and had found that what had appeared to be a wall behind it was, indeed, a flat, pine door.

She was very animated, very delighted. She looked like a girl again, Frank thought. Her eyes were wide and bright with pleasure, excitement, and anticipation. "It's locked, Frank, but I think we can get it open," she exclaimed. The pieces of the original door lay around her; she had pulled it apart with the crowbar that Frank had left in the room.

He rapped on the door once, twice, very hard.

"Do you think there's someone in there?" Allison asked, grinning.

"No," Frank answered, and shook his head earnestly, though he knew she'd been joking. "I just wanted to see what it sounded like, whether it sounded hollow or not."

"It's a hollow-core type of door, Frank," she said. "So, naturally, it's going to sound hollow if you knock on it."

"Well, yes," he said, "I know that," and rapped on it again as if to show her that he knew it. "But I can tell that there's an open area behind it, too."

"You thought there wasn't?"

"I thought it was possible, yes. Why not? Maybe it was just put here as part of the framing for the underside of the stage, I don't know. I've seen whole buildings that were made entirely of old doors."

"You're babbling, Frank."

He shrugged. "No, I wouldn't say that—"

"Let's bash it in," she suggested, and picked up the crowbar, which lay at her feet.

He put his hand on her wrist. "Allison, no, let's not do that. I mean, the door is here for a *reason*, right? If it leads into a kind of crawl space, then it's here to keep the cold air out. Your original idea was better. We'll pick the lock, okay?"

She seemed disappointed. Reluctantly, she let Frank take the crowbar from her.

They had no luck picking the lock. It was a standard key lock, and none of the keys that the realtor had provided would work in it, nor would a hairpin or a nail file. A small brass plate had been fitted over the lock area itself, so they could not simply shove a credit card in there and slip the bolt, and the hinges were on the other side of the door, so removing them was not an option.

The fact that the hinges were on the other side of the door bothered Frank. Hinges were always put on the *insides* of doors; the only conclusion he could come to, in this case, was that the other side of that flat, hollow-core pine door *was* the inside, and that didn't make any sense.

Allison didn't agree. "Maybe there aren't any hinges," she said. "Maybe it's just . . . stuck in there." She indicated the crowbar on the floor. "I still say that we should bash it in. Hell, it's pretty flimsy, Frank. It'll bust apart in no time."

He smiled at her. "You're enjoying the hell out of this, aren't you, Allison?"

"You bet I am. It's a *mystery*, Frank. It's like . . . like C. S. Lewis, or Madeleine L'Engle." She paused, continued dreamily, "Remember how Joey loved C. S. Lewis?" Another pause; her face brightened. "Only this is *real!*"

"Well," he said, "it's a real *door,* anyway." He felt like an old poop for saying it, especially when he saw Allison's face drop.

"You really know how to rain on our parade, don't you, Frank?" she snapped.

"Our parade?" he asked.

"Joey's and mine," she said, and with that, she stalked from the room.

"I'm sorry," he called after her, mystified by her overreaction and concerned that she had included Joey in her game playing. "Please, I'm sorry, Allison. Come on back. We can bash the door in. I'd *love* to bash the door in! Allison?" But it was no use.

Their third visitors at the school on Ohio Road, after Iris and Sam left in November, were Frank's mother and father. He was very surprised to see them, even though they had written two weeks earlier to say they would be visiting. The bizarre events at the school had put their upcoming visit out of his mind.

Their names were Margaret and Joseph, and they almost literally appeared at the double doors in the school's west entrance. It was early morning, not quite 7:30; Frank was walking past the doors, on his way to the showers, with only a white bath towel around his neck, and he saw them out of the corner of his eye. He lurched, grabbed the towel, threw it around himself. When he had first seen them out of the corner of his eye, he had had no idea who they were; they could have been anyone—neighbors, kids, who knew?—and there he was, flopping naked down the school hallway. Aside from the embarrassment to him, and to them, what would they think? Heaven forbid, probably the truth—that this old poop got a perverse kick out of walking naked down the school hallway.

And even when he saw that it was his mother and father, that fact still took a few seconds to register. *There* they were, smiling benignly—his mother's gaze slightly averted—behind the double glass doors.

Frank put on a big smile and opened the doors. A blast of cold air rushed in that took his breath away. "Mom, Dad!" he managed. "My God, what are you doing here? You didn't phone."

"We wrote you a letter, Frankie," his mother admonished. Frank nodded, said, "Oh. Yes, I remember."

His father extended his hand; Frank took it. His father's handshake was very firm, as it had always been. "Good to see you, boy. I didn't expect to see so *much* of you, of course." He smiled, obviously pleased with his joke. Frank's mother, her gray-blue eyes still averted, stepped forward and smacked the air near her son's cheek. She smelled of lilac perfume. "Get some clothes on now, son," she suggested in her kindly way. "We can wait for you right here."

"Mom," he protested, "that's not necessary." He stepped aside. "Come in. Please."

His mother gave him a very quick once-over, then she and her husband stepped into the school.

His father said, looking around, "You actually *live* here, Frank?"

"Yes, Dad. We do. We like it."

"I'm sure you do, Frank. But isn't it a little . . . abnormal?"

"I don't think so. It's *unusual,* I'll admit that."

"No, son," his father said matter-of-factly, as if giving him the benefit of his wisdom, "it's abnormal. It's perverse, living in a place like this. Walking around the way you do. What about your neighbors? Maybe you were something to look at twenty years ago, but you aren't anymore. You got a belly, Frank, and a little flat behind. People don't like to look at such things—"

"Dad, please," Frank interrupted, "why don't I go and get dressed, and you two can have a look around."

His father regarded him silently for a moment, then, nodding, said, "Sure, we can do that."

Frank dressed, and when he went back to the west entrance, his parents weren't there. He found them after a few minutes. They were watching a young man of fourteen or so, whom Frank had never seen before, run laps around the gym.

"Nice-looking young man," Mrs. Hitchcock said as Frank came in the gym door.

The boy was tall and thin, blond, crew cut, and wore a white T-shirt, blue sneakers, and black gym shorts. He looked, from the sheen of sweat on him, like he'd been running for quite a long time. Frank watched, astonished, as the boy rounded the far side of the gym, then—*slap, clop, slap, clop* (the sole of one sneaker seemed to be separating from the upper)—headed their way. When he was a dozen feet from them, Frank smiled and held his hand up. The boy kept running, his expression blank, mouth, impossibly, closed tight. His eyes remained focused on the floor, that bright sheen of sweat all over his face and arms. When he passed, the odor of his sweat was almost overpowering.

"Young man?" Frank called after him.

"Oh, let him run," Mrs. Hitchcock admonished.

"Best exercise in the world," Mr. Hitchcock said. "You should do a little of it yourself, Frank."

Frank called again to the boy running—who was halfway around the gym, now: "Young man, could you come here, please."

But the boy didn't acknowledge him.

"Very *firm,* isn't he?" Mrs. Hitchcock said, and Frank noted, with discomfort, the edge of pleasure in her tone. He glanced at her. Her round face, still smooth and pink although she was close to seventy-five years old, was alight with pleasure.

"Mom?" Frank said.

"Yes, Frankie?" she said, without turning to look at him; her eyes were following the boy as he moved gracefully around the gym, his blue sneakers making that rhythmic *slap/clop, slap/clop* noise.

"Nothing," Frank said, and called again, "Young man, I have to talk with you. This is a private residence—" The boy had circled and was approaching them again, his gaze on the floor, arms pumping gracefully, mouth open wide now, but oddly still, as if he weren't breathing, that bright sheen of sweat shifting and rippling with his movements.

Frank stepped out in front of him.

The boy veered around Frank without even a moment's hesitation, as if he had known what Frank was going to do.

Frank turned and looked at his retreating back. "You're going to have to stop running and talk to me sooner or later!" he yelled.

"Let him be, son," Frank's father said. "He's not doing anybody any harm."

"Dad, that's hardly the point, is it? He's *trespassing.*"

"He probably doesn't realize it. How could he know that someone's actually *living* here?"

"And *that's* not the point, either—"

"So firm," Mrs. Hitchcock breathed.

Frank glanced at her. She was following the boy with her eyes, which were wide. Her cheeks were flushed; her mouth hung open slightly.

Frank glanced at his father and saw that he was smiling paternally at her, as if in silent, amused acceptance of some perverse but pardonable eccentricity. He looked at Frank and winked. "Doesn't want to get old," he whispered. "Who does?"

Frank saw that the boy was running directly toward him. Frank stepped out of the way. The boy veered around him, through the open double doors. Frank heard the softer *slap/clop* of his sneakers on the gray linoleum. "What in the hell?" Frank breathed, and stepped out into the hallway.

He saw the boy as a thin shadow against the bright morning sunlight shining at right angles on him through the school's big windows.

The shadow weakened.

"Wait!" Frank called.

The *slap/clop* of the boy's sneakers faded to a whisper, and then to nothing.

"I said wait, Goddammit!"

The shadow thinned to a barely visible vertical line. The vertical line shimmered in the morning sunlight. It vanished. The boy was gone.

Frank moved forward a few feet. He supposed that he saw

the double doors closing, then that he saw movement down the covered walkway.

He heard his mother say, behind him, "What a nice, *firm* boy."

Frank showed his mother and father into the kitchen and made coffee for them.

Allison appeared in the kitchen doorway. She looked genuinely happy to see Frank's parents, though he knew that she wasn't. "Hello, Margaret, Joseph," she said, came forward, and kissed them both on the cheek. Mr. Hitchcock gave her a little pat on the behind, a habit she disliked, but she managed to give him a sideways, wincing smile. She was dressed in her blue nightgown and a white, floor-length, terry-cloth robe. As always, Frank's father couldn't keep his eyes off her.

"Have some of this weak tea your husband made for us," he invited. Then he said, to his wife, "Mother, maybe you could make us some real coffee. That's my girl." She was on her way to the stove before he finished his request, as he had known she would be.

As she passed him, he gave her a pat on her substantial behind, and she swiped playfully at his hand. "Oh stop that now, Joseph," she said.

They left early that afternoon. They explained that they were on their way south: "To the Virginias, Frankie," Mrs. Hitchcock said. "We're looking for a house there." He protested that they should stay for at least the night, but they would not hear of it. "Place is spooky as a tomb," Mr. Hitchcock said.

And when Frank leaned over to kiss his mother good-bye, she whispered into his ear, "It's haunted, Frankie." When he straightened, she gave him a little coy smile and a maternal nod, as if the two of them—she and her son—were now the keepers of a dark and wonderful secret.

After they had left, Allison called him to the windows that looked out on the playground and said, "Who do you think *they* are?" and gestured with a nod of her head.

He looked where she'd indicated. There were several people standing just beyond the swings and teeter-totters, maybe two hundred feet away. They were standing very still, and they were looking at the school. There was a man and a woman and two children; the man and the woman were flanked by the children. The man was holding the hand of one of the children, a girl, Frank guessed, though both children were dressed in pants, an oversized gray winter coat, and a blue ski hat, and it was all but impossible to tell their sexes from that distance because their faces were little more than pink blurs.

They started toward the school. Allison lurched a bit, startled because they had started moving all at once, as if they were a monolithic mass. "They're coming here," she whispered.

"Yes," Frank said, "I can see that." He looked at her. "We could pretend we're not home."

"I think it's too late for that. I think they've seen us." They were still a good seventy-five yards off. "Frank," Allison continued, her tone signaling a brief change of subject. "Remember the other day when we were eating, and I said I felt a vibration, like something had fallen?"

"Yes."

"I found what it was. Part of a wall in one of the rooms in the south wing."

"Good Lord. Why didn't you tell me before?"

"I just discovered it this morning. I was coming back from the showers, and I saw a door open down the south corridor, and when I went there, I saw all these cinder blocks on the floor, and daylight pouring in."

"Dammit. We'll have to have another look a little later. After we see what these people want."

|17| The man and woman and two children moved quickly and with a strange kind of grace over the lawns that separated the school from the playground. The grass was covered by a couple inches of old snow that had turned gray from ambient pollution, and as one—man, woman, child, child—they lifted their feet over it, as if it were somehow important not to shuffle through it, until the pink blurs that were their faces resolved into big, almond-shaped dark eyes, full lips, and noses red from cold. They were a family, that was obvious, and when they were within a dozen yards of where Allison and Frank stood watching, behind the windows, the man smiled and nodded and pointed at them, turning his gaze to the woman, who looked at him, then back at Frank and Allison, and smiled, too.

Allison said, "What do you think *this* is? Welcome Wagon?"

The man thrust his hand through the open doorway. Frank took it, gripped it as firmly as he could (the man seemed the kind who would appreciate such a gesture), but it wasn't enough because for a few seconds they were locked in a contest of hand strength, which, Frank realized, he would inevitably lose, so he let his hand relax, the man let his relax, gave Frank a quick, lopsided smile, and announced, "We're the Waltons, and we're your neighbors." He offered his hand to Allison. "Good to meet you," he said. Allison took his hand, which he gave one quick shake and let go of, then nodded at his wife, a fragile-looking, pretty woman, eyes wide and wary, like a doe's. "This is Dorothy," the man said. "Dorothy, these are our neighbors."

Dorothy said, "Call me Dot."

"Dot," Allison acknowledged, and, from years of living with her, Frank heard a silent and secret chuckle in the way she said the name. She offered her hand, a gesture that seemed to confuse Dot. "Oh," the woman said after a moment, then took Allison's hand and shook it with exaggerated pumping motions for several seconds.

The man put his hand on top of the head of the child standing next to him; Frank could see now that it was a little boy of eight or nine, his face narrow and ruddy from the cold, his dark eyes mischievous, sparkling with humor and intelligence. "This is Paul Junior," the man said. "My son."

Dot, as if on cue, put her arm around the child standing next to her, a girl of about the same age as Paul who looked very much like her brother, except that her dark eyes were dull, as if she were ill. Dot said, "This is Paul Junior's little sister, Paulette." She glanced at the girl. "Paulette, say hello to our new neighbors, Mr. and Mrs.—" She looked questioningly at Frank.

"Hitchcock," he said.

Allison said, "Allison and Frank."

"Mr. and Mrs. Frank Hitchcock," Dot said, returning her attention to Paulette. "Go ahead, say hello. It's okay, dear."

"Hello," Paulette managed, her voice nearly inaudible.

Allison said, "Hello, Paulette," and gave the girl a flat, concerned smile. "Aren't you feeling well?"

Dot said, "She's all right. She's shy. Girls *should* be shy, don't you think?"

"Well, I don't know. . . ." Allison answered tentatively.

Paul Jr. thrust his hand out to Frank. "Hi, Mr. Hitchcock," he said. Frank shook his hand. Again there was a moment when he thought his strength was being tested. He relaxed. Paul gave him the same lopsided grin his father had given him and let his hand go.

"Hi, Paul," Frank said.

They left a few moments later. "Just wanted to say hello to our new neighbors," Paul Sr. explained, and then they were off again, back the way they had come, through the thin snow, their legs rising up, in unison, almost as if they were doing a goose step.

When they had disappeared over the rise that the playground was on, Allison said, "My God, weren't *they* something?"

"Something *else,* actually," Frank said. He gave her a mock-concerned look. "Do you think they'll be visiting much?"

Allison shook her head gravely. "I doubt it. I don't think they liked us."

"Oh?,"

"I don't think they approved of us, actually."

"What makes you think that?"

She shrugged. "Well, look at him, for instance. Mr. Crew Cut. Parading his little family around, claiming ownership of his son, leaving his wife the responsibility of introducing the daughter. And her! My God, 'Dot'! I haven't heard anyone refer to themselves as 'Dot' for decades. It's as anachronistic as . . . as a Studebaker." She smiled, clearly pleased with her analogy. "And what was that crap about 'girls should be shy'? I didn't know anyone actually thought that way anymore."

"Clearly she does," Frank said.

"Clearly," Allison said.

They agreed that if the Waltons were to visit again, they were going to pretend not to be at home. "I don't need any fascist left over from the McCarthy hearings ruining my day," Allison said, and though Frank didn't feel as strongly about it as she obviously did, he had to agree. The Waltons would be more than welcome to stay on their side of the fence.

Frank and Allison looked into the room whose wall had collapsed, room 26, close to what had once been the principal's office. Frank opened the door—"Did you close it, Allison?" . . . "I think so. I'm not sure."—stepped into the room, stood quietly near the door, Allison beside him, and surveyed the damage. It was very bad. A man-size hole stood to the left of the room's big windows. Intact cinder blocks lay all about in front of the hole;

outside, there were bricks scattered about. Above, a finger-width crack ran from the top of the hole to the ceiling. The gray linoleum seemed oddly wavy, as if the cement slab beneath had heaved a little.

"Shit!" Frank breathed. "What a mess." He stepped forward a few feet, bent over, idly fingered one of the fallen cinder blocks. "Maybe we can just . . . you know"—he glanced at Allison, still standing near the door—"put them back where they were."

"The cinder blocks, you mean?"

"Yes. They all seem to be whole. I mean, just as a kind of temporary patch."

"And while we're doing that," Allison observed, "some more of the wall could collapse on top of us. It's not a good idea, Frank. We've got to find out what made the wall collapse in the first place."

He continued looking at her a few moments. Then, sighing, he nodded and said, "I'll call someone."

"In the meantime, we'll put some plastic over the hole. It'll help keep the cold weather out."

"Sure," Frank said. "Good idea."

Nights had become the most intriguing of times at the school. Frank felt more at home in it at night, in the hallway lined with Walt Disney night-lights, in the gym/auditorium, in the cafeteria, or simply wandering about, looking into one room, and then another, taking solace in the fact that the school was empty. He had little idea why nights at the school should have had such an effect on him. When he thought about it, he concluded that it had to do with the fact that his adolescence had been spent in such a school as this during daylight hours, and most of those hours had been uncomfortable, at best. So it was good to be a part of such a school when it was at rest, when there was no mindless chatter of a thousand young voices, no shouted commands to "Keep moving," no class bells clanging, no harsh announcements over the intercom that the buses had arrived. A building that played host to such chaos *had* to sleep, and it was good to be a part of it while it slept, when the rooms and hallways and gym could not be anything but empty. Nothing stirred in the school at night except the people who had decided to live in it. Allison and him.

It wasn't haunted.

There were no spooks shuffling down the hallways.

No young girl named Lynn appeared at odd times to beguile him.

Joey existed here, it was true, but only in their hearts and in their memories.

Those had been fantasies, his and Allison's electric imaginations making much more of the school than it was—just as his selective memory had made more of his adolescent midnight walks than they actually were.

He had to go into Danby one evening in mid-December. Allison elected to stay at home, though he asked her repeatedly to go with him. He didn't like to drive alone at night, especially on the narrow, precarious, and hilly roads in and out of Danby. Deer abounded in the area, and two sets of eyes were much better than one; often, on rides through the countryside at night, Allison had been able to spot deer before he did, and it was for that reason primarily, he told her, that he wanted her to come with him. But she complained that she wasn't feeling well—nothing she could pinpoint, she said; simply a feeling of malaise—and so he drove into Danby by himself.

It was a three-mile drive. For half a mile before the road dipped into town, it narrowed to a single lane bordered by fields on one side and tall poplar trees on the other—a pretty drive during daylight. At this time of the year, the fields were high in grass that was golden with autumn, and it rippled in a constant breeze on that flat area above the valley Danby sat in. Warm air masses might move leisurely in over the lake, and meander up the hill the road was on, but once they reached the top, and the colder air, the winds started. Frank had driven that one-lane road a couple of dozen times before this mid-December evening, and the grass had always been swaying, flashing the sunlight at him.

But he had rarely driven it at night, had never driven it alone, as he was now, and because his vision had been slowly deteriorating over the past couple of years, driving it tonight was a real chore. The headlights showed him a world that was basically gray, a world whose edges tended to shiver and flow together because his eyes, straining so hard, were tearing up.

"Dammit!" he muttered as he drove, as much in anger at his own bullheadedness for not having had his vision problems taken care of as in frustration with the narrow road and the smeary, monotone world his headlights showed him. For a few moments, he thought that a rain was falling and he turned on the windshield wipers, but when he saw that they did not help, he realized his error and turned them off.

He pulled over, his right wheels crunching on the soft shoulder and telling him there wasn't much more room. He remembered, from his daytime drives down this road, that there was a shallow ditch to either side.

He stopped the car abruptly, hesitated, shut the headlights off, put the transmission in park. Perhaps his eyes needed a rest. He'd been doing lots of reading lately, and his eyes had been giving him more trouble than usual. Maybe he just needed to rest them for a few minutes.

He turned his flashers on. Better to play it safe.

He closed his eyes lightly, put his head back against the headrest, kept his hands on the steering wheel, felt the engine humming through the bottom of the seat and through the steering wheel.

He could see the flashers working through the fronts of his closed lids; the darkness brightened slightly every few seconds. He didn't like this. It was distracting. But he didn't think it would be wise to turn the flashers off. Someone barreling down the road—which was unlikely—might smash into him; he was sure that he was still partially on the road.

He thought of turning his head away from the flashers, but that would be uncomfortable. He thought of closing his eyes tighter, but decided that that would be as distracting as the flashers were.

Dammit, everything boiled down to one poor choice or another. All he had wanted was a few moments' rest so he could continue his drive, but, at last, he resigned himself to the fact that it was not to be.

He opened his eyes.

A tall man, illuminated intermittently by the flashers, stood a dozen feet in front of the car. He was very still, his gaze fixed on the car. He wore an ill-fitting brown suit and his full head of dark hair was askew, as if he had washed it and then had slept on it while it was still wet.

Frank's pulse quickened at once when he saw the man, and a little *Urp!* of surprise escaped him.

The man smiled, as if in greeting. The flashers went off; he was gone. They came on again; he was back, still smiling. Off/gone—on/back and smiling; off/gone—on/back and smiling.

Frank watched the man appear and disappear this way for half a minute.

Then, still smiling, the man started for the car.

In one cat-quick motion, Frank turned the lights on, bathing the man in the glare of the high beams—the man put his arm up to shield his eyes—then Frank put the car in gear, floored the accelerator, and, tires spinning on the loose gravel at the side of the road, roared off.

"Hey!" he heard distantly.

18 Unlike her husband, Allison did not find it entertaining to walk the school's corridors alone at night. She thought it was passing strange, in fact, that Frank seemed to get such a kick out of sitting among all the Walt Disney night-lights in the east hallway, though she had no doubt that there were things about *her* that he found more than passing strange, as well.

So, while he was away on that mid-December evening, she spent her time in the bedroom going over the rough draft of "The Inside." She had turned the TV on, had adjusted the volume to low. It was comforting background noise, only; she could not have said, at any given moment, what show was playing. She could not have said, for that matter, what shows were currently popular because the last time she had watched TV regularly, the currently popular programs had been "Hogan's Heroes" and "Night Gallery," both of which had appealed to her.

She had the bedroom door open. This was a calculated decision. She didn't like the idea of leaving it open. Open doors (to closets, to bedrooms, to houses) invited the imagination to amuse itself, as hers did too readily, anyway. But she did not want to feel that she was a prisoner in the school, either. So she had left the door open halfway. It opened from the left, so when she looked at it from the bed—where she sat, with her back against the headboard—she could see only the plain pine door itself, not what might have been outside it, in the hallway.

She had thought at length about the whole thing and had decided that there was nothing in the hallway to see. The school was not haunted. Nothing was haunted, except her memory and her imagination, and that, of course, was as good as reality. She knew that if she wanted or willed herself to see spooks passing by the door, then she would see them, and they would be very convincing spooks. She had done it before, as a child, when spooks had been far more entertaining and far less a reminder of her own mortality. She had been immortal, then, as a child. She had known that she was going to live forever. She would see the very last days of the earth, just as the man in *The Time Machine* had. Now, at forty-five, she supposed that she would live another thirty years or so and that would be it. In the past few years, the fact of her own mortality had been weighing on her more heavily with each passing year, as the signs of aging appeared—laugh lines, gray hair at the temples, the slow loss of stamina, the bald and unattractive fact that her body had begun to droop. It was obvious, she thought, after only a casual inspection. Her breasts, which had always been larger than she liked, were beginning to point downward. (And hadn't her mother warned her about that? "Oh, Allison, I'm afraid that what might seem a godsend now will be a real burden when you're my age." And hadn't that been just like her mother, to warn her of things she had no control of?) And though her rear end remained firm, her thighs were starting to dimple, although she had been doing an hour's worth of exercise a day for the past eight or nine years. Clearly Frank still found her attractive. Other men did, too. She had felt their eyes on her. (But in five years or so, she was sure, she would be no more attractive than her own mother had been at fifty. People would probably refer to her as "handome," or, which was worse, as "dignified looking," or, worse yet, "patrician.") But, ironically, along with these—albeit still subtle—signs of aging, her sex drive had increased dramatically. Clearly it was a response to getting older, spitting in the face of age: *I might be getting older, goddammit, but I'm still ripe for a roll in the hay!* Was it as smarmy as that? she wondered. If it was, so what?

She looked up from her reading. She had heard someone knocking at the glass doors in the east hallway. She glanced at the bedside clock: 8:15. Who could be visiting now? Who *would* visit without calling first?

She wished that she could yell "Who's there?" to whoever was knocking, but it was too far, she would have to get up and go see who it was. "Alex?" she called, then shook her head self-critically; she had asked Frank to put Alex in one of the rooms in the north hallway while he was in Danby. She still did not trust the dog.

She went to the bedroom door and looked to her right down the long hallway, toward the double glass doors. It was a good fifty feet to the doors. They were lit from outside and above by a pair of small spotlights, but from her vantage point in front of the bedroom, she could see no one, only what she supposed was a shadow cast on the brown-speckled gray linoleum by someone standing at the door.

Another knock came, then another. It was a patient sort of knock, but oddly demanding, too, as if whoever was knocking knew that she was in the school but knew also that she was hesitant about coming to the door.

She called, "Yes? Who is it?"

The shadow moved slightly. What might have been its head seemed to tilt a little, as if whoever was at the door were looking her way.

"Who is it?" Allison called again.

There was another knock, then another.

"Dammit!" Allison breathed, and started down the hallway toward the door. She thought of flicking the overhead fluorescent lights on, but quickly decided against it. "Who's there?" she called.

Another knock, then, quickly, more urgently, another.

Allison's pace quickened. Maybe it was Frank. Maybe he'd lost his keys. "Frank, is that you?"

There was another knock, another, another.

She was close enough to the doors now that she could see a man's profile. He was tall. He was wearing a brown suit. "Yes?" she called, and stopped walking.

The man leaned forward. He put his face to the door and turned it toward her. His face seemed overly large, somehow, and Allison decided that the glass in the door was distorting it, refracting it. Nearly all his features were large. His lips were large, his nose, the oval of his face. Only his dark eyes were small.

He smiled. He had apparently seen her in the darkened hallway.

"Oh, my God!" Allison whispered. She stopped walking.

The man called to her, his face still pressed into the glass of the door. "Hello." He had a friendly tenor voice. It surprised Allison. It surprised her, too, how well his voice carried through the glass, as if he were actually in the school with her.

"Yes?" she called back, still cautious and hesitant.

"Hello," he said again.

Allison started walking toward the double glass doors. As she drew closer, the man's face grew smaller, until it looked as normal as any man's, and she decided that her guess about the glass distorting it had been correct.

She stopped again when she was a couple of feet to the left of the doors, just inside the little circle of yellowish light cast by the spotlights outside. The man still was looking at her. He was still smiling. His teeth were crooked and white. They seemed oversized. Then, as his broad smile grew less broad, they seemed normal again.

"Hello," he said. "Hello."

"What do you want?" Allison said, immediately regretting her unfriendly tone.

"To come in. I want to come in."

Farther down the hall, the Walt Disney night-lights cast a soft, multicolored glow into the darkness. She saw a whisper of movement there, in that hallway.

"Why do you want to come in?" she asked the man at the door.

"The phone," he answered. He was still smiling, showing all his white, crooked teeth. Clearly, he was trying to be friendly, reassuring, persuasive. "I need to use the phone." Again, Allison was surprised at how well she could hear his voice through the closed glass door.

She hesitated. She saw a hint of movement again in the north extension of the hallway. She decided that the line of night-lights was playing tricks on her eyes. "Did you have an accident?" she said to the man at the door, because his brown suit was spotted with water and what looked like mud.

He shook his head. "No, no accident." His smile flattened. "My car simply won't start." His arm moved slightly. "It's down there. It's down the road."

Allison thought that she did not much like his eyes. They were too small, too dark. They seemed to contrast sharply with his friendly smile and they bore no expression at all; they were like marbles.

"Our phone's not working," she called. "It's out of order. I'm sorry."

He nodded as if he had known that all along. "Yes. Of course it is. But perhaps you could let me in so I could get out of the cold. It's very cold. Have you been outside tonight?"

She shook her head a little. "I'm sorry, no, I can't do that. I can't let you in."

"Is your husband at home?" His smile broadened. His small eyes seemed to light up.

"My husband?" She hesitated. "Yes, of course—"

"Then it's all right. You can let me in. Your husband's at home."

"He's asleep, though."

"It's so early. He's asleep so early?"

"Yes. He works . . . he has a morning shift."

"Oh? Where?"

"Where?" She hesitated. "I'm sorry. You'll have to go back to your car. You can't come in here." She could hear the fear in her voice. She hoped the man couldn't hear it.

He stepped away from the door and was gone.

His sudden disappearance took her by surprise. It was several moments before she stepped quickly up to the door and looked out. She saw the covered walkway, nothing else.

Frank got home a half hour later and she told him about the man at the door. He assured her that she had acted prudently not letting him in; she said that she did not need his reassurance, that she knew well enough not to let strangers into the school. Then she gave him a little smile and apologized for snapping at him. "I'm still nervous about it," she said.

He didn't tell her that he had encountered the man as well, on the one-lane road that led into town. He did not want to frighten her unduly.

Later that night, when she was asleep, he went looking for the man.

19 So, just for the hell of it, you open the door.
It opens outward, toward you. You note this. You think it's important. But there's nothing very special or interesting on the other side of the door. Only the rest of the forest.

So you walk through. Again, you do it just for the hell of it.

You walk through it.

You look about. You're still in the forest.

You think, *Well, this is very strange, a door in the middle of the forest.* But, as strange as it may be, it has turned out to be nothing very interesting.

You walk on. Further into the forest.

You don't think much about the door. After a while, you forget where it was, exactly.

—Allison Hitchcock, "The Inside"

Frank had thought of calling the Danby Police, and, in fact, had dialed their number, but had hung up before they answered because he wasn't sure what he'd tell them: *Yes, that's right; the man was wearing a brown suit. My wife and I both saw him. He spoke to my wife, in fact. Apparently, he wanted to get into the school; at least, that's what he told her. He said he needed to use the phone, but she wouldn't let him. . . . Where did I see him? On Fisher's Road. I had stopped the car because I couldn't see—I'm going blind, apparently—and there he was, standing right in front of the car. . . . Did he do anything? No, I can't say that he actually did anything, but he sure as hell scared my wife, and, to tell you the truth, he scared me, too. . . . Why did he scare us? I don't know. That's hard to say. I guess he scared us because he was so much . . . there. Do you follow me? He was so present, so damned . . . big. . . . Am I a troublemaker? No, I wouldn't say I'm a troublemaker. I'm just a pretty normal guy who doesn't like being frightened by men in brown suits. . . .*

He smiled as these thoughts came to him, now, outside the school, flashlight in hand, Alex on a long leash and walking, head high and ears erect, just ahead of him.

Frank wasn't sure what he was looking for. Footprints in the shallow snow, perhaps. He'd found plenty of those. Footprints of squirrels, raccoons, chipmunks, deer. But no human footprints. No footprints of a man in a brown suit.

He had worked his way around to the front of the school when he became aware that he was being watched from the road, two hundred feet north. He couldn't make out exactly who was watching him; the night was overcast and very dark, but he could see that someone was there, near the road, facing in his direction, standing very still.

"Who's that, Alex?" he whispered.

Alex whimpered a little and gave him a quick glance.

Frank shone the flashlight toward the person watching. The light was too feeble, and he saw only what might, he thought, have been a reflection from a metal button, or a belt buckle.

He called, "What are you doing?" and felt foolish for it. What was the person doing, indeed? Simply standing quietly near the road. It was public property after all.

"*What* are you *doing?*" he repeated.

Alex shifted back and forth nervously; he clearly wanted to be free of the leash. But he did not bark; indeed, Frank had been told, he would not bark unless commanded to.

"Good boy," Frank soothed. "Steady there." Then, to the figure near the road, "Who *are* you?"

The figure did not respond.

The headlights of a car appeared far to the east, around a curve at the horizon.

Inside the school, Allison had awakened shortly after Frank had left the room. Now she was lying with her eyes wide open in the darkness. She was trembling. She was very, very afraid. She didn't know why, and that was making her more afraid.

Frank could hear the car approaching as he kept his eyes on the figure near the road. The car was noisy; it needed a muffler.

"What do you want?" Frank called to the figure on the road.

It did not respond.

Frank thought briefly of letting Alex loose. No, he decided, almost at once. Perhaps whoever it was there had a gun. Perhaps it was simply someone hitchhiking, someone who had been walking past the school who had stopped to rest, someone, at any rate, who meant him and Allison no harm. Too many unanswered questions to let Alex have his way.

Frank crossed the circular driveway in front of the school, Alex at his side, then started across the snow-covered lawns in front of the driveway. He kept his flashlight beam trained on the figure; the beam came softly back to him from that same metal button or belt buckle he had seen before.

"Dammit!" Frank shouted. "Don't just stand there, answer me."

Nothing.

He was halfway across the front lawns when the car he had noticed earlier negotiated a curve and its headlights caught the figure at the road. Frank stopped short. What in the name of heaven was this?

He watched, transfixed, as the car sped past, illuminating the figure for a few moments. Then he waited—without knowing why—until the sound of the car was only a distant ragged hum, and he approached the figure near the road, the beam of the flashlight preceding him across the shallow, gray covering of snow, Alex walking stiffly at his side.

The figure was on the shoulder of the road. Its head was a basketball that someone had painted a coy smile on, and big, hazel eyes, and brown hair with just a touch of gray at the temples. Its torso was a broomstick—one end stuck into the basketball, the other forced into the shoulder of the road. A blue satin nightgown had been draped over wires protruding from the broomstick. A necklace with an amulet hung around the neck of the effigy; it was what had been reflecting the beam of the flashlight, Frank realized.

Breasts nearly as big as the basketball had been fashioned from pillowcases stuffed with what Frank guessed was foam. They hung out the front of the nightgown. Nipples had been painted on them with bright red paint.

It was an obscene, grinning caricature of Allison.

A sheet of yellow legal paper was taped to the nightgown, below the breasts. These words, in a childish hand, had been scrawled in red ink on the paper:

BOY TOY

The Danby Police chief was a short, thin, nervous man named Peter McWilliams. He had pulled his cruiser up to the shoulder of the road so its headlights illuminated the effigy of Allison.

He said to Frank and Allison—who was dressed in her robe, a winter coat, and boots: "'Course you don't like it. I don't blame you. What's to like?"

Frank assumed it was a rhetorical question, but the man had paused, as if waiting for an answer, so Frank said, "Nothing at all. It's . . . an obscenity."

McWilliams's small head—he wore a hat, but it was clear that his black hair was very sparse—bobbed a couple of times. "It is that," he said; his voice was tinny, hard to listen to. "It is that.

But it ain't nothin' illegal, you know. Except maybe it might violate some antilittering statute."

"Anti*littering* statute?" Allison was appalled. "My God, this is . . . the person who did this is *sick!* Surely you can see that this is some kind of perverse threat."

McWilliams cocked his head, as if confused. "Threat?" he said. "To who?"

"To us, of course," Frank said.

McWilliams smiled. "Now how's that?"

"My God," Allison breathed. "Can't you see that this . . . this thing"—she glared at the figure, then at McWilliams—"is supposed to be *me?*"

McWilliams looked confused. "You're kidding? I don't see that for a moment, missus."

"Officer McWilliams," Frank began, trying to fight off the anger he was feeling.

But McWilliams cut in, "*Chief* McWilliams. I like to be called *Chief* McWilliams, sport."

"Yes. Chief," Frank acknowledged, and closed his eyes a moment; his anger was going to best him if he let it. "Do you have any idea who might have done this?"

"Sure, I do," McWilliams answered at once. "Kids."

"Kids?" Frank said, incredulous. "What kids?"

"Who knows?" McWilliams said. "Kids. They do this kind of stuff all the time. They're kids. This is what kids do."

"My God," Allison whispered.

"Where?" Frank asked.

"Where what?" McWilliams asked.

"Where in the *hell* do kids do stuff like this?"

McWilliams shrugged. "Here, of course. Danby kids. They do this kind of stuff all the time."

Allison and Frank said nothing for several moments, then McWilliams, to cut into the silence, said, "They're kids, like I said. They're blowing off steam. Hell, we all did this kind of stuff when we were kids."

"No, we didn't," Frank said, speaking for both Allison and himself.

"Sure, I know that," McWilliams said, clearly unconvinced. He gestured at the effigy. "So what do you want to do with it?"

"What do we want to *do* with it?" Frank said. "We don't want to do anything with it. My God! We want you to get rid of it. We want you to find the people responsible."

McWilliams nodded. "Okay. I can get rid of it for you. That's no problem. And I'll ask around, but I sure can't promise that I'll turn up anything—"

"We'd like to file a complaint, Chief," Frank said.

"For what? For this?" He gestured again at the effigy. He shrugged. "Okay, but I can tell you it won't do any good. Besides, I don't know what I'd call it—harassment, littering, who knows?"

Allison broke in, "You don't want to help us, do you, Chief McWilliams?"

He didn't answer at once. A slow smile spread across his thin lips. It was a smile that had the unnerving quality of being sly and lascivious at the same time. "Tell me something, missus: Do you really want people finding out about this thing? Because they will, if you file a formal complaint. They'll come around asking questions. Hell, they'll want to *see* the damned thing—"

She glared at him. "And you'd show it to them, Chief?"

He did not answer the question. He turned to Frank. "Mr. Hitchcock, why don't you and the missus just let this whole thing pass—"

Frank cut in, "My wife asked you a question, Chief."

McWilliams sighed. "You're being hysterical, missus. 'Course I understand that. You got this . . . this image of yourself, and it ain't too flattering—"

"Oh, for God's sake," Allison snapped, and turned at once and started for the school. She called back after a few moments, "And my name is *not* 'missus.'" Moments later, she was moving stiffly, with anger, across the lawn toward the circular driveway.

McWilliams smiled at her retreating figure. "You got your hands full with that one, don't you, Mr. Hitchcock!"

Again, Frank struggled to keep his temper. "Listen," he said, "why don't you just take this thing away. Allison and I will be down in the morning to file a complaint."

"You sure it's what you want?"

"Positive."

"I feel like I'm on another planet," Allison said when Frank came in fifteen minutes later. She was lying belly-down on the bed; she had her face turned toward him. "A planet for crazy people."

Frank crossed the room, sat on the bed next to her, put his hand comfortingly on her shoulder. "I told McWilliams that we'd be in in the morning."

Allison maneuvered around so she was on her back. "Let's not do that, Frank."

"You're kidding! We have to—"

"No. We don't have to. It was a prank, and it's obvious that"—she made quotes with her fingers—"'the chief' wasn't impressed. If we file a complaint, you know that he's not going to do anything about it, anyway. So why don't we let it slide, as he suggested."

Frank said nothing.

"Okay?" Allison coaxed.

"If it's really what you want."

"No, it's not what I want. Not at all." She sighed. "I just hope—" She did not go on.

"Yes," Frank agreed. "I hope so, too."

In room 22, two baby field mice had died of starvation because their mother hadn't dared to venture out beyond the desk cubbyhole where she'd made her new nest three days earlier.

The odor in the room had worsened; it was almost foglike, now, almost suffocating, and the high keening noise had risen in pitch, as if something were fomenting beneath the linoleum floor and were slowly nearing the surface.

The mother field mouse was frantic, but starvation had dulled her desperation. Her two remaining babies lay very still at her chest, their breathing quick and shallow. Now and again, she nuzzled one of them, trying to get it to suckle, but her teats were dry.

She could feel death approaching, but she had little idea what it meant because she did not think in terms of death and life.

The voice of a child rose up from somewhere in the room and startled her. Then there was silence again and her memory of the child's voice slipped away and was gone forever. Only the smell remained. And the high, keening sound, like a muffled teakettle.

And the black water. Which, she saw then through the darkness, had bubbled over to her side of the room and was lapping at the edges of the desk, threatening to spill into her cubbyhole and drown her and her two remaining infants.

She rose painfully, made her way to the lip of the cubbyhole, peered out. She saw a drab, gray-on-lighter-gray world—overturned desks, a blackboard, buckling acoustical tiles overhead.

The water was all around her. She knew that her only escape was up the desk itself, which would leave her babies at the mercy of the water.

She could not do this.

She went back to her two silent infants and spread her body around them protectively.

The first rivulets of black water curled down the desk and touched her back.

20 Late the following morning, Allison announced, "We've got a god-awful mess in one of the rooms near the gym."

Frank, who had slept late and was just then eating his breakfast, said, "What kind of mess?" He popped a forkful of scrambled egg into his mouth.

"Water," Allison told him. "I think a pipe broke. There's water everywhere. It's even coming out into the hall. And it stinks, Frank. God, it stinks!"

"Hell!" Frank whispered. "This place is falling apart around us." He got up and went with her to room 22, which was under three inches of black water.

They both peered into the room from the doorway, water trickling around their feet and finding little shallows and passageways in the hallway. The water tended to flow lazily south because the entire school had long since settled in that direction.

"Goddammit!" Frank whispered. "Isn't this a hell of a note!" He had a mental picture of a sewer pipe beneath the floor bursting—possibly from a septic tank that might not have been cleaned for years—and releasing tons of sludge and sewage. For Christ's sake, this could be ten- or fifteen-year-old shit he was seeing here; it could make the whole school uninhabitable for weeks, months! It could cost them thousands of dollars to clean up.

"What are we going to do, Frank?" Allison asked. She put her hand over her nose and mouth.

Frank glanced around the room, saw desks turned over, some papers floating in the foul water. One of the dead field mice floated past his line of sight on a little eddy, and then was hidden behind the back of a wooden chair that had fallen over.

"And look at that, Frank," Allison said grimly. She pointed at the northwest corner, where the cinder blocks had fallen, and where a wide fissure had opened in the wall. Above, the white acoustical tile had buckled; one of the tiles floated in the dark water.

Frank shook his head miserably. "I don't know what we're going to do." He paused. "We'll . . . call somebody, I guess."

"You've said that before, Frank."

"I know. I mean it this time. This is something I *know* neither of us can deal with." He pulled the door shut.

Five miles north, two young women in a vintage Mustang were lost.

"It's that damned map," one of the women said. Her name was Vicky Shephard; she was driving. She was blond, gray-eyed, and possessed an inquiring intelligence and cynicism that many young men at Brockport College—where she had graduated with a bachelor's degree in history—had found off-putting.

Before she had decided that they were lost, Vicky's thoughts had been on her boyfriend and on the quirky, perverse night of lovemaking they had enjoyed the previous evening. She had, she thought, gotten to know him a little better than she'd wanted, because she wasn't sure that she liked the side of him that he had revealed, wasn't sure that his particular sexual appetites matched hers. She was very uncomfortable, as well, with the fact that she had enjoyed their night together as much as he had.

The young woman with her—who was holding an ancient and tattered county map open on her lap—glanced over, annoyed. "This map is fine," she protested. "I've been using it for years." The young woman's name was Eileen Shute. She was small-boned, fine-featured, and confrontational.

"Well, that's the problem," Vicky said smilingly. "It's too goddamned *old*."

"This *car* is too old!" Eileen shot back.

"This *car* happens to be a classic. And its feelings are easily hurt, so watch your tone."

Eileen gave her a long-suffering smile. She had heard her friend talk about the Mustang's alleged sensitivities before, ad nauseam, and her strategy, now, was to simply ignore it. She said, "I still wish it had seat belts. I feel naked without a seat belt."

"They didn't put seat belts in cars in 1965, Eileen."

"Yes, Vicky, I'm aware of that."

Vicky sighed. "Can we please just figure out where in the hell we are?"

She had stopped the Mustang on the shoulder, near the junction of two roads. The road they were on was paved, though barely; the connecting road was gravel. She peered ahead; the road sign read CHELMSFORD ROAD. "Is that on the map?" she asked. "Chelmsford Road."

Eileen checked the map's index and shook her head. "No such beast," she said. "Must be new."

Vicky sighed. "Unlike that damned map."

"And certainly unlike this damned car," Eileen retorted.

The day was overcast. There was no snowfall here, but the fields of tall golden grass surrounding the car held a late-autumn crispness, as if they were merely renderings of fields done in stiff, bold strokes. At the horizon ahead, there was a line of trees whose limbs were all but bare; a huge barn, gray with age, and timeworn, stood solidly, like a huge gray rock, at the center of this line of trees.

"It's pretty here," Eileen said. "Maybe we should just pitch the tent and stay awhile."

Vicky was uncertain if her friend was joking. If she was, it was certainly in keeping with all of her jokes—lame. "We're not staying out in the middle of nowhere," she said.

"I was *joking*," Eileen said, and rolled her eyes in exasperation. It was unfortunate that her friend always missed her jokes. Too subtle, probably. "Besides, just because we have no idea where we are, doesn't mean we're in the middle of *nowhere*."

"And that's another joke?" Vicky asked.

"Uh-huh. A good one, too."

"We'll let posterity be the judge of that," Vicky said.

Eileen pointed toward a man walking on Chelmsford Road. "Maybe he can help us," she said.

Vicky looked at the man. She thought that anyone who was walking around in a 1950s-style brown suit in the middle of nowhere was clearly not someone from whom she wanted to ask directions.

"Well?" Eileen coaxed.

"No," Vicky said. "I don't think so."

"Why the hell not?"

The man saw them. He smiled.

The plumber, standing in the doorway of room 22, said, "My guess is that it drained back into the septic tank. It happens." He was a tall man, and thin—emaciated, Frank thought—dressed in dark gray pants and a dark gray shirt. He sported a three-day growth of reddish beard.

"It doesn't happen a lot, I'll admit," he said to Frank, then, turning his head, continued, to Allison, "It doesn't happen a lot, you know, but it happens, 'specially if it's an old system, like this one is." He turned his head and spoke to Frank again. His habit was to get close and speak directly into the face of the person he was talking to, which was unfortunate, because his breath smelled of whiskey and blood. "System hasn't been checked, probably, for a decade"—he pronounced it "dekid"—"or more. I know, because I was the one who took care of it. Bad system too. Contractor was paid off, you know. Put in a bad system. Crummy system." He turned his head and bathed Allison again in his foul breath. "You say it smelled bad?" He turned to Frank. "Smelled bad, did it, Mr. Hitchcock? Funny, I don't smell nothin'. What'd it smell like? Shit?" He turned to Allison. "Pardon my French." Back to Frank. "Shit, then? Did it smell like shit?"

Frank shook his head, which gave him a moment or two away from the man's breath. "No." He kept his head turned,

ostensibly so he could nod to indicate the room. "It didn't smell
like . . . shit. It smelled . . . it had its own sort of smell. Actually,
I can't describe it." He turned his head back. The plumber was
taller than he was by half a foot. Frank bent his head, coughed.
"Pardon me," he said, and ducked away, into the room. He was
astonished that the overpowering odor from within—which had
been an almost visible thing before—was gone completely.

Vicky said to the man in the brown suit, "I'm sorry, no,
we're okay, we were just misreading the map." She knew she
sounded nervous. She did not want to sound nervous, she wanted
to sound strong and self-confident, because the man was so . . .
present, so much . . . bigger than life, the way she remembered
thinking of presidents and movie stars, as if, should they visit, the
inside of a house would not be big enough for them. And he
smelled of formaldehyde, which seemed an odd thing for him to
smell of.

He frightened her, too, though she couldn't pinpoint why.
He seemed pleasant enough. His broad smile was continuous and
friendly, even if his teeth were crooked. His small eyes betrayed
no threat of any kind, only a bemused curiosity (as if he were
thinking, *My God, no one gets* lost *here. There are road signs, route
signs. You can see for miles*).

Eileen, in the passenger's seat, holding the map, looked over
and said, "She's lying. We're lost, and it's no sense denying it.
Maybe you can help us."

The man's smile did not waver. He was leaning over, looking through the open driver's window. "Help you?" he said. "In
what way?"

The question took Eileen aback; she did not answer for a
moment. Then she said, "Perhaps you could tell us where we
are?"

The man's smile did not waver. He leaned closer, so his
chin, which was broad and sported a couple of errant gray hairs,
poked into the car. "Where are *any* of us, miss? Have you ever
wondered about that?"

Vicky began rolling the window up. The man reached out, grabbed the edge of it, held it. Vicky's mouth dropped open. She wanted to protest, but she could say nothing. "I can tell you this," the man said, and he was still smiling bemusedly, "you're not anywhere that you *want* to be!" And he let go of the window.

Vicky hesitated.

The man straightened.

Vicky put the car in gear and floored the accelerator. Within moments, they were far down the road.

Eileen looked back wordlessly.

Vicky glanced in the rearview mirror, saw the man walking in the opposite direction, his back to them. She had expected that he'd be walking in their direction with that bemused, contradictory smile on his broad face. But he wasn't.

"My God!" she whispered.

Quietly, without knowing it, Eileen began crumpling the tattered map up in her clenched fist.

21 "I can tell you this," the plumber said as he came out of room 22, after poking around in the corner for fifteen minutes, "wherever that water came from, it wasn't no septic system. System doesn't go through here. Didn't occur to me before, but it does now. You got a problem, but it ain't nothin' *I* can fix." He pulled out a notebook, began writing figures in it, and continued, "I guess the first thing I'd do if I was you is call a mason—couple of 'em in the area do good work—and get this damned wall fixed. And that other one, too. Place'll fall down around you while you're sleepin' if you let it." He grinned. "Why the hell you buy this damned school, anyway?" He paused, though not long enough for either Frank or Allison to reply. "It's haunted, you know. Plenty'a ghosts in here. How much you pay for it? Too much'd be my guess. Five *cents* would be too much," and he ripped a sheet from the notebook he'd been writing in and handed it to Frank, who glanced at it, handed it to Allison, and said firmly, "We're not paying this. You've got to be out of your mind if you think we're going to pay this!"

The plumber's grin grew crooked. "Well, there's a lot of us pretty much out of our minds in Danby, but I guess you know that, don't you?" He nodded at the bill, which Allison was looking at, openmouthed. "You pay that, Mr. Hitchcock. You got ten days. You don't pay it, you're surely going to wish you had!" And with that, he picked up his toolbox, which had been sitting near him on the floor, and, whistling some strange, off-key tune, sauntered from the school.

Eileen said, pointing to a road only a hundred feet ahead, "There it is, County Route 36. Take it!" and Vicky, who had been doing sixty over the bad road they were on—the road on which they had stopped and had had their unsettling encounter with the man in the brown suit—punched the brake and nearly careened on two wheels around the sharper corner.

After a moment, she said, "Dammit, Eileen, don't *do* that! I'll go off the road next time. I'm on edge enough as it is."

Eileen nodded her apology. "You're right. I'm sorry." She hesitated, gauged the car's momentum over the one-lane gravel road that was County Road 36. "You're going too fast. Slow down."

Vicky slowed the car by ten miles an hour.

Eileen said, "It's still too fast, Vicky. There are deer on this road. They're everywhere. You can't see them till they're standing right in front of you." The road was bordered on both sides by old deciduous trees. Beyond them, there were hundreds of acres of tall, golden grass. Eileen nodded, to indicate the tall grass. "They hide in there and then when a car's right where they think it should be, they leap out, and that's that. Crash! One wrecked car and one messed-up driver. At night you get used to watching for any kind of movement. You get so you drive with one foot on the gas pedal and one foot over the brake, and you drive real slow. Must be a hundred people have—"

"Eileen, would you please shut up!" Vicky cut in.

Eileen looked suddenly hurt. "I'm only *talking*. I have a right to do that. That guy back there scared me every bit as much as he scared you, and I'm trying to forget about him, just like you are—"

"You're babbling," Vicky cut in, and slowed the car when she saw a large black dog, its fur glistening in the bright afternoon sunlight, cross the road several hundred feet ahead. The dog disappeared in high grass to her side of the road, and Vicky went on, "It's making me nervous as hell."

"I'm *not* babbling," Eileen protested.

Vicky sighed. She could not get the big man in the brown suit out of her head. He was like a depressing thought that simply wouldn't go away. She said, "Just tell me where we are, exactly, okay. This is *your* stomping ground, not mine."

"I wouldn't exactly call it my *stomping* ground," Eileen said. "I only lived here for a year and a half, but"—she glanced out the window, then at her map, then at Vicky, who was keeping her eyes fixed on the road—"I'd say we're pretty close. A few miles down this road, and we'll be there."

"A few miles? That's not awfully precise."

"Hell, what is?" Eileen asked.

"You sound like that creep in the brown suit."

"Sorry. I'm just saying that it's been a while, and it's hard to be precise. We've got a few miles to go. Maybe less, maybe more. There's a landmark. An abandoned gas station. A Sunoco station. If it's still up. We used to play in it, my brother and sister and me. But that was fifteen years ago. It's probably been torn down by now."

"Jesus," Vicky said, "you're about as helpful as a cold sore." She saw a figure appear at the horizon far ahead, perhaps three-quarters of a mile away, where the road peaked on a hillock. The figure seemed to be standing still in the middle of the road. It was little more than a squat black exclamation point against the bright blue sky.

"Very creative," Eileen said. "'As helpful as a cold sore.' Is that a Vicky Shephard original, or should you give credit to someone else?"

Vicky slowed the car, then brought it to a halt.

Eileen glanced quizzically at her. "I was only kidding," she said.

But Vicky was looking ahead. She nodded. "Who's that?"

Eileen continued looking quizzically at her for a few moments, then she looked where Vicky had indicated. "Who's what?" She peered through the windshield at the road ahead. The trees were casting harsh black shadows across the gravel. "I don't see anyone."

"Him!" Vicky answered, and pointed stiffly.

Eileen saw him. He was no longer merely a squat black exclamation point. "My God, it's that creep in the brown suit. How in the hell—"

Vicky shoved the car into drive, goosed the accelerator. The car lurched forward. She spun the wheel left. Within moments she had executed a K-turn and was headed, fast, in the opposite direction.

Eileen had turned around and was looking through the rear window of the Mustang. "You might be overreacting, Vicky. It might not have been him."

"Yes, it was!" Vicky snapped.

"I don't see him anymore," Eileen said. "He's gone." She turned around. "Damn, I wish this thing had seat belts."

"Iris called," Allison said to Frank, who had gotten a flashlight and was peering into the six-inch-wide hole that had belched so much black water and then had taken it back. He glanced over at her.

"Sorry?" he said.

She stepped into the room. She was clearly uncomfortable in it; she shivered, although the room wasn't cold. She told him, "I said that Iris called. She and Sam will be stopping back next week." They had gone south to see their mother, who lived in Pennsylvania, and then would be going back to their home in Vermont. Allison had offered them a place to rest before continuing their drive back. She went on, "Monday. Will we be ready for them?"

"Ready for them?" He seemed confused.

"Frank, wake up! We asked them to stop back, remember? I'm just wondering if we'll have enough food—"

"Come over here," he cut in. "I want to show you something."

She shook her head at once. "No. I can't do that, Frank. I'm sorry."

"Allison, please. There's nothing here that's going to bite you. I merely want to show you something interesting, that's all."

"Tell me about it instead. I'm not going to come over there."

He sighed, then moved his head to indicate the hole in the floor. "There's something down there."

"Oh Frank, of course there is. There's shit down there. I don't care what that crook who calls himself a plumber says."

Frank shook his head. "No. It's something else. It's very strange." He smiled awkwardly, as if at a joke he didn't understand. "Sky," he said.

"Sorry?" Allison said.

He shrugged. He looked embarrassed. "Nothing. I don't know." He looked suddenly peeved. "Would you *please* come over here, Allison. I *need* you to see this, too."

She shook her head. "No, Frank!"

He stared silently at her for a few seconds. "Okay. Forget it." He stuck his flashlight into his pants pocket. "Let's go make some dinner. I'm starved."

"Starved? After what's been going on in here? My God, *I* can't eat."

Frank took a step forward. He stopped. The dead mother field mouse was lying on her back with her mouth open at his feet. One of her infants lay nearby, grayish pink and emaciated. "Sure," he whispered. "I understand. I guess I'm not very hungry, either."

They left the room together and locked the door behind them.

Vicky was getting worried. "I think we're on that damned road again."

Eileen shook her head vehemently. "No. We're not. I'm sure of it. We can't be. I've been keeping track." She saw a route sign coming up, kept her eyes on it. The car sped past it. "Dammit, we are," she said.

"So I took a wrong turn," Vicky suggested. "I zigged when I should have zagged." She tried to smile.

Eileen did not smile back. "I say we go back to our starting point and try this again."

"Our starting point?" Vicky slowed the car. Ahead a hundred yards or so, a large black dog was crossing right to left. It occurred to Vicky that the dog looked much like the other dog she had slowed for. "Look at that dog," she said, but by then it had disappeared into the tall golden grass that crowded up to both sides of the road.

"I don't see it," Eileen said.

"It's gone," Vicky said, and added, "What do you mean, 'our starting point'?"

"Stop and turn around and I'll show you. You're going in the wrong direction."

"No, I'm not."

"Okay, tell me what direction we're going."

"We're going north. The sun's to the left, so we're going north. Simple." She picked up speed again. Far ahead, the road rose over a hillock where tall poplars crowded up to the shoulder. There was bright blue sky there, at the horizon, but overhead, clouds had moved in, so the countryside around them was in shadow.

"Will you please stop the car, Vicky. I've got to get my bearings here. I'm kind of lost."

"Shit," Vicky breathed, and pulled the car over to the shoulder. She looked pleadingly at her friend. "Eileen, you're supposed to know your way around this area."

"I do," Eileen said. "I did, anyway. It's kind of . . . changed. I don't know. It's familiar; I mean, everything *seems* familiar, but it isn't." She shook her head in frustration. "I don't know what the hell I'm talking about, Vicky. This road"—she gestured with her arm to indicate it—"was a road that my folks used all the time when we lived here. It leads into Danby. I know it. I know," she continued dogmatically, "that if we go this way a couple miles or so, then we'll come to a rise, and we'll go over it, and Danby will be there, in the valley."

Vicky sighed. "Dammit, you've told me that before. Twice.

And we've been on this road twice. And there's no Danby. How can you lose a whole *town,* Eileen? Tell me. How can you lose a whole town?"

But Eileen didn't answer. She was looking past her friend, out the driver's window. Her eyes were wide and her mouth was open slightly, as if she were on the verge of speech.

Vicky whispered desperately, "Eileen, what is it?" But she knew, even without looking, what Eileen was staring at.

There was a sharp knock at the driver's window.

Vicky screamed abruptly, turned her head, and in the moment before throwing the car into gear, she saw the broad face of the man in the brown suit, his smiling mouth, his crooked teeth.

Seconds later, she had pushed the Mustang to sixty, then to seventy. She held it there. She wept.

Sandra called Allison late that afternoon. She did not mention her strange visit to the school several nights earlier; she seemed, by turns, very excited and very elated; her voice modulated between confusion, awe, and fear, like someone describing the explosion of the sun. "You were right, Allison. That story you're writing. You were right."

"Sandra, what are you talking about?"

Sandra appeared to ignore the question. "But there are problems, Allison. Problems. Big, nasty problems. In*soluble* problems." She was speaking breathlessly, now, as if trying to get out a million facts in a minute or two. "So many things sweep back and forth." She sounded positively theatrical, Allison thought. "Back and forth, back and forth, like . . . like the tides bringing in flotsam and jetsam, and then taking it out again."

"Could you please tell me what in the hell you're talking about?" Allison pleaded.

Again, the woman seemed to ignore her. She babbled on, "So many things . . . mix together." She paused. "Imagine . . . Allison, *imagine* what we have here. On this side. What life gives us. We have . . . so much. Time. Change. Love. Hate. Beauty.

Stasis." Allison heard her take a deep breath; clearly the woman was creating what she thought of as some impossible task. "And these . . . all these things are not merely *mirrored* over there. It's not that simple. They are . . . well, just like *here,* but very differently . . . they're mixed together. I don't know why. I've never understood why. Maybe because that other place is actually the . . . the detritus—do you know what that means, Allison? Of course you do. It means what's left over. The remains. Whatever is over there is the *detritus* of what goes on here. It is the only way I can explain what happens. It may be incorrect—my explanation. I'm not sure. I don't know. But what results, you see—and I can postulate this only through observation—is a sort of dramatic, tempestuous, I don't know, *mad* inflow and outflow. Like in a channel between a lake and a bay. Inflow and outflow. And when you have that . . . I mean, imagine that this lake and this bay are composed of very similar things, but that, somehow, one is salt water, and the other is fresh water. And the inflow, in*let* and outlet between the two is very violent. There would be a sort of mixing of the two substances, of the lake and the bay in the area around that inlet and outlet, a sort of *confusion,* don't you see, a sort of *melding.* And if what you have in both is past, present, future; and life in one, and past life in the other, memory, stasis, change, all the *stuff* that makes up existence itself, then around this inlet and outlet—and actually they would be one and the same thing, of course—you would have a mixing of the basic stuff from both. And that causes stress. Do you understand that, Allison? Do you understand how *much* and what *kind* of stress I'm talking about?"

Allison said nothing for several moments. Sandra did not expect that she—Allison—would understand a word of what was being said. "No," Allison said. "What kind of stress, Sandra?"

Sandra paused dramatically, as if about to impart a great truth, a stunning revelation, "Why *stuff* stress, of course. The *stuff* that is *everything.*"

172

"Yes, I see, of course," Allison said, though she did not see.
She sighed. "It's been very, very nice having you call, Sandra—"

"And it all focuses there," Sandra interrupted. "In that
school."

"*What* focuses here?" Allison asked. There was a touch of
anger in her tone.

"What I've been talking about. The inflow and outflow. It's
there. In that school you're living in."

"I still don't understand—"

"For God's sake, Allison. Open your eyes and ears. It's all
around you. You don't understand because you don't *want* to understand, but, you see, there's really nothing to it, nothing painful,
nothing that lasts, no effects to be afraid of. It's like going to the
damned bathroom, it's so easy."

"Godammit, Sandra, you're making no sense."

"But there is the stress, of course. I've mentioned that,
haven't I? The stress. I'm afraid it's quite bad, now. And I don't
know what we can do about it."

There was a dial tone.

Sandra had never told Allison where she lived, only that she
lived close by. And she had never told Allison her last name,
either. So there was no way for Allison to call her back, or to go
to her house and demand to know what was going on, much as
she wanted to.

She would have to wait until Sandra appeared at the school
again. She hoped that when that happened, the dog would not be
roaming about; Allison wasn't sure about the dog. At first, she
had been frightened of it, and that was a normal reaction. The
dog was big, mean looking—it had been trained as a guard dog,
after all. And there had been moments, early on, when she had
encountered it while it patrolled the hallways and moments of
tension had passed between them. But the dog seemed to have
mellowed. At times, it was almost docile, and she could not explain it, nor could Frank. It still patrolled, though not as dili-

gently; it still looked fierce, but this could have been only her—Allison's—realization of the role it played here, the role it had been *trained* to play. The bottom line was that she was simply not frightened of it anymore. She was not even certain that should Sandra appear in the school while the dog was patrolling, her appearance would make any difference at all to the dog, if the dog would not simply go loping on its way, mind on whatever had taken control of it since it had arrived at the school.

Later in the afternoon, while Frank was in the kitchen and Allison was in the bedroom, trying in vain to work on her story—Sandra's strange phone call kept replaying in her head—she noticed what she thought at first was a radiator hissing. But these radiators, she reminded herself, were not the sort that hissed. Then she thought that the high-pitched noise was a distant teakettle whistling and she wondered if Frank was making himself some tea. If so, she'd join him. It was better than trying to write, especially today.

She left the room, went down the hallway toward the cafeteria. The high-pitched noise increased and she realized that it was not a teakettle. It was a noise she had never heard before.

"Frank?" she called.

"Yes?" he answered at once from within the cafeteria, just down the hallway and to her right.

"Do you hear that?"

"Sorry?"

"That noise?"

"Noise?"

"Dammit!" she whispered, and went quickly down the hallway, into the cafeteria. Frank was seated at one of the long tables. He'd made himself a snack of ginger ale, crackers, and cheese.

He looked up at her as she advanced on him across the room. "Did you say something about a noise?"

She stopped.

The noise was gone.

She turned around, went back out in the hallway. She heard
nothing. She looked back into the cafeteria; Frank was looking
quizzically at her. She hesitated, thinking that the noise would
return. After a minute, she joined Frank at the cafeteria table.
"I heard a noise," she said.
"Did you?"
She nodded. "A high-pitched noise. Did you hear it?"
"No."
She said nothing.
"How's the story coming, Allison?"
"It's coming okay. It's very . . . strange." She smiled confusedly. "I'm trying to tap into . . . well, we've talked about this,
haven't we? I'm trying to tap into my inner self. Trying to do a
lot of that automatic writing I told you about."
He nodded. He seemed only vaguely interested, she thought.
She'd told him several times about her "automatic writing"—not
automatic writing in the classic sense, where a supernatural force
guided what she wrote, but, simply enough, writing that her fingers—as if acting on their own—seemed to accomplish to a
much greater extent than did her brain.
"And," she continued now, "it's produced a lot of strange
stuff. Some of it is completely . . . inaccessible to me, I guess. I
don't know where it comes from."
"Cheese?" Frank asked, and handed her a square of yellow
cheese.
She looked blankly at it. She wondered if she should conjure
up a look of offense for his interruption, and also because he was
clearly asking her to change the subject. She took the cheese.
"Thanks," she said.
"Is Joey in it?" he asked, catching her by surprise.
She took a quick, nervous bite of the cheese. It was a very
sharp cheddar, which she disliked. She shook her head. "No," she
said. "He doesn't need to be."
"Doesn't need to be?"
"Not yet, anyway."

22 Allison announced, "Frank, I can see something through that door under the stage."

Frank was watching TV in the bedroom. He rarely watched it. Like Allison, he had little time for it, and when he did take the time, he found himself quickly becoming addicted to it, so he had decided it was good to leave it off. But he had turned it on because he needed a few quiet moments; the day had been strange, even stranger, on balance, than days at the school had tended to be, and he wanted to lose himself in someone else's world, someone else's imagination.

"Look at this," he said, and nodded at the TV; he had heard his wife speak, but had not assimilated her words. "It's 'I Love Lucy.' I didn't know that was still on."

"Of course it isn't," Allison said. "It's a repeat."

He looked at her, blinked in confusion. "You think so?"

"Of course it is."

He looked at the TV again. He said, "Cigarette commercials, too."

"Frank," Allison said, ignoring his observation, "I said that I can see something through that door under the stage."

He did not respond.

"Frank, please!"

He looked at her, surprised. "I'm sorry. What door?"

"Under the stage, dammit. I can *see* something through it."

"Is this going to be another tall tale, Allison?" He smiled, as if in forgiveness.

"Come with me," she said, "and I'll show you."

She had drilled a dime-sized hole through one of the pine doors in one of the small rooms under the stage. She had used a hand drill she'd bought years before, when she had been taken by the idea of using primitive, hand-powered tools, although this was the first time she had actually used it.

When Frank put his eye to the hole, he got the clear impression of something very large and open beyond the door, as if he were looking at a landscape under the feeble light of a crescent moon. He did not understand what he was seeing; it confused him and concerned him, which was very much the reaction he would have had if he had looked in a mirror and had not seen a reversed image, very much the reaction he would have had if, waking up from a dream, he had found himself in the landscape of the dream. The *suggestion* of what he was seeing was impossible.

Without looking away from the hole in the door, he said, "What do you think it is, Allison?"

She was standing close to him, as if waiting her turn to look through the peephole. She shook her head. "I don't know. Maybe it's some kind of painting."

He glanced quickly at her. "Painting? What do you mean?" He looked through the hole again.

She shrugged. "A painting, Frank. It's simple. It's some kind of painting. A landscape. And we're seeing part of it through this hole in the door."

He thought about that. It was possible, he decided. "But where's the light coming from?" he asked.

"What light? It's dark as a cave in there."

"No," he pointed out. "Actually, it's darker. Or it should be. It should be pitch dark in there."

"Maybe there's daylight coming in through a cellar window somewhere," Allison suggested.

He sighed. "Allison, there is no cellar. The building's sitting on a cement slab."

"Listen," Allison said, sounding a little peeved, "this is under the stage, right? Well, maybe there's light coming in from up there. It's possible."

Frank thought a moment. "Sure," he conceded. "It's possible."

Without preamble, he picked up the power saw, turned it on, and brought it up to the door. Allison, startled, backed quickly away from him. The blade ripped into the dry pine, splintering it; sawdust billowed out. "Damn!" Frank breathed. He was cutting against the grain, that's why the wood was splintering. He shut the saw off. "I should use goggles for this, Allison."

She looked quizzically at him. "Well, we don't have anything like that. Can't you just close your eyes?"

"I have to *see* what I'm doing, don't you think?"

"Sure, I guess." She hesitated. "But we don't have any goggles. I could get my reading glasses for you, if you'd like."

"Yes, why don't you. I don't want to take a chance on going blind here."

"I'll be right back," she said, and started to leave the room.

"And maybe you could bring me some gloves, too?" he called.

Eileen Shute and Vicky Shephard were on Route 36, near the corner of Chelmsford Road. Vicky had parked the Mustang on the shoulder, and for several minutes, both of them had been dead quiet, unable to assimilate what was apparently happening to them, and unwilling to accept that it *was* happening to them.

The afternoon had turned cloudy and threatened snow. A brisk, temperamental wind was pushing the tall, golden grasses about. Vicky could feel the wind on her ankle through a vent that, for the two years she had owned the Mustang, she had been unable to close.

At last, she said, "What time is it?"

Eileen checked her watch. "It's three forty-five, Vicky. It's getting late. They were expecting us an hour ago."

"Dammit!" Vicky breathed. "Give me that map, would you?"

Eileen handed her the map. She didn't know how to respond to her friend's anger. It was something new; it hinted at violence. "Do you think I should drive?" she suggested.

Vicky answered at once, "No. I don't think you should drive. *I* drive this car. No one else does!"

"Just asking," Eileen said.

Vicky tore the crumpled map open and followed Route 36 with her finger to where it met Chelmsford Road. Then she followed Chelmsford to Center Road. "It's right fucking here!" she hissed, and jabbed the map with her index finger. "It's right here on this goddamned map! Route 36 meets Chelmsford which meets Center. But when we try it—"

"Vicky, there he is!"

Vicky looked up at once through the windshield.

The man in the brown suit was fifty yards off, walking briskly toward them, that crooked smile plastered on his face.

"Bastard!" Vicky screamed. She turned the ignition key. The Mustang roared to life. "Fucking bastard!" she repeated, and jammed the car into drive. She floored the accelerator.

The man in the brown suit stopped walking at once. His smile vanished. He looked awestruck, disbelieving.

"Vicky, no!" Eileen screamed.

But it was too late. In little more than a second, the Mustang's big engine pushed the car over the fifty yards separating it from the man in the brown suit and hit him squarely, throwing him first into the windshield, then over the top of the car, then onto the road.

Vicky slammed on the brakes, craned around, saw the man lying behind the car, his body twisted into impossible angles. "Bastard!" she screamed, and threw the car into reverse.

Eileen reached out and shut the ignition off.

The engine died.

Vicky looked at her friend. "Give me those goddamned keys!" she demanded through clenched teeth, and reached for them suddenly. Eileen pulled her hand away, hit the door handle with her elbow, let out a screech of pain.

The keys dropped to the floor.

Vicky lunged for them.

Eileen scooped them up, threw her door open, and with a "No, for God's sake!" tossed them into the tall golden grasses swaying fitfully in the wind.

*   *   *

The blade of the circular saw stopped abruptly, throwing Frank's gloved hand—the one holding the saw—back. The saw dropped to the floor, *clunk*! The blade started spinning again, which sent the saw skittering about on the wooden floor. "Jesus!" Frank hissed, reached over, and tried to pick up the skittering saw.

Behind him, Allison warned, "Careful, Frank!"

"I *know* that," he said, got hold of the handle of the saw, grasped it, shut the saw off.

"What happened?" Allison asked.

Frank pushed his glasses up to his forehead, reached, and tilted the overhanging bulb toward the door. There was a three-foot-long, vertical gash in it, alive with splinters. "I hit something," he said.

"What do you think it was?" Allison said, straining to see through the cloud of fine sawdust hanging in the air.

"I don't *know* what it was," he said. "Something damned solid. It was like trying to cut through rock."

"Like something metallic?"

"I guess. Sure. It could have been something metallic. Maybe something inside the door. A frame of some kind, though I've never heard of a wooden door like this with a metal frame."

She smiled. "Oh, c'mon, Frank, what do you know about doors?" She chuckled a little, inhaled some fine sawdust, coughed it out.

He shrugged. "Not very much. I admit it." He turned the saw on and put it to the door again, on the opposite side from the vertical gash. "Wish me luck?" he said.

"What?" Allison called above the keening whine of the saw.

He held the saw to the door. The blade bit into it; splinters flew. One speared the back of his wrist, exposed beneath the glove. He flinched, but held tight to the saw. He wished he had had Allison get him some earmuffs—the whine of the saw was painfully loud in the confined space. His ears were ringing.

The face of the man in the brown suit had obviously hit the gravel road very hard. It was pulpy with blood that was clotted with tiny gray bits of gravel, especially around the opened eyes and broad forehead, which, Eileen guessed, had borne the brunt of his weight as he hit.

She did not want to look at him, but she could not look away.

Vicky was standing close by, eyes averted. "He's dead, isn't he?" she said.

Eileen didn't answer.

"*Isn't* he?" Vicky snapped.

"Yes," Eileen whispered. "Of course he is."

"Good," Vicky said. "Good."

Eileen glanced at her. She was standing very stiffly, arms crossed beneath her breasts, head turned toward the car. Eileen could not gauge her expression, only her oblique profile was visible, and Eileen could read nothing from it.

"Vicky, we've got to tell someone about this."

Vicky shook her head stiffly. "How can we do that? I hit him *on purpose,* Eileen. I ran over him *on purpose.*"

Eileen said nothing for a moment. Then, "Yes, I realize that." She wanted to add, *But who has to know that?* She said, instead, "Well, we have to do *something.*" She glanced quickly beyond her friend, beyond the Mustang, and down the road a couple of hundred yards, where movement had caught her eye. She could see nothing. Probably a bird, she thought. She looked again at Vicky. "We have to do *something,* Vicky." She felt powerless.

A snow started. It was tentative, unambitious.

"Vicky?" Eileen coaxed.

"I'm cold," Vicky said. She was dressed in a white leather fall jacket, faded jeans, and black boots. "It's cold here."

"Yes," Eileen agreed; she was starting to shiver. Probably the influence of the snow falling, she thought, because she was dressed warmly enough. "We can get back in the car in a moment, but first we have to do something with this . . . man we've killed."

Vicky glanced over at her, wide-eyed and smiling. "The man *we*'ve killed, Eileen? How generous of you." She looked away, unwilling to look at the crumpled body of the man in the brown suit. "You do something with it. I'm going to go and find the damned keys." While Eileen watched, she walked briskly to the shoulder of the road to the left of the car, and then into the tall grass where Eileen had thrown the keys. She stooped over and was almost lost to Eileen's view because the grass was so tall.

Again Eileen saw movement down the road. She snapped her attention to it. The black dog that had crossed in front of the car twice before was there, a hundred yards off, in the center of the road. He was looking in their direction. His tongue hung out as if he were breathing heavily.

It was a big dog, and its head was large. Eileen thought it was a Newfoundland, a breed she knew well because she had owned three Newfoundlands as she was growing up. Its muzzle, even from this distance, was very powerful looking. The lolling tongue looked like a red banner against his curly black coat.

"Vicky," she called, and glanced at her. Vicky was still searching for the keys; only her rear end and legs, in the faded blue jeans, were visible against the golden grass. "Vicky!" she called again, louder. But Vicky did not respond. Eileen realized that if the dog had not been a Newfoundland—or, at least, looked like one from this distance—she would have been more concerned. But the Newfoundlands she had owned as an adolescent had all been very friendly. The breed, in fact, was known for its even disposition.

The dog walked toward them, his gait slow and stiff, as if his legs would not bend properly.

23

"It must be some kind of metal frame," Frank said. He picked up the circular saw. "Goddamned blade's *bent!*"

"Do we have other blades?" Allison asked.

"I don't think so. I'll look, but I don't think so." He set the saw on the floor, gave it a little kick. "Damn thing nearly broke my arm!"

"Are you all right, Frank?"

"Yes. I guess so." He coughed; the air was thick with fine, billowing sawdust. Splinters from the door lay everywhere. There were even a few shards embedded in the back of his wrist. He gingerly picked them out.

"Why don't we forget it for now, Frank. It's not important. We'll pick it up again in the morning, okay?"

"I thought you said that Sam and Iris were coming over in the morning."

"Oh," she said, and nodded sullenly, "I did say that, didn't I?"

He took off the glasses that Allison had found for him. "The world's like a damned cloud with these things on," he said, then added, handing them to her, "And it's not much better with them off, either."

"You need glasses, Frank."

"I know I do. I just don't want to admit it." He smiled. "Let's forget this for now, like you said. Whatever's behind there will wait till we can drive a tank in here and blow that door to smithereens." His smile flattened. "Damned thing!"

"Good," Allison said, then suggested, "Want to have an early dinner?"

"Sure," he said, and realized, suddenly, that he was famished.

"It's a Newfoundland," Eileen said. "They're friendly. I had three of them when I was growing up. I know about them."

Vicky, who had—much to Eileen's surprise—found the keys that Eileen had tossed into the tall grass, was standing beside the Mustang, her eyes riveted on the dog moving stiffly in their direction. "It doesn't *look* friendly, dammit! It looks . . . dead."

"For Christ's sake," Eileen seethed, pointing behind her at the body of the man in the brown suit, "*he* looks dead!"

Vicky kept her eyes on the dog. It was less than fifty yards away, now, moving toward them down the center of the road, its huge head tilted slightly, tongue swaying left to right with each stiff step. The snow, which had begun quietly falling a few minutes earlier, had increased—half-dollar-sized flakes littered the dog's curly black fur.

Vicky said, opening the Mustang's driver's door, "I'm getting in the damned car. You do what you want with him," meaning the man in the brown suit.

She got into the car and closed the door hard. Eileen heard the engine rev, and for one terrible moment, she got a mental picture of her friend doing to her what she had done to this man. The image dissipated when she saw that the dog had turned its head toward the car and was moving in its direction.

Eileen faced the dog, bent her knees, slapped her thighs, "C'mere, now!" she called, trying to sound friendly, but her voice cracked. "C'mere, I won't hurt you," she tried again, and thought how ludicrous she sounded. *She* wasn't going to hurt this two-hundred-pound beast! But the dog paid no attention to her. His small, dark brown eyes remained fixed on the car. He was ten or fifteen yards from it, moving at a slow walking speed. She could probably make it to the car, which was a dozen feet away from her, before he could. She'd have to leave the man in the brown suit where he was. She would probably have to leave him there anyway, she decided. He was such a big man. He probably weighed half again as much as the dog did.

She heard the Mustang's V8 rev again. She looked at Vicky sitting behind the wheel. Their eyes locked. She heard the car's gears change. She shook her head in disbelief, heard the car's rear wheels spin madly on the gravel, kept her eyes on Vicky's—there was so much to be seen in a person's eyes. Love. Hate. Confusion. Desperation. But she could read nothing in Vicky's eyes.

The car shot forward.

Eileen leaped to the right, toward the shoulder, the ditch. The bumper clipped her ankle, sending an immense stab of pain through her body.

She hit the ditch and rolled, found herself covered by new snow and golden grass. Her ankle was an island of pain.

Gingerly, she parted the grasses and peered out.

She saw two things. To the left, she saw the Mustang speeding north down Route 36. And to her right, she saw the face of the Newfoundland. It was inches from hers and its teeth were bared.

The night was dark and quiet, as it always was.

Allison swung her bare feet off the bed and felt the warm air on her exposed arms. She sensed the darkness stretching out around her like a huge, docile animal.

And, just ahead, she saw a rectangle of bright light.

Frank snored raspingly on his side of the bed. The sound of his snoring was soft, distant.

Allison moved quickly toward the rectangle of bright light. She passed through it as if through fire, and as swiftly as a candle going out, she was plunged into darkness.

She was aware of warmth, and of cold, of breathing around her, as if many people were standing close by. She reached into the darkness. Her fingers found skin, muscle, hair. She withdrew her hand.

Someone said, "She's afraid."

Someone else said, "Aren't we all?"

A sudden, knife-edged kind of ecstasy that all but stole her breath away came to her. She thought that she might find herself dead from such ecstasy, and the thought gave her pleasure.

"He's here," she heard. "Within easy reach. Open your eyes. Just open your eyes."

"Joey?" she whispered.

Frank snored fitfully on his side of the bed.

Light as bright as the sun spilled over her and she gasped.

Frank snored fitfully on his side of the bed.

The glaring light abated.

Two smiling faces, each framed by darkness, appeared above her, as if she were asleep and was being looked at in her bed. She recognized one of the faces. It was Sandra's, and her eyes were bright, her features alive with contentment. The other face belonged to an older woman. It was round, pale, plump-cheeked.

Sandra said, "We are not just the moment, Allison. We are all that we were, too."

"Very nice," said the plump-cheeked woman, and her smile increased, and she turned her head to look at Sandra. "Very nice. Very well put."

"Of course you're confused," Sandra went on. "Aren't we all confused, at least a little? But in your heart, you *know* what is happening here. You *know* the possibilities. Just as you know the risks."

"Oh, yes," agreed the plump-cheeked woman, "the risks." And she nodded vigorously. "The risks." Then, with a tilt of her head, as if with some great revelation, she added, "Existence is like a Mixmaster, don't you think?"

"Excellent," Sandra said. "All that we are, and were—it's all there, Allison. Birth and life. It's all past and it's all here. Who says death is nothing? Death is everything. Death is all that is and was. The cream and the . . . the . . ."

"Oregano," said the plump-cheeked woman.

"And the chives. The dill," Sandra said.

"The dill *pickle*," said the plump-cheeked woman.

"We don't understand a moment of it, do we, Allison?"

Frank snored contentedly on his side of the bed.

24 "Well," Allison said to Iris and Sam late the following morning, "we have something of a mystery here."

"A mystery?" Iris said, and her round pink face broke into a broad smile. "I love a mystery."

"Don't we all," Sam said tiredly, "but I would really like it if we could shower and have some breakfast, first, before we look into this mystery. We had a hell of a time finding this place—"

"You were here just a week ago," Frank said, astonished.

"Yes, I'm aware of that, Frank," Sam said. "But this area is still . . . strange to us. These roads seem to meander wherever they please. I think we circled back on our own tracks a couple of times, then we saw this place from across the valley—"

"My God," Allison said, "you really were lost, weren't you? The other side of the valley is, what?—fifteen miles away. Wouldn't you say it's that far, Frank?"

"At least," Frank said.

"Never mind, though," Allison said. "Frank and I will rustle up some breakfast—you two still like French toast, right?"

As one, they nodded. "Whole wheat," Iris said.

"I remember," Allison said.

The four of them started down the hallway that led to the showers, the gym, and the cafeteria. Sam asked, "So you've really decided to stay in this place?"

"We haven't decided not to," Allison answered. "It has its charms."

It had been one of the worst nights of Eileen's life, and now it was over.

Not that the room they had given her was bad. It wasn't. It

was comfortable. A tad overdone, perhaps. A *lot* overdone, actually—a monument to pink lace and stuffed animals, something left over from "Father Knows Best"—"Kitten's" room. And they—the family that had taken her in—had seemed pleasant enough. Perhaps a little vacant, but who was she to say? Her judgment had been clouded. It still was, in fact.

What the hell time was it? She glanced to her right, toward the ticking sound of a big, brass, key-wound alarm clock on a dainty white nightstand next to the canopy bed. The clock was facing away from her; she turned it so she could read it. Eleven-thirty. Good God, she must have slept for twelve hours or more. That was no good. She had police to talk to, statements to make! First, she'd call her parents, though. Christ, if the previous half day had been awful, the next day or two or three promised to be nightmarish.

Maybe she should simply stay where she was—safely in this awful bed in this cloyingly feminine room.

But she was a realist. She could no more stay in the bed than she could journey back in time a day or so and cancel this whole insane trip altogether. She swung her legs out from under the frilly white bedspread, found, to her horror, that she was naked (she couldn't remember undressing herself; she could remember very little from the previous afternoon and evening—the dog's face, teeth bared, a shouted command, "Cloud, no! Stay!"; babbling at these people about Vicky and the man in the brown suit).

There was a sudden sharp rap at the door. "Time to wake up, dear." It was a woman's voice, as cloying as the room. "Your breakfast is getting very cold, dear."

"Yes," Eileen answered, "I'll be down in a moment."

"Very good."

"Could you tell me—" Eileen began, and the voice behind the door cut in.

"Yes, dear?"

"I was wondering about my friend. Vicky."

"We know of no friend."

"Yes, I'm sure I told you about her. I *remember* telling you about her. . . ."

"No, dear. There is no friend named Vicky."

Eileen fell silent. She didn't like the finality of the woman's statement. *There is no friend named Vicky.* It seemed too much like an odd sort of command. *You had a friend named Vicky, but not anymore.*

The voice at the door called, "The men are waiting for you, dear. We mustn't hold them up."

Iris Pfeffer had always kept her eyes open while she showered. She didn't like the idea of being—in effect—both deaf (the loud white noise of the shower) and blind (closing her eyes against the lather) at the same time. It was unnerving. What if there were something she should *see?*

As a consequence, she had always used no-tears baby shampoo—nearly half a bottle of it at each shower—simply so she could keep her eyes, and her options, open.

The idea that someone would actually be *looking* at her while she showered was mortifying to her. The very possibility made her dizzy with embarrassment. She was not, she was sure, a pleasure on the eyes while she showered. The mental picture she got of herself was of the Michelin Tire Man studded with lather and cellulite. It was an image that made her cringe, although it was unfair. She wasn't svelte, it was true, but neither was she obese. There were no rolls of flab wiggling perversely everywhere on her body. She was simply a woman who believed all the hype about being thin that the celebrity and fashion magazines had exposed her to.

And so, when she turned and saw the children staring wide-eyed at her as she showered, she shuddered, screeched, and ran from the room.

"Iris, there are no children here," Frank told her for what he supposed was the hundredth time.

Iris shook her round head earnestly and miserably. "I saw them. A dozen of them. They were all standing against that wall and they were all *looking* at me! They were all *laughing* at me." Which wasn't true. "I know what I saw, Frank." She was very upset. She was still flushed—both from embarrassment and from the hot shower—and she was trembling. "I know what I heard." She turned away. "And they were pointing. They were *pointing* at me." Which also was not true. "All twelve of them. Pointing and laughing!"

Allison came forward and put her arm around Iris. "I believe you," she said.

Iris looked at her, astonished. "You do?"

"Of course I do. I've seen them myself. That's why I had Frank build that shower stall, you know."

"I wasn't using it," Iris confessed. "I tried to, but it made me claustrophobic. You can understand why, of course."

"Certainly," Allison said. "It's small. *I* get claustrophobic in it, too." *What a stupid thing to say,* she told herself.

Iris gave her an understanding, forgiving look. Then she said, "I think we should simply go to a motel. Or a bed-and-breakfast inn. I think I'd be happier."

Sam, who had been standing by, saying nothing, distressed by what had happened—but not believing for an instant the story his sister had told; which distressed him even more, because he was not accustomed to hearing wild stories from her—said, "I don't think that's necessary, Iris. It would be expensive."

"*Damn* the expense," Iris blurted out. "I am *not* going to stay here under the eyes of those children."

Frank said, again, "There *are* no children, Iris. There really *are* no children. It's the atmosphere of the place. It makes you . . . believe things—"

"He means *see* things," Allison cut in.

"Okay," Frank agreed, nodding, "I'll admit it. It makes you see things that aren't there. I know. I've seen things, too."

*   *   *

Eileen said, "My friend, Vicky. I told you about her. I told all of you about her yesterday. I remember. And the man in the road, too. The man in the brown suit." She had dressed in the clothes she'd been wearing the day before—blue jeans, a brown, long-sleeved blouse that accented her figure nicely, and red sneakers. She was standing in the dining room doorway, staring in at the little family gathered for a late breakfast. There was a man—the father—who was grinning and sported a crew cut, and was clean-shaven; he wore a white, short-sleeved shirt and there were a number of pens and pencils in his shirt pocket. A boy of twelve or so, who could have been his father's twin, sat, grinning, beside him. A woman—the mother—thin and pretty, her eyes as round and as benign as a fawn's, sat in the chair nearest to Eileen. She wore a white apron over a billowing pastel peach dress. A little girl of ten or eleven sat near her; the girl looked painfully shy and, like the son to the father, could have been her mother's much-younger twin.

They were all grinning at Eileen, and she was trying valiantly to grin back, if only because it seemed to be the proper etiquette of the moment—vacuous grinning—but her mouth quivered, and she knew she looked foolish, so she stopped grinning. "Vicky—" she began.

And the fawn-eyed woman sitting at the table cut in, "There is no friend named Vicky. We've told you that." Her tone was maternally sweet, as if she were correcting a small child.

"And no man in a brown suit, either," said the woman's husband, still grinning. He gestured to indicate an empty chair to his right. "Sit down, now, young lady, and join us for breakfast." He lifted his cup, which was empty. "Dot," he said, and the fawn-eyed woman leaped to her feet, came quickly around the table, and took the cup from him. She poured coffee into it from a percolator sitting on a sideboard behind her, then set the cup gently in front of his plate. Some of the coffee sloshed over onto the tablecloth. The man frowned, sighed, shook his head. "I hope you're teaching your daughter better than that," he admonished.

"Sorry, Paul," Dot said sweetly.

Eileen suppressed a nervous smile.

"It's a damned good thing"—he glanced at Eileen—"pardon my French"—he looked at his wife again—"that I married you, because no one would *hire* you to work for them, clumsy as you are."

"Yes, I know that," his wife said, and still, there was only a humble sincerity in her tone. She held the gleaming percolator up to Eileen. "Do you drink coffee yet, dear?"

Elieen was still standing. *What in the name of God is going on here?* she asked herself.

"Dear?" the woman coaxed.

Eileen shook her head weakly. "Decaffeinated," she managed.

"Sorry?" the woman said.

"Decaffeinated," Eileen said, her voice shaky.

"Decaffeinated?"

"Decaffeinated."

"Without caffeine?"

"Yes."

"You mean Postum?"

Eileen shook her head vigorously. "No. Decaffeinated." Her voice was stronger, her tone firmer. "Decaffeinated. Without caffeine. Naturally decaffeinated. Decaffeinated without chemicals." She paused. "Could I use your phone, please?"

The husband said, "She means like Sanka brand, Dot." He looked at Eileen. "But where would we be without chemicals? Why, we ourselves are *made* of chemicals. Nothing but chemicals. 'Better living through chemistry,' they say, and it's true."

There was a moment's silence, then he added, "Phone's not working, sweetheart. Sorry."

She looked wide-eyed at him, then at the son, who was nodding and grinning his agreement, and at Dot, whose big fawn eyes were filled with confusion. *I don't know what he's talking about. Chemicals? It's beyond me!*

"You people are crazy," Eileen said, and as soon as the

words slipped out, she regretted them, because the four grinning faces dropped their grins and assumed looks of hurt and aggression. "I didn't mean that the way it sounded," she said. "I'm sorry. I didn't mean to say it."

She felt a strong, cold grip on her wrist. She looked. The man's hand was holding her very tightly. "Sit down now," he commanded. "Have some breakfast. Eat your breakfast." He turned his head very stiffly toward his wife. "Dot. The Rice Krispies, the pop tarts."

Eileen sat.

The man let go of her.

"I'm not hungry," Eileen whispered.

A bowl of Rice Krispies and a saucer of pop tarts were put in front of her. She stared blankly at them. She crinkled her nose up. Dot, standing expectantly beside her, grinning with expectation, smelled awful.

> This is what I saw; I saw tentacles coming out of him and wrapping him up. Smothering him. And then the tentacles grew and lengthened and moved about in the room, went through the open doorway and out the windows, and then the whole house was wrapped up by them.
>
> But they weren't tentacles. I knew that. They had no suckers on them. Tentacles, real tentacles, have suckers on them. These were not like that. These were like thick strands of his own hair.
>
> And he had *power*. He was not simply strong, not simply able to lift more weight than other men, or make love all night long, but real, geography-shattering *power*. The power to *create*, and to *change*. And to renew. He was a *magician*.
>
> He was a part of Death and he hearkened way, way back.
>
> He had come around again.
>
> —Allison Hitchcock, "The Inside"

25 It was snowing hard, and Iris was very upset. She stood in front of the double glass doors at the school's east entrance, stomped her feet, and cursed, "Dammit, goddammit!" Their Volvo wagon had no snow tires and wasn't much good in the snow, anyway. "We're *stuck* here!"

Sam, who was standing just behind her, sighed and asked Frank, "How far to the nearest motel, do you think?"

Frank shook his head. "I'm not sure." He paused. "To tell you the truth, I've never actually seen one around here. I think the closest one is in Aurora, and that's a good thirty miles. Allison and I stayed there when we were—"

"Shit!" Iris cut in. She looked at Frank. "I'm sorry, Frank. I don't mean to sound upset with you, really. But I simply can't stay here tonight, snow or not. I'm sure you understand."

Frank nodded. "Yes, we understand."

Allison put a comforting hand on Iris's wrist. "We do understand, Iris. Believe me. I told Frank just after we moved in that I thought this place was as spooky as a tomb. And it is."

Iris shook her head earnestly. "No. Spooky is not the word. It means 'fun,' I think. Spooky means *fun!*"

"I agree," Allison said, still comfortingly. "And I know what you're getting at—"

"Spooky or not," Sam cut in, "we can still stay the damned night, at least! What else are we going to do? If we go out in this weather, we're probably going to have an accident. Neither of us likes to drive in this stuff, you know." He glanced at his sister. "You know that, Iris."

Iris closed her eyes. "Yes," she whispered.

"Then we'll stay?"

Iris sighed her assent.

"Believe me," Frank said, "there are no children here. There haven't *been* any children here for ten years."

For what she supposed was the thousandth time, Eileen looked at the bedroom door and told herself that it couldn't really be locked, that these strange people hadn't actually locked her in, and again she felt the impulse to go to the door and try it, but she whispered a curse of disbelief and confusion instead.

She was locked in.

She was a prisoner in this house.

She heard a scratching noise at the door. It was not the first time she'd heard it, so it didn't startle her. It was the dog, Cloud. Soon, she knew, he'd begin to whine, and then someone would come and take him away.

She waited.

Presently, he did begin to whine. Then, from far down the hallway, someone said, "Cloud, no!" Strangely Eileen couldn't tell if the voice was male or female, a child's or an adult's.

"Let me out!" she called, as she had a dozen times already. But she got no answer. She expected none.

She went to the window, spread the pink lace curtains, looked out. She saw the dim reflection of her own face from the window glass and she gasped, startled. Then she forced herself to relax, and pressed her face to the window.

Below, light from the living room illuminated the area near the house. There were big, square patio stones lightly covered with snow, two green chaise longues, a barbecue area made of red brick.

She looked toward the horizon. She saw nothing. No lights, no stars, no snow. The landscape beyond the house was as blank as a dreamless sleep.

"And then there is Joey, whom we've lost."

"No one is ever really lost."

"But you're wrong. Some people exist for us only in our memories. We cannot ever hope to see them again, except there. Have you heard that the recently blind look forward to sleep because they can see the world again, in their dreams? And the people they love. It's the same with us, and with Joey."

"No. You're wrong. About some things you're wrong. About this you're wrong. You may believe that you have overwhelming and incontrovertible logic behind you, but you don't, because you know only a fraction of a percent of all there is to know. And that is not enough knowledge to claim that you know anything."

"I would like to believe what you're saying—"

"Then believe it. You have no choice."

—Allison Hitchcock, "The Inside"

"Do you think there's anything to read?" Iris asked her brother testily. "Something light. Or maybe we could go and watch TV."

"There's only one TV," Sam told her. "And it's in their bedroom."

"That's stupid," Iris said, pouting. "And it's discourteous, too. Why would they put the television in *their* bedroom? Why not ours? We're their guests." Iris had refused to sleep in a room by herself, so she and her brother were sharing a room.

"I don't know," Sam said vaguely. He was standing at the window. "It's still snowing. Dammit, Iris, it's still snowing."

Iris, who was sitting up in bed, said, "You don't like it here, either. I can tell by your tone."

"I don't like the damned snow. If it keeps up we're not going to be able to get out of here in the morning, either."

There were two twin beds in the room. They stood side by side; Iris was in the bed closest to the door, which was closed and locked. Light in the room was provided by an overhead fluorescent embedded in the acoustical-tile ceiling. The fluorescent tube had been flickering for some time, and Iris had been trying to ignore it, but she couldn't ignore it anymore. "Dammit to hell, Sam! Could you *please* see if you can fix that light!"

Sam glanced around at her, then up, at the light. "Oh," he said, "sure. What a pain."

The light went out, plunging the big room into darkness. "Shit!" Iris said.

"It's okay," Sam said. "I'll fix it." He started to cross the room and banged his foot into a student chair (one of many in the school), knocking it over. He picked up the chair and took it to the spot under the burned-out fluorescent, though, in the darkness, he wasn't certain he was precisely beneath it. "We have another light, don't we?" he asked.

"No," Iris answered.

"Hell." He stood on the chair, reached, found the plastic covering for the light and slid it to one side so it dropped into his hands. He lowered the covering to the floor, let it drop. It hit the linoleum with a soft *whump!* and Iris called out, "Christ, what was that?"

"Nothing," Sam said. "It's okay." He reached, jiggled the fluorescent tube, got it to flash on for a moment, jiggled it again, got it to flash once more. "I don't know, Iris. I don't think this is going to work. I don't think the tube is any good."

"Hell!" Iris whispered.

The tube flashed on again, and again, and again, as Sam jiggled it. "Maybe I can get it to work," he said.

Iris said nothing.

"Iris?"

She did not answer.

"Iris?"

"Sam . . ." Her voice was trembling.

"What's the matter?" The fluorescent tube flashed again, bathing the room in blue-white light for an instant. Sam was looking toward the bed, toward Iris. He saw, in the moment that the fluorescent tube flashed, that she was looking beyond him.

He jiggled the tube again. It flashed. "Iris?"

He looked toward the wall, where she was looking. He jiggled the tube. It flashed. And in the moment of the flash, in that pulse beat, he saw a half-dozen children standing quietly against the pastel peach cinder-block wall, their eyes wide and their mouths open into huge *O*'s of awe and surprise.

Eileen had often fantasized about doing just what she was doing now, about tying blankets and sheets together to form a ladder and then lowering herself out a second-floor window. She had imagined this because she was afraid of being caught in a house fire and having no way out. She did not know consciously that as a toddler, she had once been trapped in a house fire. The fire had killed her mother and little sister and she had been saved by her father, who had never told her the real story of her mother's death for fear that it would be traumatic, that it would release a lot of emotions and fears that were best left hidden in her subconscious, where, he had told himself, they could do her no harm.

In her imaginings she had done just what she had done tonight. She had tied the blankets together with good, tight double knots, had tied one end of the ladder to the bedpost, and had slipped out the window.

Her arms were strong, and she was supple, so it was no chore lowering herself. She was a little concerned that she seemed to have been lowering herself for quite a while without getting a lot closer to the snow-covered patio stones below, but she was certain that this was only an illusion created by her desperation to be away from this house and these people.

She was also concerned that the window below—light from within flooded the patio stones—was bare and that the people inside would see her. For this reason, she had decided that she would jump when her feet were near the top of the window. It was not a long way to jump. Eight feet, perhaps. A little more.

She heard voices from within the house. They were loud, angry voices, but she could not make out individual words. The man's voice seemed loudest and angriest, and the woman's—Dot, she remembered—seemed angry, too, but more distant, even frightened.

The fact of this argument made Eileen uncertain what to do. On the one hand, if they were arguing, then they were distracted, and she could probably slip past the window unnoticed. But if they saw her, and they were angry (for some reason, she was very fearful of receiving the brunt of that man's anger), then it might go badly for her. People could be unaccountably foolish and violent, even people who were her friends (Vicky). These people— the people in the house—were not her friends. They were strangers and they were very, very odd, and there was a real possibility that they could hurt her, and like it.

The argument from within the house intensified. Still she could make out no individual words. Perhaps there were some expletives from the man. Some whining from the woman.

"What are you doing down there?" a voice said from above, and Eileen looked up and saw a head—no more than a dark oval—sticking out of the window. "You shouldn't be doing that." the voice continued. It was the same sexless, ageless voice that had called to Cloud from the other side of the bedroom door.

Eileen did not answer the voice. She couldn't. She could only shake her head a little and wonder desperately what the person above had in mind.

"We can't have you doing this!" the voice said.

Eileen shook her head.

The voice repeated itself. "We can't have you doing this!"

Eileen shook her head again. She let go of the knotted sheet and started to fall through the cold, dark air.

(*"So many things sweep back and forth. So many things . . . mix together. Imagine . . . Allison, imagine what we have here. On this side. What life gives us. We have . . . so much. Time. Change. Love. Hate. Beauty. Stasis. And these . . . all these things are not merely mirrored over there. It's not that simple. They are . . . well, just like here, but very differently . . . they're mixed together. I don't know why. I've never understood why. Maybe because that other place is actually the . . . the detritus—"*)

26 And as Eileen fell, Frank Hitchcock, at the school on Ohio Road, was fingering the cinder-block wall where Iris and Sam Pfeffer had seen children staring and he was pointing out that there were paintings on the wall or, at least, that there once had been, but that the paint had faded over time. "Look here," he said as he touched the wall, "paintings of children." He paused. "I'll bet they were done by the children who used this classroom."

But Iris wasn't convinced. She shook her round head. "Tell them, Sam," she said, and looked dismally at her brother for support. "This is not what we saw. How could it be?"

"Well, it *could* be, if you think about it," Sam told her. "If the light was right, and obviously it was, then it would highlight these paintings and we would see what we saw."

"No!" Iris proclaimed *"This"*—she pointed stiffly at the faded paintings—"is not what we saw, and you know it."

Sam looked at her for a few moments, then shook his head. "Actually, Iris," he said. "I *don't* know it."

She looked pleadingly from one face to another—from her brother's, to Frank's, to Allison's (who looked sympathetically back at her, but said nothing), then, in frustration, she threw her plump arms into the air. "I don't believe this." She shook her head. "I don't believe this," she repeated, although she didn't go on to say exactly what she didn't believe. "I don't give two shits if it's snowing! I'm going to leave this goddamn place!" And with that, she gathered up some clothes, dragged her suitcase out from under the bed, threw the clothes into it, got her coat on, and stormed from the room.

*   *   *

She was at the east doors when Frank and Sam and Allison caught up with her. It was clear that she was having second thoughts. She had kept her hand on the knob and had watched steadily as they approached her.

"You don't really want to do this, do you, Iris?" Sam asked.

She shook her head and sighed. "No. Of course not. It's stupid." But she kept her hand on the doorknob.

"We'll give you another room if you like," Allison said, and put her hand comfortingly on Iris's wrist. "Would that be all right?"

Iris gave her a small, quivering smile. "I'm afraid of ghosts," she said.

"Aren't we all?" Allison said.

"You have to be," Frank said. "If you're any kind of a thinking person, you have to be." He saw Sam grimace.

"I don't *believe* in them, really," Iris went on. "At least I don't think that I do. But I'm afraid of them. I've always been afraid of them."

"We'll give you the TV, too," Allison said, and gripped Iris's wrist to get her to take her hand off the doorknob. Iris didn't let go of it. "Sometimes the TV is a good distraction. It gets your mind off things."

Iris let go of the doorknob. "I don't want to be in that part of the school. Give us the TV and put us in some other part of the school. Then I'll stay."

"Sure," Allison said at once. "That's no problem."

Eileen hit the patio stones feet-first. Her left ankle twisted inward, her knees buckled, and in a moment she found herself out of breath on her back, staring wide-eyed at the open window so incredibly far above her.

She had fallen through the cold dark air for a minute or more. Now the window she had come out of was only a pinpoint of light high above her, like a bright star.

There were other windows, nearer windows, on the first floor of the house. And they were like postage stamps of light.

She could not breathe. Her lungs would not work, would not take air. She thought that there was no atmosphere, that she had been demonically transported to another planet, and this landscape, this house towering thin and high and impossible above her, like an M. C. Escher creation, was something alien.

She screamed, but her voice, like her lungs, did not work, so she heard nothing.

It was then that she realized that although she could not breathe, it did not seem to matter. She wasn't growing faint, wasn't losing consciousness.

Perhaps she was already dead. Perhaps this impossible building towering high and thin above her, the black, starless sky, and the wide bowl of the horizon was all part of the landscape of death.

If so, it was hellish, nightmarish.

If so, she was obviously being punished for a life of sin and debauchery.

She smiled.

A life of sin and debauchery? What was she thinking?

She wanted to laugh. But she couldn't.

A life of sin and debauchery!

"What are you talking about?"

Her eyes moved right, left. Had she said that? Had she spoken without knowing it?

"'A life of sin and debauchery'? Where did *that* come from?"

It was Vicky's voice.

"Eileen? Are you listening to me?"

High above her, the second-floor window darkened, as if someone were looking out at her.

"Eileen?"

"Vicky?"

"I'm talking to you."

She found that she could breathe. "My God," she whispered, "I'm alive."

"And what's that? Revelation of the hour?"

"No."

"You act like you're in another world, for Christ's sake. Snap out of it."

She heard the sound of fingers snapping.

High above her, in the cold blue sky, a hawk circled. "Look at that," she said.

"Look at what?"

"That hawk." She pointed at the top of the Mustang's windshield. "Wonderful creatures."

"Yeah, sure," Vicky said.

"They are. Predators. They're predators. Wonderful."

She glanced at Vicky, who had both hands hard on the wheel and was going too fast down the narrow, one-lane road. "Something's wrong, Vicky."

Vicky glanced at her. "You bet there is. It's almost four o'clock, and you said they were expecting us at two, and I still don't know where the hell where we are."

Eileen looked ahead. The road curved, trees crowded up to the shoulder. "This is right," she said.

Vicky glanced at her. "You okay?"

"Okay?"

"Yeah. You were out of it for a few minutes."

"Was I? I don't remember." She paused. "What time is it?" She remembered that Vicky had already told her it was close to four. The dashboard clock read 4:01. "There's something wrong, Vicky."

"So you've told me," Vicky said, and slowed the Mustang around a particularly sharp curve. "Care to elaborate?"

Eileen thought about it. "Elaborate? I can't. I don't remember. . . ." She paused. "What day is it?"

"What *day* is it? It's Saturday."

"Vicky, there's something . . ." The road straightened.

Ahead a hundred yards, it crested. A man stood at the crest, in the center of the road. Eileen gasped. Vicky slowed the Mustang, brought it to a stop. They were a couple of car lengths from the man. "Well, what in the hell do you think *his* problem is?" Vicky said.

"Don't go forward!" Eileen pleaded. "Please. Don't go forward. Turn around."

Vicky looked confusedly at her. "Turn around? Why the hell should I turn around? Because of him?"

The man was very still. He was smiling a little, as if at a private joke.

"Yes," Eileen answered. "Because of him." She took a deep breath, shook her head. "No. I don't know. Dammit, Vicky, I'm confused. Something is very, very wrong!"

The man turned around and began walking away from them.

Vicky put the car in gear.

"Please, no!" Eileen pleaded.

Moments later, they passed the man.

Ten minutes after that, they arrived at their destination.

Frank said, "She's very excitable, isn't she?" He was getting into his pajamas. He had the pants on, was shrugging into the shirt.

Allison was already in bed. "Iris? Yes. I think she has low self-esteem."

Frank glanced at her, pulled the shirt down over his head. "What does that have to do with anything?"

"Simple. She thinks she's fat, unattractive, so she imagines that people are looking at her, making judgments about her. She comes here and she imagines that there are children watching her. Just *being* here, in this school, probably calls up all kinds of nasty memories."

Frank sat on his side of the bed. He was facing the windows.

The curtains were drawn. "We can't assume that her school years were nasty."

"Sure we can, Frank. *Mine* were, and I wasn't fat. I was just sort of odd looking. You remember."

He gave her an incredulous look. "You weren't odd looking, Allison. You were beautiful."

She shook her head solemnly. "*You* thought I was because you wanted to get into my pants—"

"That's not true."

"You *didn't* want to get into my pants?"

He tilted his head a little, confused. "I wouldn't put it that way, Allison. I mean, I wouldn't use that phrase. I never *thought* of it that way, to be sure. You were attractive and I was attracted to you—"

"And, anyway," Allison cut in, "fat people have a hell of a time in school. Especially high school." She paused. "She's what? Twenty-eight? Twenty-nine? So she went to high school in the mid-to-late seventies. Bad time for anyone who was fat. Even worse than when you and I went to school."

Frank glanced at her. This was a topic that he found of little interest. Especially now. He had been hoping they would make love.

"You don't agree?" Allison asked.

"With what?"

"With what I said."

He shrugged. "Sure."

"Boy, you're easy."

He nodded. "Yes. I am." He smiled.

She cocked her head. "You want to make love, don't you?"

He nodded again.

She smiled. "Well then," she said, "come convince me." And she pulled the blanket away, revealing her nakedness.

They had put Iris and Sam in a room in the north wing of the school, which was the wing they never used, the wing to which Alex had been relegated when Frank and Allison agreed that it was the most likely place where intruders could enter. ("I'll lock him up. You don't have to worry about him," Allison had assured Iris, and had put the dog, with its food and water, into room 16, two doors down.) It was cold in the room Iris and Sam were using because it faced the prevailing winds, there were no curtains on the big windows, and the night was frigid; even with the heat turned up to eighty, the air still had a chilly edge that Iris knew she'd have to contend with all night long. Doubtless, she'd wake at hourly intervals, find that some part of her body was cold, she'd adjust the blankets for it, then be unable to get back to sleep right away.

"What time is it, Sam?"

He was reading in a twin bed nearby—he and Frank had brought the beds in from the other room. He glanced at his watch on a desk near his bed. "Close to ten thirty."

"That's late," Iris whispered.

"Are you tired?"

She shook her head quickly. "No. I couldn't sleep. I'm not tired." She was staring at the big windows as she sat up in bed. She was dressed warmly, in green flannel pajamas. "I think I'm going to stay awake all night, Sam. Is that okay with you?"

"All night? You're going to leave the light on?"

She hesitated. "Well, yes. If you don't mind."

"Do you have to? I can't get to sleep with the light on. You know that."

She said nothing.

"I'm sorry," Sam said. "I know how you feel."

"No, you don't."

He thought about that. "Maybe I don't know completely how you feel. I know that's not possible—"

"You don't have this body, Sam. You don't know what it's like to be repulsive."

He said nothing. He had heard these words from his sister before and had told her countless times that she wasn't repulsive, or disgusting, or hideous—all of the words she used to describe herself.

"And to have children *staring* at you. My God, my God—"

"Dammit, Iris, there were no children staring at you. It was your imagination. Just as you imagine that you're disgusting, you imagine that people are always *looking* at you, and it's simply *not true.*"

"I *saw* them, for Christ's sake! I wasn't hallucinating, I wasn't going crazy, I wasn't . . ." She faltered. "Damn you, Sam. It's so easy for you to criticize and poke fun and—"

"I'm not criticizing and poking fun. . . ." He paused, eyes on the windows. "Jesus, look at that." The storm had intensified. "All hell is breaking loose!"

The entity in the school did not see wind-driven snow. Its eyes were blue and sparkling and it moved and reacted at the impetus of memory; it waltzed about gaily, it ran, it sang, it cursed—in its ineffectual, adolescent way—from the impetus of memory.

The rush of wind.

The crack of a willow branch.

For more than a decade it had drawn from its memories and had given itself life from them.

Soon, that would change, and the entity would move on.

The entity's existence was a paean to life. It *was* life in its purest and most unencumbered form. It knew no death, and it never had.

And that was not unusual.

For a billion years, the entity had known only change and transformation.

"What if someone had told you that they had discovered the door that led into death?"

"I think I'd laugh. There is no door into death."

"A way in, I mean. A way in to death. To what comes after. What would you say?"

"Has someone told you that?"

"No."

"Then why do you ask? Is it a literal question? Are you saying that there is actually some physical door, something I can knock on, something made of wood—"

"I'm not saying anything. I'm talking. I'm bringing up possibilities."

"But there's no point. A door into death. Death isn't something we cross into. It's a state of *non*being. It doesn't *exist;* it is *non*existence."

"You might be wrong."

"Yes, I might be wrong. But I doubt it."

—Allison Hitchcock, "The Inside"

| 27 | "Well," Frank said with a sigh and a bemused smile, "so much for that," and he rolled off Allison and stared at the acoustical-tile ceiling.

Allison said, "You're welcome to keep trying."

Frank shook his head. "I know when I'm licked."

"Pity." She sighed.

"Disappointed?"

"Yes." She sounded playful.

"I'm sorry."

She hesitated. "I'm glad."

"You're glad I'm sorry?"

"Yes." Seconds passed. "I'm tired, Frank." Her tone had changed, was less playful. "Suddenly I'm very tired."

He glanced at her. She had covered her body to her waist with the blanket. Her arms were straight at her sides, her fists loosely clenched. She did not appear to be breathing. Frank asked, "You all right?"

She nodded. "Just tired."

"I was going to go and check on Iris and Sam."

"Sure. Go ahead."

"You'll be all right?"

She did not answer. Frank got out of bed, put a robe on, glanced at her. Her eyes were closed. Again he asked her, "You'll be all right?"

She nodded.

He left the room.

He had once been on a train during a snowstorm, and he remembered it as he walked the corridor that connected the south and north wings of the school. The corridor had floor-to-ceiling windows on both sides; floodlights lit the blowing snow beyond. He hadn't realized that the floodlights were on, and as he walked he made a mental note to shut them off on his way back to the bedroom.

The corridor itself was dark, but the blowing snow reflected a creamy dull light, like the light of the full moon, and he could see well enough.

Allison thought that the bed was very inviting, that it was where she desperately wanted to be; she thought, too, as her legs carried her slowly to the door, that only a minimal willpower would take her back to the bed, where she would be out of the cold air and soon asleep.

But she was not possessed of that necessary willpower.

She was possessed of something else.

And it was pulling her from the room.

The hallway was much longer than Frank remembered. He supposed that he had been walking in it for quite some time, and from what he could see he was no closer to its end than when he had started down it minutes ago.

He stopped walking. He realized that he was suddenly in a very strange situation, a kind of dream situation, and he thought for a moment that he was still asleep.

He glanced right, left, at the tall windows that flanked the hallway, at the blowing snow lit dully from behind by spot lamps. He realized that he couldn't *hear* anything, that he could hear no wind, no soft tap-tap as the snow hit the windows, no radiators flooding with water along the hallway baseboards.

He turned around and looked in the direction he'd come. He saw the softly lit hallway, the windows, at the periphery of his vision, the blowing snow; all of it trailed off into a rectangle of blackness.

"Allison?" he called. The name was absorbed by the darkness; it did not echo, it was gone within the moment that it left his mouth.

He started back the way he had come. He was afraid. Ghastly afraid. He felt as if he were walking within the province of death itself.

In the room where Frank had found Mrs. Hastings's student reports, the slow but inexorable buildup of stress in the school caused the ceiling to crack. It was a hairline crack at first, and it let in only a hint of cold air from above. Then, in the next moment, the crack widened to finger width, and snow that had piled on the roof began filtering through to the top side of the acoustical-ceiling tile. Within the next minute, much of the acoustical-tile ceiling itself collapsed. This was not an incredibly noisy event. The ceiling tiles were held up by narrow strips of wire and a thin aluminum frame, and even if someone had been standing outside the closed door, they would not have heard the ceiling fall; the wailing of the storm outside would have masked it.

The floor cracked next, sympathetically with the crack of the huge cement slab beneath the school. The crack in the floor was as wide as an arm and it revealed beneath it a universe full of the past trying to break through.

"Nothing much comes in," Sam told Iris as he fiddled with the TV's rabbit ears. "Just snow." The TV was an aged twelve-inch Sony that they had set up on a desk a couple of feet in front of the beds.

"Yes," Iris whispered, "I can see that."

Sam did some more fiddling with the rabbit ears. "I get a little something on this channel," he said. "See. Some kind of talk show, I think. Johnny Carson?" He checked his watch. "No. Too early." He turned the sound up. A tinny, high-pitched voice filtered through the pink noise. "Maybe it's a special or something."

"Move the rabbit ears around a little bit more," Iris said irritably. "We should be able to get *something* on the damned thing."

For a few seconds Sam tried to get the picture in better. Then he shut the TV off. "Sorry," he said.

"You're giving up?"

"Sure. We can't get anything."

"It doesn't mean you stop *trying,* Sam. Now turn it on again." She was angry.

He turned the TV on. The same anemic voice came over the speaker; the small screen showed only what might have been a human form, from the waist up, in tones of gray.

"Dammit!" Iris said. She got out of bed, crossed to the TV, and slammed the side of it with her open hand. The slap caused no change in the picture or the sound.

There was a soft knock at the door. Iris turned her head sharply toward it and uttered a small curse.

"Who is it?" Sam called. He could see what he supposed was Frank's silhouette against the frosted glass. "Is that you, Frank?"

Another knock, on the glass itself, louder.

Sam went quickly to the door and threw it open. He found no one there. He stuck his head out into the hallway. It was dark except for the dull, reflected light of spot lamps outside the school; the light was filtering in through the tall windows in the hallway's north wall. In this dull light Sam could see a human form standing not far away. "Frank?" he said. "Is that you?" He didn't believe it was Frank, although he could think of no one else it could be. The school was big, though, and had lots of windows and doors; the man standing there—and Sam was certain it was a man—could easily have broken in. "Frank?" Sam said again.

The figure half in darkness moved backward a few steps. Sam heard feet shuffle on the gray linoleum.

"Who are you?" the figure said.

Sam thought, *Frank's voice.*

"Who *are* you?" the figure repeated.

"Frank? It's me. It's Sam."

"No. You aren't Sam. Liar! Get out of here! Get out!" And the figure turned and ran down the hallway, into the darkness.

*   *   *

Sam didn't go after him. He went back into the bedroom and said to Iris, "It's the strangest thing, the strangest damn thing, Iris," and told her what had happened.

"Sounds like some kind of joke," Iris said. "He's playing a joke on us. It's obvious."

Sam shook his head. "No. I don't think so. I don't believe . . ." He stopped, seemed uncertain.

"You don't believe what?" Iris coaxed.

He shrugged, smiled nervously. "I don't believe it was Frank."

The school was too quiet. And too cold. Hadn't it always been that way? Hadn't Allison complained to him enough about it? So what was he going to do? Fix the furnace? Install more lights? Track lights along the corridors? *That* was a good idea.

He touched one of the windows in the corridor and felt the soft tap-tap of the blowing snow. He could *see* the snow hitting the window.

He put his face to the glass and looked down. He could not see the grass below the window. Perhaps it was covered with snow, or maybe there was only a parking lot out there, beyond this particular window. Black parking lot and red-brick walls in the blowing snow.

In the night.

In the quiet.

The window was cold against his forehead, his nose, and chin, and fingers. He got an image of himself with his face mashed against the glass. It was an image from very long ago, when he had been a fourteen-year-old doing this same thing— experiencing the confining presence of the glass and the parking lots and the red bricks.

The image was discomforting, alien. Who was that fourteen-year-old boy? What did he have to do with the man standing here now? That young boy was dead.

Frank let the image dissipate.

The snow and wind pushed at the window. Some of the tiny flakes hit the glass hard and he felt the tap-tap of collision. Some of the snow seemed to veer off as if a wind from the glass itself were pushing at it.

He became aware that someone was standing near him in the quiet corridor.

He did not move. He wanted to close his eyes, to shield himself from this thing standing close by. If he did not see it, it would mean it wasn't there—one of the truisms of his childhood.

"Who are you?" said the thing standing in the quiet darkness.

Frank shivered. It had spoken in his voice. Perhaps *he* had spoken without realizing it. Perhaps *he* had asked "Who are you?"

"Who *are* you?"

But no, that was not him. It couldn't have been. He hadn't spoken. He would have known.

"Who in the *hell* are you?"

"I live here. This is my home."

"No. This is *my* home. *I* live here."

Frank turned his head a little so he could see the thing out of the corner of his eye. It was a tall shadow in the dull light from outside. Frank whispered, "I live here."

The thing said nothing.

"Who are you?" Frank said.

"Answer my question."

"Who *are* you?"

"I live here. This is my home."

Frank turned his head further so he could see the thing more clearly. But he did not see it clearly. It remained only a tall shadow, nothing more.

Then it was gone and he was alone again in the corridor.

28 So, just for the hell of it, you open the door.

It opens outward, toward you. You note this. You think it's important. But there's nothing very special or interesting on the other side of the door. Only the rest of the forest.

So you walk through. Again, you do it just for the hell of it.

You walk through it.

You look about. You're still in the forest.

You think, *Well, this is very strange, a door in the middle of the forest.* But as strange as it may be, it has turned out to be nothing very interesting.

You walk on. Further into the forest.

You don't think much about the door. After a while, you forget where it was, exactly.

And then you begin to notice that the leaves on the trees are green, and only minutes earlier, they were bright with the colors of autumn.

And then the leaves are merely buds, and the trees are dying, the trees are young, the sky is glazed over by the smoke of a forest fire, the ground is heavy with snow.

You realize what you've done.

You turn around to go back to the door you have come through and there you are, turning around to go back to the door you have come through, and there you are, and there you are. . . .

—Allison Hitchcock, "The Inside"

In the gym/auditorium, the overhead lights were on, in their black metal cages, and the light they produced turned the blue-green walls nearly white.

The bare oak floors—bearing a thousand gray scuff marks—reflected the light dully, their varnish unpolished for a decade. To the left of the stage, the brown, threadbare curtains—which Allison had planned on replacing; she had, in fact, written to a company in Vermont that specialized in the manufacture of stage curtains—moved a little in a breeze that snaked through a broken window, down a short hallway, and through an open doorway at the back of the gym.

Allison, standing near the stage, could feel the breeze and she wondered about it briefly, though in a detached way. Because she knew she had not been brought here to check on drafts.

She knew that she had been brought here for some other purpose.

She felt as if she were being manipulated. But she didn't mind it. Something wonderful and awe-inspiring was going to be revealed to her, she could feel it, *had* felt it all the way here from the bedroom, but now it was clear, true, inevitable.

She was going to be shown something wonderful.

She was going to be shown what Sandra had been talking about this past month.

It was as if someone were whispering in her ear, "You aren't going to believe what we're going to show you, but it's going to change your life, your future, your entire existence."

And it would make sense of the nightmare of confusion that her life had become here, at the school. And it would make sense, too, of the grief that had rekindled in her over Joey's death so many years ago.

She bent down, put her hand against the little door that led to the rooms beneath the stage. The door opened. She peered in. The underside of the stage was empty. She had known it would be. That little voice had told her. "There's nothing to see here," it had said.

She went in.

She realized again that she was being manipulated. It was all right.

Frank did not go to check on Iris and Sam after the encounter in the corridor. He went back to the bedroom instead. He intended to share news of the encounter with Allison so they could add it to the already long list of odd occurrences at the school. He would phone the police, he supposed, although he didn't like the idea of trying to deal with Peter McWilliams again.

But when he went into the bedroom, he found that Allison wasn't there. It annoyed him.

"Allison?" he called, first inside the bedroom—as if she really was in the room, but for some reason, he couldn't see her—and then down the corridor that led to the gym. But he got no answer.

It was past twelve. He was tired, cold, angry, and confused about the encounter with the man in the corridor (he wasn't at all sure anymore that there actually *had been* a man; he wasn't at all sure that the school itself wasn't causing him to hallucinate. He thought that whatever slop was oozing into the school from the crack in the floor in room 22 might be causing a slow but insidious realignment of his brain chemistry—Allison's too, and possibly Iris's and Sam's; it was not impossible—far stranger things had happened), and what he very much wanted was to go to bed.

But now there was Allison to locate.

The police to call.

In the room where the mother field mouse and her brood had died, where the ceiling had collapsed and the floor had cracked from the slow buildup of stress in the school, the windows blew out simultaneously, raining bits of plate glass onto the snow-covered lawns. The event was very quick and very loud, and four rooms away, in room 18, Iris and Sam heard it and supposed it was simply a strong gust of wind. In room 16, Alex, who had been trying to nod off but was finding it very hard, indeed—not only because storms had always bothered him, but because his senses were being assaulted from every angle by strange new sights and smells and sounds and his dog brain was trying to fit them into his dog world—cocked his head and whimpered a little, aware, in some primitive way, that something unusual and alarming was happening.

Frank tried to call the Danby Police first. It wasn't critical that Allison was not in the bedroom. Certainly she was *somewhere* in the school, possibly with Iris and Sam, and if there was an intruder on the premises, then calling the local police was his top priority.

He let the phone ring a dozen times, then hung up. "Dammit!" he whispered. He stared at the phone. Perhaps he had somehow gotten the wrong number out of the phone book. He dialed again. Again he let it ring a number of times and then hung up.

He dialed the operator. "Could you give me the number for the Danby Police Department?" he asked. The operator gave him the number; he looked in the book again; it was the same number, the number he'd been dialing. "Dammit!" he whispered again. Why in the hell wasn't the police department available to him? What kind of town *was* this? Did the police take their nights off?

At last, he decided that it was probably good that he hadn't been able to get hold of the local police. It gave him an excuse to call the county sheriff's department. Certainly *they* would answer the phone.

They did.

Frank told the man who answered, "I'd like to report an intruder in my house."

"Yes, sir. Is he still there?"

"The intruder?" Frank asked.

"Yes."

"I don't know. Possibly. That's why I'm calling. It's possible he's still in the school somewhere?"

"The school?"

"Yes. We live in a school. The school on Ohio Road."

"What number on Ohio Road is that?"

"Number? I don't know. It's . . . our address is an RFD number. Is that important?"

"Yes, sir. I believe you may be outside our jurisdiction."

"No, I'm not." He paused, flustered. "I mean . . . I don't understand how someone can be outside your jurisdiction. I'm *in* the county."

"No, sir. Ohio Road bisects the county line. That's why I need to know where you are on Ohio Road."

"This is ludicrous. Can't you give me the benefit of the doubt and send a car over? My God, we might be in trouble here—"

"I'm sorry, sir, but we don't operate that way. Now if you could find your correct house number I could tell you whether or not you're in our jurisdiction. If you are, then yes, of course we'll send a car over immediately. If you're not, then my advice would be to call the Ontario County Sheriff's Office. Better yet, sir, perhaps you could call the *local* police. What town are you near—"

Frank hung up.

Iris said to Sam, with a nod toward the TV, "I don't like this. It's too old. What is it, anyway?"

But Sam didn't know what the program was either. It had appeared on the screen out of a layer of snow. "'Leave It to Beaver,' maybe," he guessed. He hoped it was "Leave It to Beaver" because he had a fondness for it.

"No, Sam. This isn't 'Leave It to Beaver,'" Iris said, miffed. "Look at that woman. That's not Barbara Billingsley."

Sam looked. He had to agree. The blond woman who was playing the woman of the house wasn't Barbara Billingsley. She was too chunky. She wore too much makeup. She looked like an overfed doll. "Then I don't know what it is, Iris," he said glumly.

The picture vanished. It was replaced, again, by snow. "Shit!" Iris hissed.

"Listen," Sam suggested, "maybe we should just go to sleep."

Iris shook her head, annoyed. "Sleep? Who can sleep? If we go to sleep, who knows what the hell is going to happen? *I'm* not going to sleep."

Sam sighed, got out of his bed, went to the TV, and touched the rabbit ears. They gave him a small electrical shock and he yanked his hand back. "Jesus, what the hell was that?"

"Static," Iris said. "Pick your feet up when you walk across the floor and it won't happen."

He gave her an annoyed look. "You don't get a shock from a bare floor, Iris."

There was a knock at the door.

The dark figure of a man appeared behind the frosted glass.

For all her confusion and awe and, beneath it, her terror— lurking like some vile disease in its first stages—Allison knew that this wasn't her first visit to this place.

It wasn't a feeling of déjà vu. It was more concrete than that. Déjà vu was always nebulous, unformed; there was always question in it—*Well I've done this before, haven't I?* or *I've been here before, I think*. Déjà vu carried with it the seeds of its own discredit. You *knew* that people experienced it, and that you were experiencing it, and however real it seemed, it was still only an absorbing illusion, nothing more.

This was different.

She *had* been here before.

In this place.

When she was a child? she wondered. Had she been here as a child, during what she had supposed then was a shimmering fantasy that came to her between wakefulness and sleep? Had she glimpsed this place then? Yes. For only moments at a time, it was true, but long enough that she could know it for what it was.

Exactly what it was. But then did she forget when, in the next moment, it dissipated, gone until the next time, the next night?

Yes, she had been here then. As a child. More than once, more than a few times.

But she had been here much more recently, too. And more than once.

As if it, this place, was preparing her, showing her itself.

She had never guessed that it was an actual, physical place. A place that she could touch and smell and hear as easily, as surely, as concretely as she could hear herself speak, and experience her own pain.

And she had never guessed—how could she have guessed it?—that there was a way *in,* an *entrance* to this place. An entrance that was real, not fanciful, not the stuff of dreams. But real, tangible. Like going into a supermarket, or over a footbridge and into the woods, or driving onto a turnpike.

An actual, physical way in to this actual, physical place.

Under the stage.

Through the doors that Frank had mutilated with his power saw.

It was so easy.

Like going from one room to another, from one building to the next.

To be where Joey was.

The crack in the gym wall widened, from finger width to arm width; half a hundred cinder blocks toppled onto the lacquered blond wood. Several of the black wire cages holding the gym's bright lights separated from the ceiling and clattered to the floor.

The floor itself split, one side to the other. The split was narrow—in the dark it was invisible.

29

"Have you seen Allison?"

"No, Frank, I haven't," Sam said. There was something strange about Frank, Sam thought. Something a little askew, something off-key.

"I seem to have . . . misplaced her." An embarrassed smile. "I've looked everywhere. You're sure you haven't seen her?" The man shifted his attention to Iris. "How about you? Have you seen her?"

"No, Frank," Iris answered. "I'm sorry. But she's got to be in the school *some*where. It's a big place. Maybe we could help you look for her." Iris noticed it, too. Something strange about Frank.

"No, no, that's all right," the man said. "It's no problem, really. It's hard to say that I've actually looked *every*where. I mean . . . I haven't looked in the cellar."

"The cellar? This place has a cellar?"

The man looked confused, then he answered, "No, it doesn't. It was just a figure of speech, Sam. I haven't looked on the roof, either, have I?" He smiled again, this time as if amused. "And I haven't looked in *any* of the closets." He cocked his head, as if with revelation. "I think I'll do that. I think that's a *good* idea." And he turned and moved off down the corridor.

Sam stepped out into the corridor and called, "Frank, what the hell is going on?" But he got no answer.

He stepped back into the room.

Iris said, "I don't give a damn about the snowstorm, Sam. If this bullshit keeps up, I'm leaving. It's getting *very* weird, here."

She curled her leg so she could see the bottom of her foot. She picked at the encrusted dead skin there with her fingernails and flicked off pinkish gray flakes so they settled onto the floor like snow.

"That's pretty disgusting, Iris," Sam told her.

"Yeah," she said, unconcerned, "I know."

Allison thought, *How can there be stars?* But there were, and they were in familiar groupings—the Big Dipper, Cassiopeia, Orion. Their light was steady, unwinking, white against a field of gray, as if they were tiny mirrors reflecting some great light hidden somewhere in the ground beneath her. And they looked impossibly close, as if she could pull them from the sky, as if the sky itself were within arm's reach.

The trees were dark spiky clumps on the darker landscape, and they made a soft, swishing sound, like skirts rustling, though she could feel no breeze.

She thought, *If this really is the place I* know *it is, then where is Joey? He should be here.*

But there was no one. Only the gray sky, the dark trees, the stars that were too close.

Her terror bubbled up from inside her and made her lips move, but no sound came out.

Being here was suddenly like being under a heavy blanket and losing air.

She was going to suffocate.

She turned. She saw a rectangle of bright light far behind her. "Frank?" she wanted to yell, but she could only gasp.

She ran toward the rectangle of light.

Her steps soon slowed.

The air was gone.

She couldn't breathe.

Frank saw himself putting all those cinder blocks back. Erecting a scaffold and hauling the cinder blocks up with a rope and putting them back. Saving his home.

But the image was ludicrous, and he knew it.

The school was coming apart. Something was making it come apart. Something he had smelled, perhaps, and caught quick glimpses of, perhaps. Something alien. Something real.

"Allison?" he called, but he got no answer. He called to her again.

It was very cold. A few of the ceiling lights in their black wire cages were on, and in the gray light they cast, he could see that the drab brown curtains on stage were moving in reaction to the storm being let in through the fissure in the gym wall.

He called to Allison a third time, with a mounting sense of urgency, now, as he made his way across the gym floor. But still he got no answer, and he decided that she must be outside. He went up on the stage, through the side exit, down the corridor, and out a door that led to the side lawns and parking lots. He stood on a cement porch that was midcalf deep in fine new snow.

There were spotlights on the wall to his left and right and they lit much of the sprawling lawn area. The wind was fierce and biting; it pushed the fine snow about as if it were hair. The snowfall itself had stopped, and the wind had created complex, shifting patterns on the snow cover.

Frank hugged himself for warmth. He could see no footprints in the snow, although this meant little, he thought, because the wind could easily have covered Allison's footprints within minutes.

He sniffled, felt suddenly dizzy—the transition from warmth to bitter cold, he realized—and he stepped back, put his hand on the doorjamb, recoiled from the touch of the frigid metal.

He heard a *whump*. He turned, looked. The door had closed. He looked for a doorknob. There was none. The door had been designed so that it could not be opened from the outside.

"Goddammit!" he whispered. He stepped back and looked right and left for a window to go in. But there were no windows, only a solid brick wall. He'd have to go around to the front of the school, through the deep snow and biting winds.

*   *   *

Iris said, "It's not as if she could really have *gone* anywhere, Sam."

And Sam, who was still trying to get a picture on the TV, nodded and said, "Where's she going to *go*?" He smiled and whacked the side of the TV with his open hand.

"Nowhere, of course," Iris said.

"This is no use," Sam grumbled. "I say give it up."

She looked confusedly at him. "Give it up? Give what up?"

"This." He inclined his head sharply toward the TV. "It's useless. And if we do manage to get a picture, it probably won't be worth watching anyway."

"Don't be so negative. What else have we got to do?"

Sam thought a moment. "We could help Frank look for Allison."

Iris nodded solemnly. "I think we should do that, Sam. This is a big place, after all. She might have . . . I don't know, she might be in trouble."

"Yes," Sam agreed thoughtfully, "that's a possibility."

Iris swung her legs off the bed. When her feet hit the floor, she recoiled. "God, but it's cold," she said, and put her pink fuzzy slippers on.

The cement slab the school had been built on cracked in a million places, like a car window on a very hot day. The cracks were very fine, but very deep. They reached all the way through the slab to the ground beneath.

In reaction, the school itself swayed two inches this way, two inches that way. A hundred ceiling tiles fell. A thousand square feet of linoleum buckled. In the south corridor, a brown ceramic drinking fountain exploded.

In room 16, Alex rose to his feet and urinated spontaneously.

Overhead, the roof began to separate from the walls.

Allison was on her hands and knees, and her head was lowered. She could faintly see the dark tendrils of her hair swaying leadenly around her face; and she could see her hands, dull red against the black earth.

She wanted to scream, wanted help, wanted to be pulled from this place. But she couldn't scream, and her muscles were in pain and nearly useless from lack of oxygen.

The air seemed as thick as water, and it was all but impossible to breathe, as if someone had stuffed a washcloth into her mouth and had pinched her nostrils shut. Her body felt bloated, and her bladder, full from coffee she had drunk with Frank an hour earlier, threatened to let go. That possibility made her cringe with embarrassment.

For she was certain that she was being watched.

Certain that there were people all around her in the darkness. Countless people watching her creep toward the light with her bladder about to let go and her nostrils pinched shut and her hair damp and stringy from sweat.

They could see her. They could see in the dark because the dark was their element, the dark was where they spent their time, where they *existed*. Hadn't she written about them? Didn't she *know* them. Hadn't she been here, in this place, more than once in her forty-five years?

But she could not see them because she was on her hands and knees, and her head was lowered, and her mouth was full of the awful, thick air.

And she was dying.

In this place that was surely the place of the dead, she was dying.

The first door that Frank tried was like the one he'd come out of, not designed to be opened from the outside. He cursed. The bitter wind was making him numb, dizzy. He was wearing only a cotton shirt, light pants, penny loafers, and the temperature was probably near zero, he guessed, the windchill somewhere precipitously below that, and his anger and frustration were mounting geometrically. What a foolish design for a door. Especially a school door! What if there should be a fire, people trapped or

hurt, unable to get out because they couldn't move, and these one-
way doors were the only doors available? It would be curtains for
a lot of unlucky and innocent kids.

"Goddammit!" he screamed, and slammed the metal door
with the side of his fist. The cold, hard metal hurt his numb skin
and he cursed again.

"It's only the storm," Sam said.

"I hope you're right," Iris said. "I just don't think a little bit
of wind can make a building like this move the way it did."

"Well, I think it can," Sam said. "And you know what else I
think? I think you're just being nosy."

He and Iris were in the school's cold north wing, where the
heat had been turned off. There were ten rooms in the north
wing—they were numbered 8 through 17 in tarnished chromed
script—and all of their doors were shut, though not locked.

They had looked into rooms 8, 9, and 10 and were heading
for room number 11. All of the rooms were on the south side of
the corridor. The north side was composed of floor-to-ceiling
windows and solid brick walls. They could see nothing out the
windows except a vague cream-colored horizon and, for a brief
moment, the faint headlights of a car on some distant road.

"What I'm *doing*," Iris said testily, "is looking for my friend.
I am *not* the nosy type, and you know it."

The corridor was dark, except for illumination from its west
end, where they had come from; it provided a soft, greenish light
that was close to phosphorescence.

Iris opened the door to room number 11, reached to her left
for the light switch, found it, flicked it on.

The room was much like the ones they had already looked
in. It was bare of furniture, except for a light oak teacher's desk
that had been pushed up against a wall, beneath the green blackboard, and the battered remains of a student's desk nearby.

Half the ceiling, on the opposite side of the room, had cav-
ed in.

That part of the room was deep in snow, sections of tarred roof, and acoustical-ceiling tile.

"Damn!" Sam whispered.

"I told you it wasn't the wind," Iris said.

"It looks worse than it is," Sam suggested. "It's just this room. The roof's probably been bad for years. It just gave way under the weight of the snow."

"I hope you're right."

"Of course I am. It's just this room. Believe me."

They backed out of the room. Sam closed the door behind them.

30

Allison lay facedown, her arms splayed out so her palms pointed backward.

She was aware of her cheek, her breasts, her knees, and the tops of her feet because they were what connected her most solidly with the dark earth, and the earth was so cold that it sent tremors through her that would have become shivers, had she been breathing.

She was in awe of what was happening. She had wondered more than once how long death would take to overcome her, because she had thought that what might seem instantaneous to an observer could easily be a very, very long time. A car is hit head-on by a semi, the glass splinters, the metal shrieks. Then there is an awesome silence. But for the people involved, the ones who die, that awful moment encompasses a day, a week, a month. Forever. It had always seemed a grim and fanciful notion to her. Now she was proof of it, and she was in awe of it. Christ, Christ, the universe really was unpredictable, it really was unknown and unknowable, people really did fool themselves when they believed they understood even a small part of it—for instance, why water froze, or why the sun set, or why bodies aged ("They know that dogs think of their homes as their dens because of years and years of study and observation," Frank had said). But it was all just best-guesswork, and people were smug because of it, people thought they could extrapolate from what they were sure they knew in order to find answers to the unknowable. But it was *all* unknowable, Christ, *all* of it—

(What had Sandra said? "But there are problems, Allison. Problems. Big, nasty problems. In*soluble* problems. So many things sweep back and forth. So many things . . . mix together. . . . So there is stress, *stuff* stress—")

*   *   *

She belched. It was long and loud. A rolling, tumbling, rumbling belch that made her cheeks quiver and her nostrils twitch.

Then she did it again.

And again.

And, nearby, in the darkness, a wheezing, tenor male voice, said, "Overet. They do that."

And a female voice, harsh and high-pitched, laughed sharply, like hail hitting a tin bucket.

And younger voices, the voices of teenagers, sang a shrill chorus: "Boy toy, boy toy!"

The children had come quickly and woodenly into room 13 as Sam and Iris backed away from them, and now the children stood quietly, side by side, backs of hands touching, mouths open slightly, eyes as wide as silver dollars—blue and brown and green pupils afloat in yellow corneas, in faces as gray as a winter sky.

The children were humming. A long, extended note, high and precise.

A dozen children.

The boys sported crew cuts that were black, brown, blond, ash white; gray skin clear, gray skin bearing brown marks that could have been freckles. One tall, thin boy had downy white hair above his pale lips—the beginnings of a mustache.

There were cowlicks here and there, and they looked wet.

The boys wore black pants, brown pants, some with cuffs, all with belts tied tightly, some so tight that the end looped down over the fly, some so tight that the short-sleeved Oxford shirt wrinkled and bunched out over the top of the pants.

And they all continued humming. They all strained on one high note without change.

They were twelve years old, eleven years old.

The girls were dressed in taffeta, in frills and pink and bows, in patent leather, in gloves, some of them, and their hair was long, was black, was brown, was blond.

The boys wore black Oxford shoes, brown Oxford shoes,

penny loafers, and crew cuts and light-colored shirts covering skin as gray as winter, eyes as wide and unmoving as the locked jaws of snakes.

And the girls hummed.

And the boys hummed.

One long extended note without change. Precise and impossible from those open mouths.

Then it changed.

It became lower, louder.

And stayed this way for whole minutes.

Then changed again.

(*"So many things sweep back and forth. So many things . . . mix together. Imagine . . . Allison,* imagine *what we have here. On this side. What life gives us. We have . . . so much. Time. Change. Love. Hate. Beauty. Stasis. And these . . . all these things are not merely* mirrored *over there. It's not that simple. They are . . . well, just like here, but very differently . . . they're mixed together. I don't know why. I've never understood why. Maybe because that other place is actually the . . . the detritus—"*)

The eyes fixed, the mouths wide and unmoving, the gray skin, crew cuts, and taffeta and pink lace—all of it stuck unchanging in eternity, like the smallest particles of matter.

The children were singing.

The children were starting their dark morning with a song. In slow motion. In real time.

("We have all that is and all that was," Sandra said.)

Their time.

The moment.

Eternity.

<table>
<tr><td>

31

</td><td>

The naked woman in the school said, "Frank, I think there are people out there."

"People?" said the man in the bed. "What people?" He got up and joined his wife at the window.

</td></tr>
</table>

"What would people be doing out there at this time of night?" He peered out with her—two naked bodies recently satisfied in their hunger for one another; and now, as they looked, their hunger returned.

A spotlight illuminated much of the parking lot. The man saw moving shadows just beyond the perimeter of the light. "It could be deer, Allison," he suggested, and his hand went to the woman's waist, and then to her buttocks.

The woman shook her head quickly, as if annoyed. "No. It's not deer. How could it be deer? Deer aren't that tall."

The man put his face to the window and cupped his hands around his eyes to block reflections from the room behind him. "I'm sorry, Allison," he declared after a moment, "but I don't see as much as you apparently do." He stepped back from the window. "Let's get back in bed. It's cold. Aren't you cold?"

"It's your damned eyes," she told him. "You're going blind, and you won't admit it."

"I am *not* going blind," he said, and his tone betrayed his sudden anger.

"There!" the woman cut in. "There they are!"

The man looked again. "Yes," he whispered, because he could see them now, and though they were still little more than shadows, he could tell that they were indeed human. "What the hell do you think they're doing, Allison?"

The woman shook her head, bewildered. "I don't know. I

don't know." She paused, looked at her husband. "I think they're coming here, Frank. I think they're coming to the school."

"Yes," the man said, "I believe you're right—"

The woman gasped.

The man glanced quickly at her, then out the window again, then, once more, at his wife. "Allison? What is it?"

She shook her head in sudden confusion and fear. "Can't you *see*, Frank! Damn you! Can't you see!"

He looked again.

He saw.

He backed away from the window, head shaking, sweat starting, throat dry. "It can't *be*," he whispered.

The decay started. It was very quick. As quick as a moment passing.

And the room was empty.

> "We are watched and judged and manipulated by other people all of our lives, but I think the people who most watch and judge and manipulate us are the people we once were, the people we were twenty years ago, ten years ago—the children we were, the adolescents, the people we were yesterday, this morning. They're all there, invisible to us, watching and judging and manipulating."
>
> "But why would they do that?"
>
> "Because they have a stake in us."
>
> "I'm sorry, I don't understand."
>
> "Because everything comes around again. Everything starts and restarts and restarts and changes. And they—the people we once were—are only looking out for their own pleasure, of course, caught as they are in their moment of eternity."
>
> —Allison Hitchcock, "The Inside"

Frank had found a door that would open, but he did not go in. The school wouldn't let him. It allowed its door to be opened by him, it allowed him to enter, but it did not allow him to breathe once he was inside.

"Allison!" he screamed, because, in his mind's eye, he could see her struggling for breath somewhere in the school. But the only sound he heard in response was a mute cracking noise above him, on the brick wall.

He screamed her name again, and again.

He heard a louder cracking noise to his right, as if a large tree were splitting in a wind.

"Allison!" A stab of pain pushed through his throat from the effort of his scream.

He heard the squeal of brakes from behind him. He looked. A yellow school bus stood in the parking lot, engine running, fifty sets of dark eyes in fifty pink faces fixed on him.

Then it was gone. Lost in the chill night like a pulse of vapor.

"Frank, there are people out there," said the naked woman.

"People? What people?" He joined his wife at the window. "What would people be doing out there at this time of night?" He peered out with her—two naked bodies recently satisfied.

The man saw moving shadows beyond the window. "It could be deer."

"No. It's not deer. Deer aren't that tall."

The man put his face to the window. "I don't see as much as you do," he whined, and stepped back from the window. "Let's get back in bed. It's cold. Aren't you cold?"

"You're going blind," she said.

"I'm not, I'm not!" he protested.

"I think they're coming here, Frank. I think they're coming to the school."

"It can't *be*," he whispered, watching himself approach from beyond the windows. "Hold me, Allison."

She turned toward him and she held him.

"We are forever," she said.

"We are forever," he said.

The decay started. It was very quick. As quick as a moment that has passed.

And the room was empty.

It was as if the school was on fire. As if Frank could only watch it being consumed.

But it was not being consumed by fire. It was being consumed by the past. He knew this, though he could not have expressed it.

He had no choice but to leave.

No choice but to go to his car, around the far side of the school, get in, drive away.

He was going to leave Allison to the mercy of the school. And Iris too. And Sam.

What could he do for them, after all? What could he do for anyone?

He got a hundred yards from the school. He stopped, looked back. All the windows were lighted. The light was pale green, the color of ocean water.

The wellspring of life, he thought.

Did he really *know* what the school wanted, what it was up to? Did he know anything of the virus it was churning out? The changes it was making. *Would* make! (What could he do about it? He might as well try to stop an earthquake.)

"Allison!" he screamed, because his love for her, and his need of her in his life, had struck him hard again. "Allison!" he screamed.

Gentle Allison. Loving Allison. Allison and her special sorrows and insights.

"Allison! Oh, God, I'm sorry!" he screamed. And he was. He knew that he was. *Sorry.* He did not want to be doing what he was doing. Abandoning her.

He heard the squeal of brakes from behind him, in the chill

dark. He looked. A school bus stood in the parking lot with its engine running and fifty sets of dark eyes in fifty pink faces fixed on him.

Then, as quickly as a pulse of vapor, it was gone.

The woman said, "One of them is going away, Frank."

The man had backed halfway across the room, so he was near the bed. Above, the fluorescent ceiling fixture had begun to flicker, and it was making him breathless. He said, "One of them is going away?"

"Yes." The woman glanced at him. "Are you all right, Frank? You look pale."

"It's the light. It's flickering."

The woman looked at the ceiling fixture, then at her husband again. "Don't stand under it. It's your eyes, Frank. There's something wrong with your eyes."

The man nodded stiffly. "I know that."

The woman looked out the window again. "The other one's coming to the school," she said.

"Which one?" the man asked.

"The man."

"Frank?"

"The man."

The ceiling fixture went out.

The man shrieked. It was a low, guttural noise, but clearly a shriek. The woman giggled. Her husband's fear and anxiety were amusing.

He was *sorry*. It was true. He was so awfully sorry!

He started back to the school.

How could he really be sorry and continue to do the thing he was sorry for? It didn't make sense. It was a lecture that he and Allison used to give to Joey when Joey said "I'm sorry," and it was clear that he didn't mean it.

*   *   *

The entity in the school did not see wind-driven snow. It saw a churning expanse of ocean, and bits of willow wood to be collected and stored in some secret place in its bedroom, and wind blowing the leaves and saw grass about.

The entity saw a closed door.

"Dad?" it pleaded.

"Later," it heard. "I'm working."

The entity's eyes were blue and sparkling and it moved and reacted at the impetus of memory; it waltzed about gaily, it ran, it sang, it cursed—in its ineffectual, adolescent way—from the impetus of memory.

It pleaded from the impetus of memory.

It heard the rush of wind.

The crack of a willow branch.

For more than a decade it had drawn from its very recent memories and had given itself life from them.

But soon, that would change, and the entity would move on.

The entity's existence was a paean to life. It *was* life in its purest and most unencumbered form. It knew no death, and it never had.

And that was not unusual.

For a billion years, it had known only change and transformation. It had become very old in a universe of the similarly old.

Allison felt hands on her in the moist darkness. There were hands on her back, and on her buttocks, on her legs, too.

And a voice said, "Feel her, touch her."

And another voice said, "She's a good-looking woman."

Allison listened, hoped desperately for Joey's voice, which she remembered so well—his sweet young soprano. And now it was caught in growing up forever. It would always be his voice, would always be her son's sweet and imperfect voice.

But she heard the harsh voices of men she did not know, and the men touched her, caressed her with hands that were

hard and unkind, and their voices muttered obscene things—
"Nice, titties, eh?" "Ass round and smooth and firm. Get a nice
ride, for sure."

She thought that it had been a very long time since she had
last drawn breath.

She felt her legs being pulled apart, as if she were a chicken,
and she did not think of protesting because she was beginning to
feel disconnected from her body; and that, she thought happily,
was the kind and gentle part of dying—being freed from the
confinement of the body, freed from being a part of it, one with
it, identical with the soft, moist and open areas, the areas that
responded to touch and were alive.

Those areas did not give her life. *She* gave life to *them,* and
now she was taking it away, gathering life back into herself in
preparation for the journey to come.

Let these men do as they pleased.

She would be elsewhere. Free of them.

Free of herself.

Forever.

The ceiling in room 21 collapsed.

And in room 16.

And in the north corridor, the floors heaved up three feet
under the pressure of the slab beneath.

The stress was everywhere.

It was magnificent.

Frank looked back at the elongated footprints he'd left in the
snow cover and watched as the wind began filling the footprints
up with snow as it erased evidence of his passage from there—a
hundred yards off—to here, the glass doors at the west entrance
to the school.

He reached, put his bare hand on the metal door handle,
recoiled.

He was as cold as he had ever been.

                          *   *   *

Allison could breathe again.

She was no longer being touched, manipulated, handled.

And around her, there was silence, near darkness. As if a half-moon had risen.

This was invitation, she realized.

She stood.

"Joey?" she called. She could hear her own voice, and it startled her.

"Joey?" she called again, her voice louder, trembling on the edge of joy, because she *knew* that she would find him. She had been promised. Sandra had promised her. It was a simple thing. Going back and forth. Like going from the living room into the kitchen into the dining room into the foyer.

As simple as taking two steps.

"Joey?" she called.

She was on a brightly sunlit landscape and there were smells about that were comforting and familiar.

The odor of spring flowers.

Hay newly mown.

Leaves burning.

Worms after a rain.

The rain.

The landscape cascaded, tumbled, plunged, rose to giddy and tumultuous heights. It was brown and green, a patchwork, an anarchy of weeds and moving water.

"Joey? I'm here!" she called.

Like swells on an ocean, the landscape moved and changed. Clouds like ink spilling covered the sun and blocked the light.

The landscape became a landscape of shadows.

She saw movement. Gray light playing amid the mounds of dark earth. And she heard a moment of laughter, sharp and real.

"Joey?" she called. She saw the movements of dark air that her voice made and they were like movements of water. "Joey?" she called.

A willow sprang up close to her from the black earth. She could see its yellow leaves hanging in the dark. They moved. They brushed her face. Tickled her. She laughed suddenly, quickly, alarmingly.

A willow had killed her son.

Joey laughed.

She saw his face.

It vanished.

The willow vanished.

She had the sun again, and the patchwork landscape, the anarchy of weeds and moving water, the smells—worms after a rain.

The rain.

"Joey?" she called.

She walked. The landscape rushed beneath her. A cartoon landscape rising and falling. Mickey Mouse, Goofy, Donald Duck, Pluto danced about her, mouths agape, cartoon eyes wide and friendly, and then they were gone and

a willow rose up and its leaves touched her face and she laughed.

"Detritus," Sandra said.

She cast about, her head moving left, right, left.

No Sandra. No willow.

"Detritus," Sandra said.

And the clouds, like ink spilling, moved in and blocked the light and she was being touched in the darkness by a billion hands.

"Mama?" Joey said.

"Joey?" she cried. "Joey?" she cried. And she wept.

"Joey?" she wept into the darkness.

"Detritus," Sandra said. "It doesn't work anymore. Allison."

And Sandra was there. Her face aglow in the darkness. Her face in agony. "It doesn't work anymore, Allison. It's coming apart," she said. "My own sweet Michael is moving away from me," she said.

"William!" cried the plump-cheeked woman. "My William!"

And there was Joey.

On a hill in the darkness.

Fleetingly, on a hill in the darkness.

Like a memory that prods the senses and is gone.

"Joey!" Allison called, and started after him.

Hands stopped her.

One hand took hers. It was cold, strong, demanding. "This way," Sandra said.

Allison moved quickly toward the rectangle of bright light. She passed through it as if through fire, and as swiftly as a candle going out, she was plunged into darkness.

She was aware of warmth, and of cold, of breathing around her, as if many people were standing close by. She reached into the darkness. Her fingers found skin, muscle, hair. She withdrew her hand.

Someone said, "She's afraid."

Someone else said, "Aren't we all!"

"Sandra?" she pleaded. Where was she? Where was Sandra—her protector and her guide through this place?

A sudden, knife-edged kind of ecstasy came to her, and it all but stole her breath away. She thought that she might find herself dead from such ecstasy, and the thought gave her pleasure.

"He's here," she heard. "Open your eyes. Just open your eyes."

"Joey?" she whispered.

Light spilled over her and she gasped.

Sandra's face appeared before her. And the face of the plump-cheeked woman.

"We are not just the moment," Sandra said. "We are all that we were, and all that we are. Of course you're confused. Aren't we all confused? But in your heart, you *know* what's happening here. You *know* the possibilities. Just as you know the risks."

"Oh, yes," agreed the plump-cheeked woman, "the risks."

She nodded vigorously. "The risks." She tilted her head, as if with some great revelation, she added, "Existence is like a Mixmaster, don't you think?"

"Excellent," Sandra said. "All that we are, and were—it's all there, Allison. Birth and life. It's all past and it's all here. Who says death is nothing? Death is everything. Death is all that is and was. And we don't understand a moment of it, do we?"

Frank breathed in quick, pain-filled gasps. He wanted to yell to Allison, to Iris and Sam, even to Alex. He wanted to save them all from this place. But his breathing was too shallow, his movements too slow. He felt dizzy. He felt as if he were going to vomit.

And the school was falling down around him.

Allison was no longer being touched, manipulated, handled in the darkness.

A half-moon had risen.

She stood.

She called to her son.

She *knew* that she would find him. Sandra had promised her.

Sandra had said it would be as simple as taking two steps.

"Joey?" Allison called.

She was on a brightly sunlit landscape and there were smells about.

The odor of spring flowers.

Hay.

Leaves.

Worms after a rain.

The rain.

The landscape was brown and green, a patchwork, an anarchy of weeds and moving water.

"Joey? I'm here!" she called.

The landscape moved and changed. Clouds spilled over the sun and the landscape became a landscape of shadows.

*   *   *

Frank strained to see the gym doors in the pitch dark.

He saw them. They were open wide.

He went through, into the gym.

Allison saw movement—gray light playing amid the mounds of dark earth. And she heard a moment of laughter, sharp and adolescent and real.

"Joey?" she called.

A willow sprang up close to her from the black earth. Its yellow leaves tickled her face and she screamed.

A willow had killed her son.

She saw his face. Oval. Bright. Happy.

It vanished.

The willow vanished.

And she had the smells again—worms after a rain.

The rain.

"Joey?" she called.

She walked and the landscape rushed beneath her like a cartoon landscape rising and falling. Mickey Mouse, Goofy, Donald Duck, Pluto stood by

their mouths agape and their cartoon eyes wide and unseeing and then they were gone and

a willow rose up and its leaves touched her face and she laughed.

"Detritus," Sandra said.

But there was no Sandra and there was no willow.

"Detritus," Sandra said.

And the clouds moved in and blocked the light and she was being touched again and again and again and again in the darkness.

"Mama?" Joey cried.

"Joey?" Allison cried. "Joey?" she wept.

"Joey?" she wept.

"Detritus," Sandra said. "It doesn't work anymore. Allison, it doesn't work anymore. We can't come here anymore. The stress!"

And Sandra was there, her face showing agony. "It doesn't work anymore, Allison. It's coming apart," she said. "My own sweet Michael is moving away from me," she said.

"William!" cried the plump-cheeked woman. "My William!"

And Allison saw Joey.

On a hill that rose gray out of the darkness.

Fleetingly.

Like a memory that prods the senses and is gone.

She felt a hand in hers. It was warm and strong. She heard a voice.

Frank's voice.

"My God, Allison, push!"

The stress was everywhere. Curling about in the cold dark, sweeping over the landscape, changing, restructuring. The stress was magnificent.

"Push, dammit!"

"Help me, Frank! I can't breathe."

"Push! Push hard! Harder!" He pulled. He wheezed. His wife's hand was very cold. He was afraid for her. Afraid for himself.

The stress swept past standing trees and pushed them over. It tore the tiles off roofs. It tumbled night creatures about, leaving them still and confused, or dead. It whipped the new snow into fantastic swirling clouds and then turned the clouds to steam and the steam to ice.

"This way," Iris said to Sam, and held her plump hand out to her brother in the darkness. She had found a path through the rubble. "Can you hear me?" she yelled.

"I can hear you," he yelled back.

And Iris saw that the outer wall was gone and that the horizon bore the rust of dawn.

*   *   *

The stress had been relieved.

The four friends huddled together outside the school, near the playgrounds, and watched the sun rise. It was not a particularly good sunrise. It was light blue and faded gold, covered over by wispy clouds. But it held their quiet attention, and when it was done and the day had started, they looked back at the school and they said nothing for a long while.

The school had most of its walls. But seen from the outside, its windows and empty doorways peeked at the sky.

Allison was the first to speak. She said, "I saw him."

Frank said nothing. He had his arm around her and he squeezed her a little to show that he understood.

"Saw who?" Iris said.

Allison thought a moment, then she said, "Someone I knew once. A long time ago."

A male cardinal, red and dashing, flew over and landed in a pine tree not far away.

"I don't know what's happened here," Sam said, apparently to himself.

Allison said, "Sandra's in there. With her son."

"And we're here," Frank said. "With each other."

The female cardinal joined its mate in the pine tree.

"Winter birds," Sam said.

"Rhymes," Frank said.

Eventually, they all walked to a farmhouse a half mile off and used the phone there to contact the local police.

"What was all that *racket* over there last night?" said Bowerman, the man who lived by himself in the farmhouse.

"Worlds colliding," Allison said.

"Thunder," Frank said.

A Day Later

She did not like pulling away from the school. She wanted

to tell Frank, *No, turn back. We're doing the wrong thing. This is too logical, too rational. Sometimes we have to do what our insides tell us to do. Joey* needs *us, our son needs us, and we're abandoning him.* But she said nothing because she wasn't sure how much of that would be true. Perhaps none of it.

Did Joey need them? No. It was obvious. He had grown beyond them. If anything, *they* needed him.

What wonder and wisdom there had been on that cherubic face! Though she had seen it only for an instant. He was caught up in such a great adventure, and he *knew* it. After only six years on the earth, he had learned how to leave it without fear, and how to journey outward.

And what did she and Frank know? Only how to grieve. Only how to plead with the maker of them all to give their son back. To let them be together, no matter what the cost. Just as Sandra and the plump-cheeked woman had.

Such things could not be, she realized.

The car bucked a little, its engine still not warmed enough from the night of bitter cold.

She glanced at Frank. "Will we come back here?" she asked.

He looked at her. His face bore no emotion that she could read at first. Then his mouth drew into a little smile, and he blinked a couple of times and looked at the road again. He did not answer her question.

She turned her attention once again to the school. She could see only the top few feet of its brick walls now. The car was beginning its long descent into Danby.

In moments the school was gone.

She turned around, sat quietly for a few moments. She wanted to say something, wanted to put some words to what had happened, wanted to give it an ending statement. It was the way that literature worked. Wasn't it the way that life worked, too? She said, "I feel better."

"Than what?" Frank asked.

"Than I ever have before," she answered.